# A Deadly Obsession

## The Obsessed Duet Part One

Vi Carter

# Contents

Other Books by VI CARTER      V

PROLOGUE      1

1. CHAPTER ONE      5

2. CHAPTER TWO      12

3. CHAPTER THREE      19

4. CHAPTER FOUR      27

5. CHAPTER FIVE      34

6. CHAPTER SIX      42

7. CHAPTER SEVEN      50

8. CHAPTER EIGHT      58

9. CHAPTER NINE      66

10. CHAPTER TEN      74

11. CHAPTER ELEVEN      83

12. CHAPTER TWELVE      91

13. CHAPTER THIRTEEN      101

14. CHAPTER FOURTEEN      110

15. CHAPTER FIFTEEN 118

16. CHAPTER SIXTEEN 125

17. CHAPTER SEVENTEEN 132

18. CHAPTER EIGHTEEN 140

19. CHAPTER NINETEEN 148

20. CHAPTER TWENTY 156

21. CHAPTER TWENTY-ONE 163

22. CHAPTER TWENTY-TWO 172

23. CHAPTER TWENTY-THREE 179

24. CHAPTER TWENTY-FOUR 186

25. CHAPTER TWENTY FIVE 193

26. CHAPTER TWENTY-SIX 203

27. CHAPTER TWENTY-SEVEN 212

28. CHAPTER TWENTY EIGHT 220

29. CHAPTER TWENTY NINE 228

30. CHAPTER THIRTY 235

31. CHAPTER THIRTY-ONE 244

32. CHAPTER THIRTY-TWO 252

33. CHAPTER THIRTY-THREE 259

34. CHAPTER THIRTY-FOUR 267

35. CHAPTER THIRTY-FIVE 274

About The Author 281

# Other Books by VI CARTER

Other Books by VI CARTER

**WILD IRISH SERIES**

FATHER (FREE)

VICIOUS #1

RECKLESS # 2

RUTHLESS #3

FEARLESS #4

HEARTLESS #5

**THE BOYNE CLUB**

DARK #1

DARKER # 2

DARKEST #3

PITCH BLACK #4

**THE OBSESSED DUET**

A DEADLY OBSESSION #1

A CRUEL CONFESSION #2

## YOUNG IRISH REBELS

MAFIA PRINCE #1

MAFIA KING #2

MAFIA GAMES #3

MAFIA BOSS #4

## MURPHY'S MAFIA MADE MEN

SINNER'S VOW #1

SAVAGE MARRIAGE #2

SCANDALOUS PLEDGE #3

# PROLOGUE

## ELLA

THE COLD CONCRETE UNDER my hands penetrates my skin and worms its way into my veins. Small pebbles feel harsh against the sensitive area of my hands as I scramble up the steps. All I can focus on is two black wooden doors ahead of me.

*Freedom*, they scream.

My bare foot slips on the edge of a step in my haste to get away from the madness behind me. My chin takes the impact of my fall as it hits the concrete slab, but I don't stop as a metallic taste fills my mouth. I need to reach those doors before he reaches me.

My palms cry out as I slam them repeatedly against the black doors, but they don't budge. My frantic heart sends my temperature spiking, sending the cold that I briefly felt racing away. A sob I can't keep down trembles on my lips before it forms fully. I blink, allowing the tears to fall as I push with my shoulder. Something shifts under me, and the smallest breeze that escapes the crack of the door has me pushing harder. With every ounce of strength I have, I manage to get the doors open and spring from the basement.

Grass still covered in dew blankets my feet as I race across the front lawn. I don't dare look back; I don't dare let that final image flood my mind. I want to scream for help; I want to beg someone to help me. But no one is around. Holding up my white bloodied nightgown, I continue my race for freedom across the lawn, which feels more like an endless meadow. The wind whips hair across my face, the feel of it is frozen and harsh against my skin.

My fingers dig into the wooden fence as I pull myself over it. The shouts from the house, along with lights being turned on along the porch, have my heart fluttering and my vision tinges with black along the edges. Dread pools in my stomach as I fear I might pass out. The shouts mingle along with the blood that pounds in my ears as I fall across the fence and onto a hard surface. My fingers race across the tarmac.

A road.

I'm on a road. Standing, I wobble as I spin around. More tarmac, more trees. My tongue feels heavy in my mouth, and I wonder when it was I last had something to drink. I can't remember. My feet start to move again.

I freeze. The noise of someone coming has the blood running cold in my veins. My chin scrapes against the tarmac as I throw myself down on the ground. Fear is consuming me; something I can't control, my vision blurs and wavers. Feet appear out onto the road. A whimper pulls at me, and I close my eyes tightly. Warm liquid rushes down my face.

*He can't see me. He can't see me.*

My skin crawls, and I'm too afraid to open my eyes. Another part of me wants to scream so this will end. I open my eyes slowly, and the feet race past me. My heart hammers in my chest as I wait for them to stop and come back, but they don't. Another whimper leaves my chattering lips.

*Get up, Ella.*

Pushing myself up on shaky arms, I spring from the ditch and run in the opposite direction the other person went. My eyes shoot around the landscape as my mind tries to push the images back in front of me. Like a detective sliding a gruesome image in front of the murderer to make him crack.

He wanted me to break.

He wanted to break me.

My lungs burn as I race around a bend in the road. I don't know how long I've been running for, but I haven't seen a car. My mind won't decide if that's a good thing or a bad thing.

*Thin red lips.* I cover my mouth to keep the scream in, the scream that's building inside me and wants out.

The noise of a vehicle cracks through my thoughts, and without slowing down, I throw my body to the left of the road, where most of the undergrowth is. My skin burns from the sharp thorns that pierce my skin and drink my blood.

As I lie still once again, the cold ground becomes comforting, reminding me that I'm out here and not in there with that monster.

The one blond curl wrapped in red. Stained in blood. I tighten my eyes as my mind tries to conjure the rest of the image.

*Move, Ella.*

I leave the road completely and start to run across an open field.

*Help me.*

My frantic mind won't slow as my feet dig deep into the grass. I don't remember how I got here, but when I stop and look up, I'm standing outside my house.

"Mam." My lip trembles as my voice cries for my mother. My body shakes and dips like it's giving up. I'm a yard from my own front door. A yard from my home.

"Mam," I shout louder as I find the use of my legs and start to run.

"Mam." My roar is said with a pounding heart. How long has it been—weeks, months, a year?

"Mam!" My fists hit the door. The overhead porch light burns my eyes from the darkness of the night.

When the door opens, I collapse to my knees at my mother's feet.

# CHAPTER ONE

## (BEFORE)-ELLA

M Y MOTHER SWIPES THE yellow dress right out of my hands.

"That color does nothing for you, and we want him to pick you." She finishes her sentence while holding my face in her hands, her touch gentle but her words firm.

"I like that dress." My words fall flat as I face her back. She's been packing these bags for most of my life, waiting for the day I'm swept away to Lucas Andrew the third. Honestly, so have I. He's been my bedtime story since I was a child, my reward when I complied, my punishment when I didn't.

They made him whatever they needed to at the time, and all I knew was that I was raised for him and only him.

I tighten my legs together as I remember the uncomfortable examination I had to go through, only days ago, to prove I was a virgin.

"Ella, you're slouching."

My spine straightens at my mother's words. It takes me a moment to catch up with her.

"Sorry, Mother."

A quick nod and I return to the dresses laid out on my single bed. So many green ones. "Just like your eyes," my mother has always said.

I glance at her now and can see her excitement in how quickly she moves about the room. Our eyes clash and she stops, folding a snow-white nightdress in her hands.

"Don't be nervous."

These are her first words of encouragement, and my lips tug up into a smile that she mirrors. She loves when I smile. She's told me a thousand times it's my best asset.

"I'm excited." I want to gush about how handsome he is, but this is my mother. Another brief nod of her head sends me back to work, packing.

"I think that's it." Her cheeks are red as she glances around the room and over the five suitcases we have packed. My stomach tightens. This was it.

Our eyes meet over the suitcases, and her brown ones soften. "My baby is now a woman."

I hate the sadness that fills her eyes. "Mam, once he picks me"—she smiles at my confidence—"we can see each other."

Her smile slips, but she recovers by giving me a nod and counting the suitcases. "I'll get Larry up here."

I stare at her back as she leaves me in my room for the final time. I wonder now, as I look around at my neatly made bed, when I will lie in it again. I walk over to my dressing table and sit down, picking up a brush that still has some long black hairs in it from this morning's brushing. Automatically, I start to pull them out and place the loose strands into the bin.

I meet my gaze in the mirror, wide green eyes full of hope. Smiling at myself, I inhale and exhale a deep breath.

"Ella, stop admiring yourself and come along."

"Yes, Mam." I glance away from the innocent girl in the mirror and follow my mother and Larry outside. All my suitcases are now being stowed into the back of the car.

No one speaks as Larry opens the back door for us. Once everyone is in, Larry starts the engine, and I use this final moment to stare up at our two-story family home. It's perfect, from its white walls to the manicured lawns on either side of us. The shiny red front door moves past us, and my stomach jerks.

"Remember, there are rules, Ella." My mother speaks like she's on autopilot.

"Mam, I know. I've been listening to them for the past nineteen years. Always mind my P's and Q's. Never eat everything on my plate. Smile. Be respectful. Don't befriend the other girls."

"Don't slump. You have a tendency to slump, and it's very unattractive."

My spine straightens once again.

The car slows down, and I'm surprised at how quickly we arrived. I knew we lived close by, but it felt too quick. Nineteen years of waiting have boiled down to this moment.

Two large white steel gates face us now. Larry rolls down the window to speak to a man in a small hut. I pull myself forward, trying to see who he's speaking to. A hand on my shoulder pulls me back.

"Ella, sit back. A lady doesn't get excited like a child." I sit back and try to contain my excitement.

"He can't see me right now." My lippy words have my mother's eyebrows rising in unison.

But I stay seated and glance out the window as we're ushered into his estate. It's just as I pictured. Endless lawns, all freshly cut. Flowers of every color weaved in sync on both sides. Trees are sporadically planted throughout the lawns. I can see me and Lucas having a picnic under one of the trees. A giggle threatens to burst from my lips, but I swallow it.

I keep shifting as we make our way up the winding driveway; the house at the end has me looking up and up. I smash my hands against the window, ignoring my mother's earlier warning.

"Wow!" It's like a castle. Forbidding, intimidating, marvelous.

My mother's tut has me leaning back in the seat as I watch my handprints disappear from the glass.

The large black double doors open, and my heart does a dance. Is it him? Will he greet me? I sit straighter and want to touch my hair, but I don't. I don't want him to think I'm a fidget.

My mother's hand wraps around my upper arm as I reach for the door handle. When I look at her from over my shoulder, I end up fully facing her.

"What's wrong?"

She looks... odd. Like a captain standing on a sinking ship. I blink the image away, and as I do, she lowers her lashes. When she looks at me again, she doesn't wear that terrified look.

She pushes a piece of hair back behind my shoulder. Her actions tell me everything.

"Mam?" I question.

"Nothing. Just... I will miss you."

I let out a relieved laugh. "I will miss you too, Mam." I will, but I'm also eager to start this stage of my life. I've waited forever for this. When I reach for the door handle again, my mother doesn't stop me, and I step out on the tarmac.

Two men dressed in tailored suits take my bags from Larry, who helps them. I inhale the fresh air, the smell of a new beginning. My mother doesn't get out of the car.

"This is goodbye, Ella," she says as I lean back inside the door. She won't look at me. The trunk is closed and has me glancing at Larry through the back window. He circles around and gets into the driver's seat.

"Good bye, Mam," I say, and wait.

She doesn't turn, and when Larry starts the engine, I close the door gently. I watch the car as it leaves, but my mother never looks back at me.

I'm the first girl to have arrived. This gives me the upper hand. I'm led from one enormous room to another. This place is just as I pictured it. I try to contain my excitement as Mark gives me a tour.

"This is the drawing room."

Something inside me sings. This is a fairy tale come to life. I run my hand along the velvet chaise lounge. My hand touches air, then the fabric under my fingers changes as I run them along a high-back leather chair. I'm not focused on what I'm touching. My focus is on a large image hung between two bookcases. It has my cheeks coloring while my heart beats a bit faster.

"That is Master Lucas."

I glanced over my shoulder to Mark, who just spoke. He's standing close to the door, his hands held in front of him.

I turn back to Master Lucas. "I know," I say as I stop at the picture. I could draw him with my eyes closed. My mother gave me a picture of him only two years ago. In this one, he's slightly older. His shoulders are wider. My stomach tightens.

He's so handsome.

He's a prince.

An exhale behind me has me swinging around.

"He's perfect, isn't he?"

Red hair, so much red hair—that's what I see when I look at the girl who's staring up at my Lucas.

"I'm Hannah, but you can call me Ann." She reaches out her hand, a wide smile on her face. Her white teeth flash against her plump lips. She's beautiful.

I take her hand slowly. "Ella."

"Like Bella?" Hannah bites her lip, hiding a smile.

"Just Ella." I remove my hand from hers and glance up at Mark, who watches us.

"So, are we the first two?" she asks but doesn't wait for an answer as she glances back up at Lucas. I have the urge to step in front of her and block her view.

Instead, I stare up at him. The image captures him perfectly. A small amount of light is cast across half his face, and it showcases his strong jaw, straight nose, and lips. He's flawless. Inky-colored hair reflects in his deep black eyes. The right side of his face is cast in shadows, where the light doesn't touch it, and there's almost something sinister in his right eye.

The high black polo neck stretches across wide shoulders, and I can almost see the definition of his chest muscles. His arms hang on either side of his perfect body.

"I wonder when we get to meet him." I say the words but curse myself when Hannah smiles at me. I'm here only five minutes, and I'm already breaking my mother's rules. I'm not to befriend any of these girls.

"Soon, I hope." Hannah doesn't seem to notice the change in my attitude as I walk away from her. I keep taking peeks at Mark, who lets us roam around the room. He's watching us with interest.

Hannah continues staring up at Lucas, and I want to stay beside her. I ache for friendship as badly as I ache for Lucas. But I can't have both, I know that. If I befriend one of these girls, I'll get distracted.

The horrible thought of not becoming Lucas's wife has everything inside me freezing. I wouldn't know what to do. He has been everything my entire life. I push the thought away like it's a dirty thing.

Movement beyond the drawing room has me glancing at Mark, who's looking out into the hall. I stand a bit straighter. It must be another girl.

My spine straightens as my whole body buzzes and vibrates. He is so much more than any picture or painting could capture. His presence is felt in every cell of my body.

Lucas has just stepped into the room, and he doesn't look happy.

# CHAPTER TWO

## LUCAS

"MASTER LUCAS." MARK NODS at me as I enter the drawing room. His pasty white face and washed-out eyes have me wanting to step back out of the room.

"Where is he?" I glance over the room. "Who are they?" I ask, turning to Mark. Why the hell are there two women in the drawing room?

"The ladies have started to arrive, Master Lucas." His monotone voice has me gritting my teeth. Instead of reacting to Mark, I take a second glance at them. One of them is wearing an emerald green dress the same color as her large innocent eyes. She stares at me like a deer in headlights.

"For what?" I bark at Mark but keep my eyes on the deer. At my raised voice, she jumps slightly. I grin at her reaction.

"They're here for the selection as your future wife, Master Lucas."

I exhale loudly and release the deer from my stare, giving Mark my attention. I take a step toward him. "I told you to reschedule that for another week." Another year, or forever.

He has the nerve to puff out his tiny chest, which I want to crush. "The orders came from your father."

I tighten my fists. Mark's a snake. He's my father's servant, not mine. Always watching, always running back with his tales. I have no argument and can't change the arrival of these women, so I return to my reason for being in this room.

"Where is Henry?"

"I'm afraid I don't know, Master Lucas."

I sneer at him. He knows. He's just protecting him like always.

I lean in closer and watch fear slowly creep its way into his gray eyes. "Don't worry," I whisper. "I'll find him."

I glance once more at the two women, who haven't moved a muscle. Puppets for the show my father is sure to have. One way or another, he will get the ending he wants. I don't understand the whole point of this charade.

The idea that I'll have to marry one of them gives me a headache. It shouldn't be me. It should be Henry. But Henry doesn't want to, so Henry doesn't have to.

I leave the room and make my way to the stairs as two more women enter the foyer, both stopping dead in their tracks. One steps toward me, her arm rising in a waving gesture. The stupid smile dissolves off her face as I pass her by and take the stairs two steps at a time.

I stay silent until the stairs open onto a large landing.

"Henry." I call his name slowly. He hates when I do that. I wait and don't hear anything back. I'm pretty sure I know where he is. I continue to walk, taking small controlled steps.

"Don't make me come looking for you," I call as I peek into his room, which is perfectly made. The small single bed in the giant room looks ridiculous. He refused a large bed, told father it took too long to warm up.

Movement above my head has me grinning as I make my way to the end of the hallway. Tucked behind large plants is winding gold stairs that lead to the open third floor. It was once divided into servant quarters, but since they don't live in the house, Henry claimed it and demolished every wall. It is now Henry's domain.

"What are you doing hiding in the attic?" I ask the moment I see him sitting on a red-and-green rug. Whatever he's playing with, he tucks behind his back before pushing his black glasses up on his face. Everyone says we look alike. I don't see it. All I see is a weirdo I don't want anyone associating with me.

"What do you want, Lucas?" He tries to sound bored, but I know better. He hates when I refer to his space as the attic. The fact that he didn't correct me tells me he's up to no good again.

I deliberately walk around him while touching things. An ugly floor lamp. The cream tassels pass easily through my fingers. I glance down to see a small wooden box behind his back.

"What poor creature are you torturing?" I glance at Henry as I touch a blue hanging chair suspended from the ceiling. The white stripes along the arms are pure white, like no one has ever used the chair. I run my hands along the white fabric.

His nostrils flare. "What do you want?" He's still sitting, his hands gripping his crossed legs.

"I want my weird brother to stay out of my business." I stop in front of him, folding my arms across my chest.

"I don't know what you're talking about." His smirk has me clenching my fists.

I pretend to think. He knew exactly what I was talking about.

He shifts and pushes his glasses up on his nose again, his irritation noticeably growing.

"Where is your weird friend?"

His cheeks grow red with anger, and I grin.

"It's Alex, and you know his name." Henry gets up off the floor. I'm still a foot taller than him, even though he's the older of us. "He isn't weird. He's different. Not like all you carbon copies."

I snort. "He's weird. Just keep out of my business."

"Or what?" He's excited at the prospect of my next words. He has a devious smile worming its way across his face.

I smile at my brother, and his excitement dwindles. "I won't tell father. He won't take my word over yours."

I know that. He knows that. That is what he expects me to fire at him.

"So what?" He curls his nose up as he speaks, eyes widening.

I shrug. "Let me think about it."

"Lucas. You can't make a threat without actually making one."

*He is so easy to annoy.*

I turn around. "But I just did," I say, glancing over my shoulder.

A muscle twitches in his jaw. "It doesn't matter what you do. You can't hurt me."

I walk slowly and shrug. He's right. I can never hurt him. I pause at the stairs.

"No. But I can hurt Alex."

He's stomping like a wild boar across the floor as I duck out of the attic and make my way down the stairs. He's on my heels, and I pretend like I don't notice.

"If you so much as look at Alex..."

I let a laugh linger as I turn to Henry and smile. Taking a step toward my brother, he reins in some of that anger. His shoulders are slumped forward, his head slightly tilted as he watches me from the corner of his eye. He looks wrong. He looks fucking weird.

"What will you do?"

I take another step toward him, and he hunches forward even more.

"No one is watching, Henry. So you don't have to act like a victim."

He grins up at me before returning to his full height. "But sometimes people are watching. Do you know what they see when they watch us?"

This time, he takes a step toward me. "They see you, Lucas—the bully. And then they see me." He grins. "What will I let them see this time?"

I clench my fists. "Are you threatening me?"

He grins and shrugs just as I did to him. Only, I'm not stupid enough to call after him as he turns and heads back up to the attic.

I make my way down the stairs and stop abruptly on the last step. More girls, more giggles, more smiles. How many are due to arrive?

"Master Lucas." George greets me as he helps carry in their bags. His back is bent. He needs to retire, but my father refused to let him go. I want to bark at the three women and tell them to get their own bags.

I continue to the back of the house, passing the drawing room, where I hear more voices. I don't pause as I keep heading toward a place I will find silence.

Turning up the knob of my stereo, I blare my music in my soundproof room. I pull off my navy jumper and place it on the wooden bench. After switching my trousers and shoes for black jogging pants and sneakers, I wrap my hands.

I don't hold back as my punching bag becomes Henry. I punch it, picturing his glasses crumbling under my fist. The impact of my next punch sends the bag sailing back, and I'm ready for the impact when it returns. I jab my fist into the side of the bag, and Henry's ribs crack, but not before I get a sickening hit into his other side. The bag swings back, and when it returns again, I focus on Henry's face, hit after hit, bones smashing and crushing under my fists.

I'm panting hard, sweat coating my naked torso, but I still have more. All the faces melt together—each punch is Henry, my father, even Mark. I keep hitting until the image changes to nameless faces. My fists are raw and no longer enough.

My knee impacts, swinging the bag back. I keep going until exhaustion has me puffing and holding onto the bag for support. The music pounds into my head, not allowing anything else in there. Just the way I like it. My fists cry out, and my knee stings. I focus on the pain.

My ears ring for a moment, even as the music ends. I straighten and look over at Mark, who stands up straight.

"All seven ladies have arrived, Master Lucas."

"Turn my music back on." I don't have much energy left, but I return to punching the bag. It's not as vicious as it was before, but with Mark's presence here, it fuels me.

"Your father left me instructions."

I turn and stretch out my hands. Fresh blood seeps into the bandages. Mark's eyes flicker to my damaged hands, and his lips curl up in disgust. He doesn't budge.

The fabric comes away easily as I unravel it from my hands. "My father isn't here and won't be for four weeks." I take a step toward

Mark. "So why don't you and George occupy the ladies. In any way at all." I wink.

His eyes widen. "That isn't my role, Master Lucas."

"What? Sleeping with them?"

His eyes grow hard.

"I promise I would never tell. Take your pick."

"This is not a joke, Master Lucas."

"Master Lucas," I repeat while throwing the bloodied bandages into the bin. "If I was your Master, you wouldn't be here."

I grin up at Mark, and he holds firm in his stance.

"Your father will be expecting a report, Master Lucas."

I sense a tone in how he says my name now. I want to point it out, pull him up on it, but I'm getting tired.

"What did you come here for?"

"You need to greet all the ladies."

"Let me shower first."

His eyes roam my bare torso. "Yes, that would be best."

Mark turns to leave but stops. "I would suggest a pair of gloves, Master Lucas."

I would suggest he leaves quickly before I lose my temper.

The door closes, and I glance down at my damaged hands. I grin.

I have no intention of making this easy for them.

# CHAPTER THREE

## ELLA

Five suitcases. I keep counting them as if the numbers might dwindle.

*"Who are they?"* His words are on repeat in my head. The way he looked at us... My cheeks darken even now, and my eyes sting. It was him from the picture, but he didn't seem happy to see us. He wasn't what I had thought he would be.

I sit on the edge of the four-poster bed and look around my room. It's how I pictured it. At least something has turned out right. The lush cream carpet gathers around my bare feet. I wiggle my pink-painted toenails.

I thought one look at me, and it would be love at first sight. It's how it always goes in the fairy tales. I felt ... scared. His raised voice was harsh; his eyes held something that was so dark. I shiver now and get off the bed. I know the cold isn't coming from the soft breeze that pours in through the open double windows, but I'm going to pretend it is.

The window bay is large, and one single reading chair sits in a stream of light. Like someone took the time to watch what way the sun fell and positioned it there. Red velvet curtains hang on either side, reminding me of the curtains on a stage. I close the windows and stare out onto the gardens. They're endless, a maze of plants and flowers. I see an actual maze made from a hedge far beyond the lawns. It's just like the one I've seen in the storybook *Alice in Wonderland*.

"Hi, Ella, who isn't Bella." Hannah knocks softly on my door as she speaks. Her smile is still wide. "May I come in?"

She bites down on a plump red lip after she speaks. I know I shouldn't, but I also have to watch my p's and q's. Mother's orders.

"Of course." I turn away from the window fully and slip on my beige heels. I don't want to appear sloppy. I need all the girls to know that I'm a real threat in this competition.

"All the girls are talking about Lucas." She wiggles her eyebrows as she kicks off her shoes and sits on my bed. She's messing up my room.

I can't help but bend down and pick up her shoes before placing them alongside the high skirting board. That is much better.

"What are they saying?" I can't stop my curiosity.

"How gorgeous is he? Vicky said she's going to sleep with him first."

My stomach sours at her words. "Who is Vicky?"

"Oh yeah. You haven't met the other girls. All seven of us are here now. So Vicky is the tall one. You can't miss her." She bites her lip again as she smiles. It's like she's trying to contain herself.

"I thought Lucas was rude." I quickly cover my mouth once the words leave them. *Oh my God.* "Please don't..."

She's laughing. "Don't worry. I think he was rude too. But he's still hot."

A smile pulls at my lips. "He is very handsome."

The silence in the room feels uncomfortable. I don't want to break it. I shouldn't be speaking to her in the first place. I can't encourage this. Whatever *this* actually is.

A small blonde head pops around my open door. "Ladies. We finally get to meet him."

She steps fully into the room. She's pretty too, with a wave in her blonde hair that reaches her shoulders. She isn't in a dress like Hannah and me. Instead, she wears a pair of high-waist white trousers, and tucked into the waistband is a simple black shirt. She looks sophisticated and older. All of a sudden, I feel childish in my green dress.

Hannah slides off the bed, her cheeks flushed. "Well, Ella and I have already met him."

I glance at Hannah, wondering why I've been brought into this conversation.

"Is that so?" The blonde-haired girl stares at me, and her once soft blue eyes now seem a bit sharper.

"Well, he walked into the drawing room when we were there."

I glance behind the blonde girl as four more girls wait to hear what I have to say. My stomach twists and I curse Hannah.

"What did he say?" A brunette steps into my room, who's so tall.

"That's Vicky," Hannah says with a wink.

So she's the one who's going to sleep with him first. I stand straighter now and focus on Vicky. But I'm no match for her height. She has to be over six feet.

"He was busy, so he didn't say much," I answer honestly.

"He was angry and it was so hot." Hannah takes over, and all the girls smile and giggle at her expression. Before, they just stared at me like I was boring them to death.

"He was up in Mark's face. I thought it was going to turn into a fistfight. Ella and I witnessed the whole thing."

I glare at Hannah and her nonsense.

She winks. "Anyway. He was only looking for Henry."

"Who's Henry?" two girls ask at once.

Hannah shrugs. "A mystery we will have to solve, girls." She claps and they all giggle again.

"Well, we better get down to the drawing room. Now we all get to meet Lucas." The blonde bats her lashes dramatically, and more giggles burst forth.

I wait until everyone has left my room before running to the mirror. I look terrified. Oh God. I take a few deep breaths before leaving my room.

We enter the drawing room again. Vicky and another brunette sit on the chaise lounge. I opt for a high-back leather seat. Hannah quickly sits across from me, while the blonde and another two brunettes sit on a large couch at the back. We're spaced out but still close to each other. My heart drums as I sit straight and cross my legs, only to uncross them again.

*Don't fidget.*

A man dressed in the same black suit that Mark wore enters the room. He must be in his eighties. He smiles kindly at us all, and I relax instantly.

"Thank you, ladies, for gathering. Master Lucas will be with you shortly." Two more ladies arrive, dressed in black skirts and tops. They hold trays high above their heads.

I accept the drink that is offered to me, but I can't take my eyes off the door, waiting and hoping we get to see Master Lucas, the gentleman. Everyone has bad moments. Maybe Henry, whoever he is, really upset Master Lucas. Maybe that's why he was so angry.

Once everyone has a drink, the ladies leave the room, the door closes behind them, and the old man still stands at the head of the room. I place my drink on a small table to my right. My stomach is too queasy to accept the liquid.

"A few rules before we get started." Everyone quiets down. "We don't allow phones or any other technological devices during the selection period."

I don't have a phone to begin with, so that rule doesn't bother me. As I glance at the other girls, I see their eyes widen.

"Will we hand them over now?" Vicky asks.

"All will be collected after your first meeting with Master Lucas. The second rule is that you can't leave the property without permission."

No one says anything.

"Thirdly, you are only allowed into your assigned rooms, which are your own quarters, the drawing room, the library, and the main kitchen. Any questions?"

"Can we watch TV?" This is from the brunette who sits beside the blonde girl. Once again, I notice how pretty she is. Chocolate brown hair with matching eyes. Even her skin looks like light chocolate. Her voice is soft.

"Yes, TV is permitted."

I face forward, looking away from the girl just as the door opens. My heart beats too fast, and my hand flutters to my throat to try to calm it down as Lucas steps into the room.

"Master Lucas. I was just informing the ladies of the rules." The old man smiles at Lucas, but Lucas doesn't smile back.

He looks as angry as he did earlier. When he stares up at us, his dark eyes are tight with irritation, like he really doesn't want us here.

"You told them not to wander around my home." His voice is deep and hostile.

I want to look at the other girls to see if their hearts are beating as hard as mine is.

"Yes, Master Lucas." The old man sounds disappointed as he speaks.

Lucas glares at us all like we're the enemy in a war I'm not aware of. I try to smile when his dark eyes land on me, but they narrow. He rubs his jaw, and my breath catches at his damaged hands. I can hear someone inhale quickly, so I'm not the only one who noticed the cuts.

He grins, but it's sinister and filled with loathing. *For us?* I'm not sure what's going on. But right now, I'm caught in a trap as he continues to stare at me.

"Anyone have any questions?" His deep voice rumbles through me, and his words sound more like a dare.

Two beats pass and no one speaks.

"Let me introduce the ladies, Master Lucas." The old man sweeps his arm toward us.

"If you insist, George." Lucas's drawl sounds bored. Each time he opens his mouth, my dreams disappear at an alarming rate.

"This is Vicky O'Sullivan."

Vicky stands at the mention of her name, but Lucas doesn't take the hand she raises slightly. He gives her a sharp nod, and my stomach twists as she sits back down.

"This is Mary Walsh."

Mary stands and straightens her red knee-length dress. She looks pale, like she might pass out. Lucas gives another nod while placing his damaged hands in front of him. I think we are all distracted by them.

"This is Ella O'Leary."

My heart thumps as I rise and face Lucas. This moment was meant to be perfect. It was meant to be everything I spent all my nights dreaming about, but instead, he gives me a nod just like he had the other girls. Even as my heart beats wildly, and I see George open his mouth to introduce the next girl, I take a step toward Lucas and reach out my hand.

"Pleased to meet you." I try to smile. I try to pretend this moment is the perfect moment. He stares at my hand and my smile wobbles. I pray that he takes it.

A large warm hand encases mine, and my eyes snap up to Lucas's. He tightens his fingers around my hand, igniting pain. I pull back, but he won't release my hand. I try again, and this time, he lets me go. I stumble back but catch my balance.

Giggles erupt from the room and my eyes burn. Why would he do that? I'm staring at him as I sit down in a daze.

"This is Sandra Crowley." George continues as if nothing happened. The only blonde amongst us stands. She sits the minute he nods. She doesn't try, like me, to shake his hand.

"This is Hannah Fitzgerald."

I don't look at Hannah as she stands.

"You can call me Ann." She doesn't sound as happy as she normally does, and when I glance at her, our eyes meet. Her plump red lips are turned down. Hannah sits without looking at him.

"This is Jessie O'Connor."

The beautiful girl with the chocolate skin stands, and then the final girl is introduced.

"This is Bernie Collins."

Bernie rises and quickly sits back down. Lucas doesn't miss a beat. He's out the door, and the silence that's left in the drawing room is suffocating.

# CHAPTER FOUR

## LUCAS

T HE LIGHTS ARE DIM as I enter the basement. Chairs are being set up in a circle. Half of the floor is slated, and the recent coat of fresh gloss is making my shadow stretch out in front of me.

A fresh coat of paint was recently given to the one wall that isn't stone. Yet it still doesn't disguise the smell that I think will forever remind me of Declan.

George is here. He glances at me as I enter the room. He doesn't speak. I was hoping we could avoid this painful conversation. George is old school and wouldn't have liked how I treated the ladies. The servants, who are setting up the room, don't raise their heads as I walk past. They continue to keep setting up the room, yet they stiffen as I pass. With my father not here, I'm now their leader. Not everyone likes it, especially the older members, but they have no power to say otherwise.

George walks to the far side of the room. We don't speak as I make my way to the back of the space. I take the three steps, then climb up onto the podium and push the curtain that hangs on the wall behind it. Beyond the curtain is a room.

Bending down, I open the safe and remove the phone from it. Switching it on, I wait for it to power up. Once it does, I check to see if I have any messages from my father. Nothing. Turning it off, I place it back into the safe. I could keep it on me, but I don't want anyone to know that I still take orders from my father. That kind of knowledge could undermine my authority, and one day, I will lead.

George enters the room, his timing perfect once I have the safe door closed. He must have been waiting outside until he heard the safe close.

I wash my hands slowly—thirty seconds to be exact—letting him wait a bit longer, hoping this conversation won't happen. Turning to George, he's waiting with a red hand towel, which I take to dry my hands with. The cuts sting, but I ignore the pain.

"In life, there are only a few things we must do." His words are low; they're meant for my ears only. No one else is back here with us, but years of being in our family has taught him to be careful. "One of those is respecting tradition."

"I greeted them, didn't I?" I hand the towel back to George. A part of me knows I have the power to end this charade, but I don't.

"You terrified them." George speaks with his back to me, and I hate how old he has gotten. I hate how his fingers twist slightly inward. The wrinkles on his hands remind me of his age.

I exhale and look away from him. "Why do you care, George? You did as my father requested. My reaction doesn't affect you."

He turns around, his smile quick. "This isn't about me, Lucas."

I hate when he refers to me as Lucas, instead of Master Lucas. It means he's serious. It means he cares. In this world, caring is dangerous and foolish.

"This is about you, my boy. You will have to marry one of those ladies, no matter what. So don't make it hard on yourself."

I clap George gently on the arm. "When you retire, I'll stop rebelling," I tell him.

His smile is sad. He can't retire; only my father can release him of his duties, which he won't do. George will leave this house in a wooden casket. The depressing thought has me stepping away from him. George gives a jerk of his chin, like he sees the change in me. He seems to try to stand a bit straighter, but his old body doesn't do much. Yet his eyes hold the youth I often see in him.

"The Lewises collected the body," he informs me while opening a press and taking out large white pillar candles.

I rub my jaw. "I hope you gave our condolences." It's a messy situation.

"Of course, Master Lucas." George places the pillar candles on the top of the wooden cabinet before reaching back in and taking out a box of large matches.

"Has a verdict come back on what caused his death?"

I can still see him convulsing in the chair. He was choking on his own screams. We stood and watched, unable to do much as his body slowly stopped jerking and he came to an abrupt stop. Smoke had filled the glass box, and no one spoke. When the shock wore off, everyone looked to me like I had an answer to what we had witnessed. All I thought about was my father. I would never live it down, even if it was an electrical malfunction. Somehow, he would make it my fault.

"The electrician said the trip wire was removed."

A part of me is surprised that the answer is what I thought. "So if it was removed, someone had to do it?"

George looks at me with weariness in his eyes. "Yes, Master Lucas."

Who? I don't think any of the other members held a grudge against Declan. I leave the small room and cross the podium. The chairs are set up in a circle. The servants are gone.

I walk to the left of the room, where one large glass cube sits. It's the judgment room. It's fair. It's always been the way of our kind. We don't get authorities involved in our troubles. We deal with it ourselves. We've just never had a punishment go so wrong. Someone had to do that before the punishment commenced. Someone who had access to the back rooms, where the switchboard is.

It was meant to be five shocks of electricity. That was Declan's punishment for disobeying my father. No more. No less. But the switch never kicked in. The current never stopped.

George stands beside me now, both of us on the edge of the red rope that stops us from touching the glass cube. It's a warning to everyone not to interfere with the punishment. Even if it is a family member or a lover, it doesn't matter. No one has a right to stop it. In my lifetime, I've never heard of anyone trying to stop a punishment.

"There is something else, Master Lucas."

I focus on George in the glass. I know he's going to start in about picking a wife again. His intentions are good, but he has to know it won't change anything.

"It won't matter, George. I can pick one if I want, but my father will always have the final say. Anyway, I have no interest in a wife."

It looks like he's smiling in the glass, so I glance at him, but he isn't. "It's not the matter of you selecting a wife, Master Lucas. It's the matter in regard to Declan Lewis's remains."

I wait and George faces me. "He seemed to be missing a finger."

I rub my jaw, wanting to ask if he's sure. "Would the force of the electrocution have done it?"

This is something that will bring my father home, and I want him to stay away for as long as possible.

"That was my thought when I first heard, but no. It was severed with a sharp object—postmortem."

"What was the Lewis family told?" My skin prickles at wondering who would do this. It must be someone who had access, and my mind immediately jumps to Henry, with his little wooden box. Is the finger inside it? He hid it when I arrived. Had he been admiring his handiwork?

"They were told it was due to the electricity." George flickers a glance to the left before looking back at me. "They did request the finger, but we can't seem to find it."

"Does my father know what happened?" I cross my arms over my chest. I want to leave right now and find out if the finger is in the box Henry had been playing with. I want it to be him so I can forget about this situation, but another part of me doesn't want it to be my brother, no matter how much I hate him. He has no dealings with this part of the family, so why would he hurt Declan? What punishment would my father give him if he is responsible? Would he turn a blind eye?

My main thought is why would anyone hurt Declan?

"Yes, and he said he's leaving it in your hands to find out who has committed this crime, and to punish them with how you see fit."

I raise a brow at that. I get to pick the punishment? That's a first. It's normally his rules, or should I say *their* rules, which are read from a book passed down from one generation to another.

"Did he give any other instructions?"

George shakes his head.

"Like how creative I can be in delving out my punishment?"

"No, Master Lucas." Worry worms its way around George's words.

I need to find Henry and question him. If it is him, I get to punish him how I see fit. A smile grows slowly across my face, and when I glance at George, his worry has turned to dread.

I step away from the glass cube. "The meeting is at eight tonight, Master Lucas," George calls after me, like I might forget.

"I will be there, George."

I take the concrete steps two at a time, then open the doors that lead to the gardens from the basement. Henry favors a part of the garden. If he were to bury something, it would be there. He isn't stupid enough to still have the box after I saw it in the attic. And now is the time to strike—when he doesn't suspect I'm looking for it. The soil would be freshly dug and easy to spot.

It's warm out, and I pull at the collar of my black shirt, which feels restricting. The black sweatshirt over it isn't helping. I try to ignore my discomfort and move quickly through the garden, all the way to the back where the maze is.

*Henry's domain.*

I'm standing on the edge of what I sometimes think is Henry's mind. I hated this maze as a child. He loved it. Even now, as a fully grown man, I teeter on entering. I know it by heart. I memorized the maze so I could never get trapped in it again.

This is Henry's playground. I just need to take that first step, and I can move quickly. I won't let the memories of being lost flood me. I was just a child. A frightened child at the time.

Tightening my fists, I move, but voices to the left of the maze have me pausing. I leave the mouth of the maze and move carefully along the edge of the hedge.

*Alex.*

He's smiling while looking up at someone. His beige suit is stupid looking and hangs on his thin frame. It's like something from the turn of the century. His blond hair is spiked all over his head, and the smile displays the gap between his large teeth.

A female laughs at whatever he's saying. I can't see who, but I don't let my guard down for one second and take my eyes off Alex. He's the whispers in my brother's ear. To my father, he's a fitting best friend. He's from good stock, so Father would say.

The female's hand appears as she touches Alex's arm. A flash of emerald green. When she comes into view and sees me, her smile disappears. Alex's face pales.

I grin. This is perfect.

# CHAPTER FIVE

## ELLA

After Lucas leaves the drawing room, the silence stretches, and I'm fumbling with my hands. My mind is jumping from the picture I had painted of him to what I got. I glance at the other girls, who don't say anything.

"Does anyone have any questions?" George asks, grabbing our attention. Questions? Did he not just witness what we all went through?

"Yes." I stumble across the word, swallowing. I peek at Hannah, feeling her eyes on me. Her cheeks are flushed, and I wonder if I have that same lost look in my eyes that she does.

I stretch out my sore hand again. Did he mean to squeeze it so tightly? He couldn't have hurt me intentionally. I had done nothing wrong.

"You have a question, Ella?" George prods gently.

The fluttering in my stomach won't settle, and the room is starting to feel stifling. "May I get some fresh air in the garden?"

George nods. "Of course." George looks over the rest of the girls. "Does anyone else have a question?" His voice holds a note of hope that no one does, and he gets lucky. Everyone remains silent, and he excuses himself from the room.

I straighten my dress as I stand. My hands flutter across the soft material.

"Would you like some company?"

*Yes. Company sounds wonderful.* "No. Thank you."

Hannah's eyes widen like I've hurt her. Before I feel any more guilt, I leave the room and make my way outside to the gardens I saw from my window. I want to find the maze. I want to get lost, and maybe like Alice, I can fall down a rabbit hole. Maybe I already have. This isn't how it was meant to be. My Prince Charming is mean and cruel, and I have nothing to fight for. My chest tightens at the thought.

The day is warm outside as I pass several flowerbeds of beautiful plants. The colors are a little bit of salve to my soul. I find my chest loosening a bit the deeper I walk into the garden.

I flex my fingers again and glance down at my hand. His was so large and warm around mine. He looked like he was enjoying it, but my heart refuses to believe that he would want to hurt me, or anyone for that matter. What kind of person does that make him?

What would my mother think if I told her how he treated me?

"Hello."

I have been so consumed with my thoughts that I hadn't noticed a man sitting on a brown bench amongst the flowers.

"Hello," I say to him. Once again, I question if I have fallen down a rabbit hole. He looks eccentric. I've never seen anyone like him before. A beige top hat is beside him, and he removes it from the bench.

"A penny for your thoughts." He taps the seat for me to join him.

My mother said I'm not allowed to make friends with the girls, but she never said anything about other people here. Right now, having company would be nice. After stepping over the flowers, I sit down beside him. He's smiling, revealing a large gap between his front teeth.

"Only a penny?" I ask and his smile widens.

"Name your price."

I exhale on a smile. "Tell me a joke."

"Jokes aren't my forte, but for the beautiful lady in green, I will try." He gives me a wink, and I smile again.

"What's brown and sticky?" he asks.

I don't like the sound of that. "Clay?"

He shakes his head. "A stick."

"A stick," I repeat.

His laughter is musical. "I told you I was bad. Let me try again." He sits and taps his chin with a long finger. "Ah, I got one. This will make you laugh."

I raise both eyebrows.

"What do you call bears with no ears?"

"A deaf bear?" That sounds silly. "An earless bear?" That sounds even worse.

He laughs again. "*B*. Take the ear off the bear, and you get *B*."

"Okay, you are officially the worst at telling jokes."

"So are you going to tell me your thoughts?"

I don't know this man, so the answer is no. But I won't be rude.

"Yes, I'm looking for the maze."

He picks up his hat and places it on his head. "I will lead the way." As he rises, he extends his hand and helps me up. A lump forms in my throat. He's what I thought Lucas would be. Charming.

"Thank you," I say once I'm standing. He holds his hat as he walks. The beige tailcoat is velvet and way too large for his frame, but when he glances at me and smiles, I find it all enchanting.

"My name is Alex."

"Ella," I offer as we walk.

"It suits you, Ella. Do you know what your name means?"

I shake my head.

"Ella means light, or beautiful fairy woman." We stop.

I laugh. "You're making that up."

He smiles. "No. It's the truth."

A large shadow casts across us, and my heart stills as Lucas stands in front of us. As he glares at Alex, a slow, devilish grin forms on his lips.

"What have we got here?" His question is directed at Alex. He's barely given me a second glance, and I don't want to be in his company.

"Lucas." Alex's voice has hardened, and I take a peek up at him. The distaste for Lucas is evident on his face.

"Master Lucas." Lucas says the correction with a tilt of his chin.

Lucas, who is dressed all in black, looks like a fallen angel. The light hits him perfectly, emphasizing all his angles, making him look harsh, yet beautiful. I don't want to admire him. I want to say goodbye to Alex, but I don't want to draw any more attention to myself. Maybe I will see him again in the gardens. I hope so. He is a bit of light in this dark place.

I take a soft step forward, then two. I'm nearly past Lucas when he reaches out. His large hand wraps around my wrist. I freeze at his touch, my eyes flickering to his dark ones, which are pinning me in place.

"I never said you could leave."

I pull away from his touch, but I don't leave.

"Master Lucas. I was just speaking to Ella. She hasn't done anything wrong."

Wrong? What's being implied?

"Ella." Lucas tries my name out, and a shiver weaves its way through my body.

"I have no idea what you two were doing out here. Rules are rules, Alex."

Alex takes an angry step toward Lucas. He releases his hat easily, and it falls to the ground. "You know damn well nothing has gone on here, so don't you dare accuse me of touching her."

My cheeks burn. I'm at a loss for words.

"Your word means nothing to me. If I say you touched her, then you touched her." Lucas raises his chin.

My skin feels hot and sticky. I glance at Alex, but he hasn't looked away from Lucas.

"You've always had it out for me," Alex says.

Lucas takes a step toward Alex. "How will I punish you for your crime?"

I don't know what passes between these two, but this is ridiculous. What he's accusing him of, and me for that matter, is outrageous. He might be Master Lucas Andrew O'Faolain the third, but I still have my integrity to protect. I take a step toward Lucas. Alex flickers me a worried glance.

"I was out looking for the maze and—"

"Stop speaking." Lucas cuts me with a lethal stare, and my heart beats against my chest.

"It's okay, Ella." Alex speaks gently to me before looking back at Lucas. "Do your best." He grins and my heart hurts for him. I don't know either of them, but what I can see is that Lucas will do his best, and he will hurt Alex. Alex is one of those people for whom life didn't give a chance to. I hate the injustice of standing here while Lucas speaks down to him.

"Since my father isn't here, I'm allowed to pick the punishment. So what punishment fits this crime?" Lucas walks around Alex, intimidating him.

Alex surprises me when he laughs.

"Do you find something amusing?" Lucas's words are angry, and I want to tell Alex to stop smiling. I glance around the garden to see if anyone else is near, but we're alone.

"Henry was right about you. You're afraid of what you can't control."

Alex hits the ground hard as Lucas shoves him to his knees. The action is rough, but Lucas looks calmly down at Alex. My heart has picked a different beat. Black spots dance around the edge of my vision.

"I control everything." Lucas kneels beside Alex. "I control Henry. I control you. I control this situation."

Alex's face is red with embarrassment and anger. I feel terrible standing here doing nothing. My chest aches.

Alex is staring at his hand on the ground, and I'm waiting for the world to shatter. It feels so tense when he looks back up at Lucas and smiles.

"I see you still have your strings. Daddy still controls you."

A startled scream tears from my lips as Lucas hits Alex in the mouth. The red liquid dribbles from his lips, and I'm moving. I know I shouldn't.

I don't care when the ground tears at my bare knees. I grab Lucas's closed fist in hopes of stopping him from hitting Alex again. It works for a moment. I want to smile in triumph, until my eyes travel from Lucas's fist all the way up to his eyes.

I swallow. But I've come this far; I'm not backing down. "He has done nothing wrong," I say. My voice betrays me by shaking.

"You will regret that." He removes his large fist from my hand and rises easily. I'm stumbling off my knees to my feet.

"What?"

His hand tightens around my upper arm, and I'm being pulled toward the house.

"Let me go." Panic has me yanking away from his touch, but he only tightens his grip on me.

"You're hurting me." I glance back at Alex, who's standing now, his hat back in his hand. I'm wondering why he isn't following us. Why he's not coming to my aid, like I came to his. Instead, he gives me a wave.

*What the hell?*

"Lucas, let me go now."

He releases me, and I feel a sense of triumph for the second time, only to have it demolished as he turns to me.

"It's Master Lucas. We are here now."

When he releases me from his stare, I look up at the house, feeling confused.

I follow him in with a sense of trepidation in every step I take. I try to look back at the gardens but can't see them from this angle.

I'm not sure what just happened. Why Alex isn't trying to fight in my corner. Maybe he's gone to get help.

Mark, who brought me into the house, greets me with a nod as Lucas marches me into a library. I glance around, but it's short-lived as Lucas clears his throat. The moment our eyes meet, he speaks.

"I want her tested again."

Mark's head snaps up to mine, confusion marring his face. I'm as confused as he is. I want to ask what he means, but his glare has me rooted to the spot.

"Tested? Master Lucas."

Lucas releases a breath. "Yes, Mark. Tested. I found her in the gardens with Alex. So I would like her tested again."

Mortification burns me. "I did nothing." My bravery is born from the shame of this moment.

Lucas takes a step toward me, towering above me. "If you did nothing, then you won't mind being tested."

The test was horrible and uncomfortable. My stomach twists painfully. If it will stop this charade.

"Fine," I bark too loudly.

"You keep speaking out of turn. So I will be present, to make sure it's done."

My knees wobble. I keep my mouth closed. He's punishing me for speaking. If I answer again, how much further would he go? Anger burns my skin, and I can feel the heat travel across my chest and along my neck. When I don't say anything, Lucas smiles.

"You are learning." He steps out of the room, and my eyes meet Mark's, but he isn't going to help me. No one is.

# CHAPTER SIX

## LUCAS

I GLANCE AT ELLA in the rearview mirror. She's staring out the window, her cheeks still red. She has quite the temper. I refocus on the road as I drive us to the clinic. I glance at Ella again; this time our eyes clash. Emerald green eyes reflect her anger—they're wide and focused. She doesn't look away from me, her chin held high in defiance. I clench the steering wheel in my hands and look back to the road. No one has ever defied me so much. I want to put out the fire that burns too brightly inside her. She is young and naïve and doesn't seem to know her place.

"If you keep looking at me like that, Ella, I'll take it as an invitation." I glance at her in the mirror. Her eyes widen even further, her mouth forms an *O*, and her chest rises and falls quicker.

"It's not an invitation."

I look away before I grin at her blatant disregard for my authority. She grows angrier.

"That temper of yours is going to get you into trouble."

She's back to staring out the window.

We arrive at the clinic. They have a room set up and are waiting for us.

Doctor Paige greets us at the door. "Mr. O'Faolain, Right in here."

I glance at Ella, who's standing rod straight.

"Ladies first," I offer with an outstretched hand. For a moment, she looks like she might attack me as she inhales a sharp breath. She snaps her head forward and marches into the room. Her shoulders slump forward as I close the door behind us. She glances over her shoulder and when her eyes meet mine, some of that fire is gone. Her eyes darken as she looks away.

Doctor Paige glances at me over the rim of his thick glasses. "Are you staying for the examination, Mr. O'Faolain?" The question is delivered with a sense of disbelief.

"Yes. Proceed." I flick a hand at Ella, and Doctor Paige looks at her, his eyes softening around the edges.

"Okay, Ella, you want to pop up on the bed?"

Her whole body is screaming *no*. I lean against the wall. She glances at me, and I hope she's starting to understand her place in this situation. I'm not leaving.

Her chest is flushed as she stares at me, fighting some internal battle. One I will squash for her.

"I don't have all day."

That seems to settle her internal debate. Whatever she wanted to say is gone as she climbs up on the bed. I do notice her tightened fists.

"You need to relax." Doctor Paige's voice is gentle, and he smiles at her. I can see Ella's body visibly relaxing.

"You need to do your job, Doctor Paige. I have other things to do today." I bite the words out, and both of them stiffen.

No one speaks and as Doctor Paige gets ready to do his examination, I focus on the photos on his desk. His wife and three kids are smiling up at the camera, which no doubt, he's behind. Ella exhales loudly.

"It will be uncomfortable for a few more minutes," Doctor Paige tells her.

"That's okay. I remember." She sounds so vulnerable. Like she didn't back herself into this corner. Like she didn't put herself in front of me and ask for my attention.

I grit my teeth. Well, she has my attention now whether she wants it or not. I keep focusing on everything but Ella. A part of me can't take that bit of privacy away from her. Me being in the room is a large enough statement.

A calendar on the wall has the seventh of April circled in pink marker. I wonder if it's a birthday. Maybe one of his smiling daughters did it.

Ella hisses again.

"We're nearly finished." Doctor Paige is using that soft voice again, trying to reassure Ella.

"Okay. All done. Just lie there for a few minutes."

I wait until Doctor Paige leaves Ella before glancing at her. She's staring at the ceiling, her clothes back in place, her legs firmly closed. She's beautiful. Her face is youthful and innocent—until she looks at me.

I grin. Her eyes show everything. Right now, they shine with hate, and I'm happy to see it. I push off the wall and walk to her. With each step, I get closer, and I can see her body tense, but she doesn't look away from me.

"I hope your results are the same as before," I warn, knowing they are.

Her jaw clenches, and I wonder again where this fire comes from in her. How do I put it out? What fuels it?

*Fascinating.*

I lean in closer and watch her pulse flicker in her neck. "Your eyes give away what you feel, Ella."

Her pulse jumps and her eyes flutter closed, cutting me off from those stunning green eyes.

I don't move away. She smells of soap.

"She is still a virgin, Mr. O'Faolain."

Doctor Paige stands behind me, and I lean out from Ella. Her eyes snap up to me, and she looks smug with her results.

"I know," I answer, watching her eyes widen. The anger returns, and I know I've driven my point home.

Once again, Ella doesn't speak as I drive us back to the house. Even when I glance at her in the rearview mirror, she doesn't look up.

When we arrive into the house, three of the other girls are lounging in the hall. No doubt, they saw us arrive, but now they're pretending they're having a chat in the hall. All eyes are on me, a mix of lust and fear. It's what I'm used to.

When I look at Ella, she stares at me with her head held high.

So defiant.

The girls are waiting and watching to see what will happen. I could embarrass her.

I lean in and lower my voice but make sure it's loud enough so the other girls can hear.

"I enjoyed myself. I hope you did too." I brush my lips against her cheek, and when I lean out, I'm expecting anger to burn in her eyes. Instead, they swim in a mist that she's fighting not to let out.

"Can I go to my room?" She's holding back the emotions that I'm sure will spill within the next second.

I could let her cry here in front of everyone. The girls are still watching; their tongues will soon be wagging.

I nod my head, and she's past me in a blur of green. I take a quick look as she flees up the stairs. I stare at the other three, who still stand in the hall.

One of them starts to smile at me. I walk past the blonde and make my way outside. I still need to check the maze.

When I enter the garden, I don't encounter anyone. I still stall at the mouth of the maze. My fingers sizzle, and I tighten my fists. Once I take my first step, that fear that wants to grow disappears. I know this maze. I focus on the ground as I walk, looking for traces of turned soil. I find nothing. Time passes quickly in the maze, and when I emerge, the skies have darkened.

I check my watch to find it's close to eight. I need to get ready for the meeting.

There are only four of us today. All are seated and talking. When I enter, the chatter ceases.

I take the seat, leaving one empty on either side of me.

Aine is the first to greet me, as usual. "Master Lucas." Her high cheekbones and small chin have had too much work. At first it's hard to think why she looks so formidable. The more you take her in, the more work you see. Her nose looks thinner today. It could be more work or a trick of the light.

"Aine." Her white shirt has more ruffles on it than I can count.

"Brendan, Cathal, Sean." I welcome each member. They are all a lot older than me. Cathal and Brendan don't like that I'm in charge, but Sean doesn't seem to mind.

"What happened to Declan?" Brendan speaks with pursed lips.

I don't answer.

"Master Lucas," he adds begrudgingly.

"We are still looking into the cause of his death, but I'm sure you have all heard that he lost a finger during the electrocution." I know father won't approve of me lying to the members, but to me, any of them could be guilty. I need to be careful, yet convincing with my words.

"The moment I find out more, I will promptly let you know."

"Debbie was devastated." Aine holds a manicured hand to her chest.

"Of course she was." Brendan's sarcastic remark is delivered with a smirk. The light bounces off his bald head, distracting me. "Her husband was electrocuted to death. She was hardly happy."

"How do we know it wasn't on purpose, Master Lucas?" Sean speaks, while Aine and Brendan glare at each other.

"We don't." Now all eyes are on me.

"So it's best for everyone to be careful." I make sure I direct this to Cathal and Brendan.

There's a smile in Brendan's eyes, like he knows something I don't. It makes me nervous. He's a clever man, and as much as I loathe him, I still need to be careful around him.

"Congratulations on your upcoming wedding, Master Lucas." Aine speaks up, a clear way of trying to release some of the tension from the room. Only, my upcoming wedding isn't a topic I want to discuss.

"Thank you, Aine."

"My son is also in his selection process, Master Lucas."

"I hope he finds what he's looking for."

There's a moment of confusion from the other members, and it reminds me how new I am to this.

"The selection for him is perfect," Sean offers with a smile. "I have no doubt any of them will make a stunning bride, Master Lucas."

I wonder what my father would have said if he was speaking about me.

"The reason we called the meeting, Master Lucas, is because a local has been repeatedly striking his wife." Brendan folds his arms across his chest.

"Bring him in." That's what's meant to be done. His punishment will be in the glass box.

"Are you sure that's wise, Master Lucas?" Brendan is questioning my authority, and I grit my teeth.

I'm ready to dismiss his question, but once again, I'm all too aware of how clever he is, and also how the other members seem to lean toward him, like he should lead.

"It's just, with what happened with Declan, I'm sure we don't want a repeat."

"I completely agree, Brendan."

He raises both eyebrows in surprise.

"I think we will have to add a new chapter in our book."

Confusion mars their faces. It's time we change our ways. Shocking people is such a barbaric way to discipline.

I look to Aine. "What do you think is a fitting punishment for a man who strikes his wife?"

Aine's painted lips stretch out, and it makes me think of the joker. "Cut his dick off."

I think we all tighten our legs, but I grin. I have to hand it to Aine for her boldness.

"Master Lucas." She dips her head, still smiling.

"Outrageous." Cathal speaks up for the first time, staring at Aine. "The chair has always worked, so I don't see why we would stop using it." He speaks to Aine and not me. It's another blatant disregard for my authority. I know Brendan is watching me, enjoying my discomfort far too much.

I stand up. "Leave it with me, and I'll let you all know what I decide." I meet each of their eyes, and none of them answer me back, but all rise as I leave the room.

I had no idea of what my father would say to me changing the rules they have followed for generations, but if I am to lead one day, things have to change.

# CHAPTER SEVEN

## ELLA

I LEAN AGAINST MY closed bedroom door. My heart threatens to rip through my chest. My fingers touch my cheek where he kissed me. His lips were surprisingly soft. I tighten my eyes as a knock vibrates through my back.

"Ella, it's Hannah."

Another knock has me pushing away from the door. I don't have a lock on it, and she knows I'm here. Taking a deep breath, I open the door, but don't let her in.

"Yes, Hannah."

She tilts her head with furrowed brows. "Are you okay?"

I'm staring at her wide-eyed, terrified if I blink or speak, I'll cry. I can't show weakness.

"I'm rather tired. I'm going to bed." I hold the door, not ready to close it.

"Okay." She nods her head with pursed lips, her eyes looking troubled. "I'm here if you need to talk." She smiles softly. "We are sisters now." She sounds so sincere.

Sisters. God, it sounds so nice.

"Good night." I close the door and don't let go of the handle until I can hear her receding footsteps.

I take a step away from the door but stare at it. I don't know what I want. To scream or cry. How did this go so wrong? Should I ring my mother? Do I want to leave?

I'm not one to admit defeat, but this isn't what I signed up for. A knock to my door has me closing my eyes again.

She isn't going to give up. I open the door, but I'm surprised to see Mark standing in my doorway.

"May I come in?"

"No," I say immediately. I can only imagine the rumors that would spread if anyone saw him come into my room. I don't want to think about what Lucas would do.

He doesn't seem put out by my response. "Okay, I will make it quick. I believe you were found with Alex today."

I gape at him, wondering where this is going. I want to tell him I already received my punishment.

"You should keep away from all males."

I force a smile. "Great. Does that include Lucas?"

His nostrils flair. "It's *Master* Lucas, and of course not."

My cheeks burn. I need to control my mouth. What is wrong with me? "I apologize. Of course, I didn't really mean Master Lucas, but Alex was in the garden, and we just said hello to each other."

"Take the warning, Ella," he says before giving me a curt nod and closing the door. I'm left feeling confused and staring at the door again.

\*\*\*

Sometimes the morning brings more clarity, and I often wake up with a new lease on life. Not this morning. Everything feels dimmer.

I woke up hoping I would be in my own bed, not in this nightmare. I want to return to the days I spent blissfully daydreaming about Lucas.

I throw the covers off me and climb out of bed. The soft pink nightdress is cool against my hot skin. There's a lot of commotion outside my room. Opening the door, I see three girls chattering. They turn to me, and all talk ceases.

Sandra smiles at me, but it doesn't reach her eyes. Her blonde hair is in a messy bun, but she still looks stunning. Her blue eyes narrow at me.

"I hear you stole the first date with Master Lucas."

First date? Is that the lie he spread? I have no idea what to say.

The tallest girl steps forward. *Vicky*, I remember now. The one who declared she was going to sleep with him first.

"Did you do it with him? You know, have sex?"

"Absolutely not," I grind out.

She smirks. "I know we can't go the whole way, but we can do other things." She winks.

I shiver.

The thoughts of Lucas putting his hands on me sends a shiver racing throughout my body. I hate how my skin burns.

"Look, she's going red," Vicky points at me like I'm a zoo exhibit.

"Leave her alone." Jessie looks like she stepped out of a magazine promoting morning wear.

"I better get dressed." I leave them knowing I shouldn't be speaking to any of them anyway.

As I step into the shower, I think that maybe having friends will be allowed now, since I'm no longer fighting for Master Lucas's hand. Maybe once I explain to my mother what a brute he is, she'll understand.

I finally get that feeling as I step out of the shower—a new lease on life. A new purpose.

Ninety percent of my clothes are dresses, which I had thought enchanting, but now they all look stupid, like a girl playing dress-up. My mother forbids trousers, so I pick up a long black full-length skirt and a green shirt. "The same color as your eyes." I mimic my mother's voice as I put it on.

God, I couldn't wait to get away from her. Guilt churns in my stomach. Now, all I want is to hear her voice. I swallow as I let my black hair fall down my back. Minimal makeup and I'm ready to go downstairs.

I check to make sure my room is tidy. I know we have maids to clean our rooms, but at home, my mother always made me keep my space clean. She always told me no matter what, never leave the house without making your bed.

My mother swore it helped your brain function better for the day and also taught you self-discipline.

My brain obviously isn't running on full steam yet. I didn't notice Lucas standing outside my room.

"How did you sleep?" My heart gallops and I turn, gawking at him like he just stepped out of the wall.

He takes a step toward me, and I'm searching the landing for the other girls, but the area is empty.

I'm flustered as I stare at him. He is dangerously gorgeous. Once again, he wears all black, and with inky hair and dark eyes, I know I should run. I lock my knees and raise my chin, hoping my fear isn't showing.

"Fantastic," I lie.

He smirks and steps closer. I want to run, but I force myself to hold still.

"You look nervous." He comes closer now, and I keep my hands clenched behind my back so he can't see the tremble in them.

"No," I say quickly.

His smirk widens. "Now, now, Ella, you can't lie. I told you that already." He's reached me now, and I flinch as he takes my chin in his hand. "Your eyes tell me what you feel."

*Oh God.* I tighten my legs so I don't fall down.

"Good." I fake a smile and hope he can read my eyes now as I force as much hate into them as I can.

His laughter has me flinching again. My heart races faster.

"Can I go?" I bite out each word.

His smile dies on his face, and my stomach hollows as he releases my chin.

I've angered him; his eyes grow darker. "You need to remember who you're speaking to."

I grit my teeth. "Yes, Master Lucas."

His smirk is back. "That wasn't so hard, was it?"

My heart is in my throat as I stare at him. "No, Master Lucas." I hope the sarcasm doesn't fill my words.

"Now you're overdoing it, Ella." His smirk is still present, so I haven't pissed him off completely.

Footsteps have me looking away from Lucas and toward someone who looks just like him. I quickly look back to Lucas to see his jaw clenched. Turning back to the one who looks just like Lucas, I can't stop staring. The difference is this one has glasses and a smaller frame, but he is no doubt related to Lucas. He glares at Lucas as he quickly moves down the stairs. Lucas moves past me swiftly and follows, leaving me feeling weak.

It takes me another few moments before I'm able to go downstairs. All the girls are sitting at a large dining table. It runs the full length of the room. They're all seated at the end, which is positioned half in a conservatory that captures all the sun that shines today. The room smells of maple syrup and pancakes. I'm the last one to arrive and feel anxious as I approach the table. Hannah looks up and smiles at me. She's wearing a red top the same color as her hair. It makes her stand out.

"I saved you a seat." She pats the seat beside her and I hesitate.

I notice Sandra is watching me, her eyes calculating. I force a smile and sit down beside Hannah. "Thank you, Hannah."

Her smile widens, her white teeth a flash against her plump red lips.

"What are friends for, Ella, who isn't Bella?" She chews on her lips like she can't contain her excitement.

Once I'm seated, I don't get a menu. One of the servers places a full plate of pancakes covered in icing and strawberries in front of me.

"Tea or coffee?"

"Tea, please." I glance at the server over my shoulder, and she nods.

"So Ella, you have been keeping very tight-lipped about your date with Master Lucas."

I cut my pancake before looking up at Sandra. "It wasn't a date."

"Oh, I heard it was." Vicky is seated beside Sandra. Two peas in a pod.

"You heard wrong, Vicky."

I return to my food.

"I was there with Sandra and Mary when you arrived back from your date. I saw him kiss you on the cheek." Bernie speaks from the end of the table. I have to lean in to see her. Mary is bobbing her head in agreement.

I tighten my legs as I think about what I had been doing. Something outside the conservatory catches my eye. It's Alex, walking along the window. He's wearing another top hat. This one is purple, the same as his suit. He looks just like the character from the old *Charlie and the Chocolate Factory*. He has a black stick with a gold ball on top. He twirls the stick in his hands.

Alex looks up. I don't know why—he can't possibly know I'm looking at him—but he smiles, his eyes meeting mine. I don't return his smile. I still don't understand why he didn't do anything yesterday.

Hannah's elbow digs into my side, and when I look away from Alex and to her, she widens her eyes. "Are you okay?"

I glance at all the girls who are watching me. Like there's something wrong with me.

"Yes." I cut the pancake with no intention of eating it, my appetite gone.

"You look so pale." Hannah moves her head closer to me. Her worry seems genuine. But it's hard to know in this place. A lump forms in my throat. It's all too much.

"Excuse me." I stand up after excusing myself and make my way across the room, feeling all eyes on me.

"She's just an attention seeker." Vicky's voice follows me, and I walk faster with my head down, just wanting to be away from them. I want to be away from this place.

Someone clears their throat ahead of me and I stop, nearly walking into Mark.

"If you could please take your seat, Miss O'Leary."

Now it's Miss O'Leary. I'm staring at Mark, just asking him for a break without asking.

"Miss O'Leary. Take a seat." He rewords his sentence, like I might understand it better.

I turn on my heel and make my way back to the table. I try not to look at Vicky. I can feel her joy at me being told to go back. I sit down and once I do, Mark addresses us all.

"I have some fantastic news. The first ball will be held tonight."

A squeal of excitement sounds around the table.

"Game on, girls." Vicky grins at everyone, like she has it in the bag.

I give a very unladylike snort and get everyone's attention again.

"You think he's yours?" Vicky challenges me.

I've had enough. Everything in me tightens and grinds to a halt. I snap. I can feel the burn traveling along my chest and up my neck. "He's all yours. Trust me, I don't want him." My words come out louder than I intended.

I glance at Hannah, who looks as white as a ghost. Now that I think about it, all the girls do. The silence in the room could only mean one thing. I turn slowly to where everyone's eyes keep flickering and meet a very dark pair of breathtaking eyes.

Lucas is staring at me.

# CHAPTER EIGHT

## LUCAS

I soak up Ella's fear. I don't blink as she swallows. Her mouth opens and closes. It's a perfect mouth—pouty, kissable.

When her lids flutter closed, cutting me off from her wide eyes, I glance at the other girls. As my eyes find each of them, they seem to sink back further into their chairs. Turning on my heel, I walk out of the room at a leisurely pace, grappling for control of my emotions.

No one has ever refused me. That's what I do best—shut people down Ella's words were filled with a venom I'm not used to. People may think bad things, but to announce them out so brazenly isn't very nice at all.

"Close the door." A cold chill runs down my spine at my father's words. I meet his dark eyes briefly before closing the study door behind me.

I try to reel in my confusion and fear at his arrival. "I wasn't aware you would be home so soon. If I had known..." I trail off and let him fill in the blanks. I would have welcomed you. I would have tried harder to clean up the mess with Declan. I would have run a fucking mile.

"You left me no choice." My father leans against my desk, his eyes darting from the mail on my desk to me.

"Declan was killed by someone we know and his finger cut off. You didn't think I needed to know that."

I finally let the air trickle back into my body, like it's defrosting. I take a step toward my desk. "Clearly, I didn't need to tell you since you already know."

His finger jabs the envelopes. "I wanted to hear it from you." My father doesn't raise his voice. He doesn't need to.

"Yes, sir." I grab for more control over my emotions and sit down in my desk chair.

He stares at me. I'm waiting for him to pounce. He pushes off my desk and moves around my study like he hasn't stood in it a million times. It was his when he was a young man.

"Tell me your thoughts."

With him not looking at me, I can finally gather my thoughts. I wasn't going to point out that I thought Henry did it. He would brush it off. I don't think it's love he has for Henry. It's hard to explain. He is like a pet you keep hidden but secretly like it.

"It must be a member."

He takes a snap look at me before turning back to the bookcase. "Which one?"

"Aine," I state.

His eyes look murky as he stares at me, and I have no idea what he's thinking.

He nods his head. "Female, small, friendly. No one would suspect her."

"But why?" He stops now and faces me.

"I don't know," I answer honestly. It isn't Áinc. It didn't make sense to me.

"Thirty years ago, we had a member die." He feeds this knowledge to me with his back turned once again.

"The same way?"

"Yes." My father folds his arms across his chest. His black suit makes him look formidable. He isn't someone you disobey. That's why he leads all of us.

"Did you find out who was responsible?"

I can see the trouble rising to the surface in his murky eyes. "No."

I raise both eyebrows and sit forward. "You think the person that did this also killed thirty years ago?"

If that's the case, it rules out Henry.

"We will have to look into it more."

"Who was the member who died?"

My father stares at me longer than necessary. "Why?"

"There might be a connection."

"There isn't." His answer is abrupt, but I know better than to ask any more questions.

"I hear you're changing the way our punishment system works."

I swear I see a smile in his eyes. The only person who could be feeding him information is Brendan. "I think it's time for a change," I say carefully.

My father stares at me again before unfolding his arms. "I don't want anyone to know I'm back."

I nod.

"Meet me in the sheds. I want to show you something." My father turns, and I'm waiting for him to leave through the door, only he pushes in a panel along the wall.

A breeze sweeps in as a secret door I was unaware of opens. He walks through it without looking back at me.

I leave the study. Two of the girls are in the hall, and they don't giggle when they see me. They're wary and that's good.

The gravel crunches under my shoes as I walk out back to the sheds. The shed is used mostly for storage of my father's collection of vintage cars. It's always been off limits, but something tells me I'm about to find out the real reason I was never allowed in without my father's permission.

I open the small door in the bigger one on the shed. I step in and search for my father, waiting for someone to scream at me. I spot him at the back of the shed. His eyes clash with mine.

Closing the door behind me, I don't speak. I walk forward, but before I reach him, he walks off to the left and descends down a set of concrete steps. I follow him and when my father glances back at me, there is a dark glint in his eyes.

I have so many questions, but I wisely keep them to myself as we stand in a corridor. A large wooden door to our left is our destination. My father opens the door, and I pause while swallowing around a lump that forms in my throat.

"Come in." The command has me passing the threshold as my father closes the door behind me.

Once again, I don't ask any questions. A man is strung up by his hands. His naked torso is painted in splashes of purple and black. My father puts a pair of leather gloves on. The man's wild eyes flicker from me and my father. He starts to shout only to have his words jumbled from the cloth in his mouth.

"This may seem barbaric to you, but sometimes it takes this." He points at the man who tries to push his swinging body closer to my father. His arms look extremely long, like they might be dislocated. "To make a point," he finishes.

My stomach tightens. My father turns away from me and hits the man repeatedly in the ribs. The man cries out in pain. When my father stops, he's breathless.

"Do you remember when you were a child and your dog died?" A cruel smile crosses my father's face. How could I forget?

"Yes." I speak my first word. The man whimpers in pain, but I focus on my father.

"You wouldn't stop crying. It was... irritating."

I tighten my fists, wanting to drive them into his face. How could I forget that day? I had let my guard down, allowed my emotions to spill over, only to have him laugh at me.

"What did I tell you that day?"

"To turn it off."

He nods like a proud father. "Exactly. Now turn it off and hit him." He points at the man who still whimpers in pain.

I've never disobeyed my father before. I glance at him. "I've got a punching bag in the house," I answer.

The look in my father's eyes is murderous as he takes a step toward me.

"Turn it off."

"I can't."

"You're weak." The taunt comes with another cruel smile. "He's a drug dealer, infecting people, tearing down our youth. Does he not deserve to die?"

I'm picturing my emotions like he taught me—a swirl of colors for each feeling. I grab them all but leave red and black swirling inside me. Taking the rest, I push them into a box and lock it.

Hate and Anger fill me up.

Anger trickles into my veins, and I clench my fists. I take a step toward the man, and he tries to swing away but like my punching bag, he will swing forward.

I don't hold back.

\*\*\*

Under the instruction of my father, I wear gloves to the ball. I tore my knuckles nearly down to the bone. They ache, but I use the pain as a crutch to carry me through tonight.

As I enter the room full of people, I know all the ladies will be to my right. My eyes immediately seek out Ella. She is wearing another emerald dress, only this one is to the floor; it catches her in all the right places. Wide, wild eyes stare back at me, and I give her a cold smile. With her black hair swept back off her face, she can't hide from me.

I see her heavy inhale as I release her from my stare. When I become the real Master, this tradition will be banished. It's not just the ladies here tonight; members of the community and their families are here, too. The room is full, but I don't seek anyone else out.

I sit in a chair like an imposter. I hate it. I hate the clothes I wear. I stretch my hands and hiss as the pain travels up my arms.

Mark walks to me. "Master Lucas, shall we commence?"

I nod at him and grind my teeth in irritation. I want this over with now.

Each girl presents herself in front of me, giving her name. I know I'm meant to say something nice about them, but I can't find one thing to say about all the pretty things that are dangled in front of me.

They all curtsy and smile sweetly, and when I don't return their smiles, Mark hurries on to the next one.

Ella is presented and she refuses to meet my eye. Her curtsy is the shortest one, like she'd rather spit on me. I tighten my fingers around the claw of the chair. Pain races up my arm.

"Look at me."

Her eyes snap to me, and her pulse pounds in her neck. I rise from the chair, knowing we've captured the room. Making slow precise steps to Ella, I stop only a foot from her. Mark looks at me wearily.

"I'm starting to think you like me, Ella." She bristles at my words. I close the distance between us and speak low, just for her.

"You say you don't want me, yet at every chance, you crave my attention."

"What are you talking about?" Her eyes grow wider, and I see that temper rising.

"Of course I'll dance with you," I speak loudly and while she's in a moment of confusion, I take her hand and lead her to the floor. I don't know why I'm doing this.

Pulling her close to my body, she releases a hard breath, her body flush with mine. Her small hand in mine looks tiny, and I think of how easy it would be to crush it. Another voice in my head tells me not to hurt her. She's stiff and I tighten my hold on her waist. She tenses. Her hand barely touches my shoulder.

Now that I have her in my hands, I don't know what to say. Striking green eyes flicker up to me, and I find my gaze trailing down to her lips. The box with my emotions in it is opening. I slam it shut and tighten my hand on hers—not tightly enough to hurt her but to hurt me.

"I would like to ask permission to go home."

I look down at her now. "Did someone die?" What could her reason be?

With furrowed brows, she looks confused, before she shakes her head. "No. I would just like a pardon. Please."

Now it's my turn to be confused. "A pardon from what?"

She raises her head even higher, but I see the fear trickle into her eyes. I stop dancing but don't release her.

"A pardon from marrying you."

# CHAPTER NINE

## ELLA

H IS EYES HOLD EMPTINESS like I've never seen before. He's beautiful and terrifying all at once. I'm on a tightrope as he stares at me, and I'm not sure if I'll fall and hit the ground hard. I want to take my words back; I want to grab them and shove them down my throat. I don't know how long we stand in that frozen state while he radiates pure anger, and my own fear grows with each second.

"No." His hands tighten on me, and his face tenses as he continues dancing, breaking us from our frozen stance only to enter a more dangerous phase. His anger is tightening around my throat.

"There are six others," I challenge, keeping my voice low. I hate how my voice shakes, betraying me. He works a muscle in his jaw before releasing a hard sigh. His eyes snap to mine, and my heart beats wildly in my chest. All my bravery withers away with the look he gives me.

I drop my gaze. The dance feels so long. I'm aware of everywhere our bodies touch; I'm aware of his fisted hand on my hip. His hold on my hand has loosened. My chest aches and I close my eyes, allowing him to lead me around the room.

My treacherous body loves the feel of him so close. His breath brushes my face, and I slowly raise my lashes to find him looking at me. The dance stops and he releases me like I've burned him. I curtsy, but he turns his back on me and walks away. The dismissal is shown to everyone in the room. I can hear the girls behind me start to chirp.

As I turn, all eyes are on me, some gleeful in Lucas's dismissal, some watching me wondering how I snagged the first dance. Vicky looks like she's ready to chew me up and spit me out. I seek out Hannah with her soft blue eyes.

"Are you okay?" she mouths.

*No, I'm not.*

I nod and walk completely off the dance floor and to the bar, away from Hannah's prodding eyes, away from all the curious stares. I refuse to cry. I refuse to let anyone see the turmoil that thrashes through my veins.

The bar area is empty as I arrive, and I grip the counter to center myself.

"What can I get you?"

I glance up at the bartender. "Water, please." I wait, not thinking, and focus on the feel of the wood under my fingers. It's cool and sleek. Maybe it was recently polished. Was it polished to have this room looking perfect for the first ball? A twisted fairy tale, that's what this turned out to be.

One, two, three, four—I count the bottles on the top shelf. I don't want to think anymore.

"Ella." Alex says my name like he's pained.

I accept my water from the bartender. "Please, Alex. Leave me alone." I take a sip slowly, without looking at him.

"I just wanted to make sure you were okay."

I peer at him sideways. My stomach tightens. "Go away," I hiss. Is he trying to get me into trouble? If Lucas saw us talking, what would he do? And especially now that I've asked to go home.

"He left the room." Alex has the cheek to move closer to me. "Did he hurt you?" His question is delivered with sincerity.

He's sporting a mustard and dark green suit. It's ugly, but he makes it look fun.

"No." *Yes.*

"I..." He pulls his lip between his teeth before releasing it. "I should have tried to help you."

My anger with him splinters, and I find my frame softening. "Are you afraid of him?" Of course he is. I'm afraid of him. Who wouldn't be? Lucas is dangerous.

His smile showcases the gap between his teeth, which just adds to the quirkiness of Alex.

"Not quite. I'm afraid of the power he holds. If it was just Lucas, I think I could take him on." He ducks his head, his blond eyebrows drawing down.

My smile fades as I think about the complications of even talking to him. Alex is someone I could really see a friendship blossoming with. There's something about him that just puts me at ease, but it would be cruel to both of us to try.

"I don't think we should be seen talking."

The words snuff out the light in his eyes and he nods, leaning away from me. "I know, but I needed to apologize for being such a coward."

I reach out to touch his arm. My fingers curl into a fist and I withdraw. "Apology accepted." I smile and Alex's face lights up.

"If I could, I would offer you a dance."

I face the bar and smile into my glass. "You better go, Alex." I don't look at him, but I can feel the burn of his eyes on me.

One, two, three, four—I count the bottles on the top shelf again as I drink my water, allowing the cold liquid to douse the flames inside me. From the corner of my eye, I see the space beside me become vacant. My stomach twists painfully, so I continue to count until another figure lands beside me. This one isn't wanted at all.

"So you stole the first dance." Vicky speaks while calling the bartender by waving two of her fingers.

"Vodka." She leans against the bar so she's looking out on the dance floor. Her full-length black dress hits the floor and trails out behind her.

"I didn't ask for the first dance." I wonder why I'm bothering, but I don't want them thinking I asked when I didn't.

"You said you didn't want him?" Her drink arrives and she takes it, turning to me with raised eyebrows. Her red lipstick leaves a print on the glass.

"I don't." I look away from her, hoping she'll leave.

She takes another drink before sneering. "I hate liars. I know it's a competition, but you're such a liar. Playing this innocent facade like 'he won't leave me alone.'" Her face changes, and she flutters her lids like she's trying to mimic me.

I place my glass of water back onto the counter and make my way to the main doors of the ballroom. Mark is close to them, and I stare at him, daring him to stop me.

He reads my warning loud and clear and opens the door for me. I don't pass him untouched. He stops me without looking at me. "Tread carefully, Miss O'Leary."

I hear his warning. Right now, I can't afford to snap in front of everyone.

I just want a moment alone in my room that isn't even my room. The cool banister under my hand is what I focus on.

"What are you running for?" Vicky follows me up the stairs. "Trying to run away now and look like a victim? You think he'll follow you?"

I spin on the stairs and have the most horrible thought about pushing her down the steps. My hands instantly go behind my back so I don't touch her.

"I just want to be alone, Vicky."

Her nose curls up, and she closes the distance between us until there's only one step left.

"Alone with him, you mean?"

"Now you sound crazy. I'm alone." I look around the space before training my stare on Vicky.

"You sound crazy."

I turn on my heel and march the rest of the way up the stairs. She's hot on my heels, and I don't know what she wants. The moment my foot touches the wooden floor, she's beside me. The burn erupts across my scalp as she digs her hands into my hair.

I find myself on the floor, staring up at a very pissed-off Vicky. I'm in shock. No one has ever put their hands on me.

"You're so ugly," she sneers, standing over me.

My fingers prod at my head. My hair is all lopsided now, but it's intact on my head. I rise slowly. Vicky towers over me as I raise my head.

"I will report you." I make each word clear. She has no right to put her hands on me, but I'm giving her the warning, as I don't want to go that far. I just want this to end.

Her hand moves quickly, and the sting across my cheek is instant. "Vicky."

I hold my face as I glance at Hannah, who's racing up the stairs, holding up her gold dress.

"Get away from her." Hannah continues to shout until she reaches me. "You can't hit Ella." She looks bewildered.

Vicky purses her lips before calmly leaving like she did nothing wrong.

"Are you okay? She broke the skin. Come on." Hannah leads me into my room.

I feel a little fractured as Hannah directs me to the bed. I sit down while she goes into the bathroom; I start removing pins from my hair.

The running water stops, and Hannah returns with a washcloth. "Put this on. It might stop the swelling."

The moment the cloth touches my face, I hiss. "Thank you."

Hannah chews her lip, her eyes filled with worry.

"I'm okay, Hannah. Really, it wasn't that bad." I try to give her a reassuring smile.

She exhales loudly and plonks down beside me. "You know she's just jealous that he favors you."

Oh God. She has no idea.

"He hates me," I say matter-of-factly.

When I look at Hannah, she smiles sweetly at me. "Nope. Not from where I was standing. You looked perfect dancing together. Like you were made for each other." Her face is full of light.

I take the washcloth away from my cheek. There's no point explaining to her what's really happening, how I've requested to leave.

I take another look at Hannah. "Why are you being so kind?" I'm her competition. Didn't her mother tell her not to befriend any of us?

She shrugs while smiling. "When you can be anything, why not be kind?"

I'm nodding at her so I don't cry. I swallow around the lump that's forming in my throat. "Please don't tell anyone about this. I just don't need the hassle." I put the cloth back up to my face.

Hannah chews on her lip. "You won't be able to hide it. Take a look at your face."

I'm off the bed and sitting down at the dressing table. Taking the cloth away, I curse Vicky. Hannah's eyes widen at my unladylike language.

My face is red and slightly swollen, but that will go down. It's the scratch across my cheek that will take a few days to clear.

I meet Hannah's eyes in the mirror. "Just keep it to yourself about how this happened. Okay?"

"Of course."

I divert my eyes from the mirror. "Thanks for helping me." I speak to my hands.

"You're welcome, Ella, who isn't Bella."

I glance up at Hannah and give her a genuine smile. She is too good for this place. But I'm glad she's here.

\*\*\*

I toss and turn. My dreams are filled with Vicky growing taller, her lanky body bending around me. Alex is in the background, laughing maniacally, and Lucas lurks in the shadows, watching me with dark, empty eyes.

I open my eyes, and they all turn to shadows that dissolve slowly. All except for one shadow. The blood in my veins turns to ice as I become fully awake. A large frame is standing in the corner of my room watching me.

# CHAPTER TEN

## LUCAS

HER EYES ARE TRAINED on me as she clutches the quilt in her hands. I don't know how I ended up here, but after hearing that Vicky hurt her, I just had a primal need to make sure she's okay.

"Hello." Her voice trembles.

I smile. She can't see my features; the room is cast in shadows, but she knows I'm here. I step forward like this is normal, like me being in her room isn't strange.

"I heard one of the girls attacked you," I say frankly.

She pushes the quilt fully off her, and her small feet touch the carpeted floor. "Lucas?" Outrage tinges her words.

She's standing up now, but she doesn't come any closer, so I take a step toward her.

"What are you doing in my room?"

"This is my room," I inform her, and her brows draw down. She's standing in a pool of light that's filtered in from the window, and she's a vision in her white nightdress. My trousers tighten as my eyes roam across her body.

"I'd like you to leave, please."

I tighten my fist at her dismissal.

"I'll leave when I'm ready." I bite back the anger that's starting to swirl inside me, feeding my words. I take another step toward her, and she flinches when our eyes meet. As half my face comes into view, I want to ask her what she sees, what frightens her so much.

Being this close to her, I can see the mark left on her porcelain skin. I close the distance and touch her cheek. She flinches again like I might hurt her. When I don't move, she remains still, and I stroke my thumb across the scratch.

I don't have to ask why one of the girls hurt her. I know why.

"She will be removed from the house." My eyes trail up to Ella's large green ones. Her mouth opens and my focus moves to her lips. The pulse in her neck jumps. I want to kiss her neck and see what happens.

"It wasn't her fault." Her words are low but grab my attention. She swallows. "If anyone is to blame, it's you."

Her neck, which I wanted to kiss only moments ago, looks so fragile, like If I wrapped my hands around it, I could break it so easily. I take a step away from her.

"How is it my fault?" I tilt my head and wait as patiently as I can as she chews on her lip. My trousers grow tighter. Is she doing that on purpose? Is she trying to tease me?

"You made it seem like I had asked for the dance when I hadn't." Her chest rises and falls faster the longer I look at her. Her lips tug down at the edges like she might cry.

My fists clench. I hadn't done anything wrong. I'm only here to make sure she's okay. I have no idea why she's always so hostile toward me.

"I said I'll have her removed." My words carry my anger, and her body recoils from me.

She's afraid, but not enough. "No, I don't want that."

I'm in front of her now, moving quickly. "Stop answering me back."

She drops her gaze and focuses on the floor. Her breathing is heavy, and real fear is gripping her. I close my eyes and inhale. She smells of soap and something feminine. I clench my fists, causing the pain to pulse up my arms, and I soak it up.

I hate her silence.

"I saw you with Alex."

Her head shoots up, and something settles around me now that I have her attention.

She's shaking her head. "I barely spoke to him."

I raise both eyebrows. "But you spoke to him." The smile grows on my face as she clutches her chest.

"What are you going to do?" She sounds so resigned that I'm going to punish her.

I exhale loudly and she shivers. "I don't know yet." I focus on her lips. I could kiss her. The thought pops into my head quickly.

"You could kiss me." I speak my mind.

Her mouth falls open, and color splashes her cheeks. "No." she says the word, but I can see how her eyes keep flickering to my lips.

"I told you before, Ella, your eyes give away too much." I take a step toward her as she takes a step back. I keep moving forward until her back hits the wall and she's trapped, just where I want her. I place a hand on either side of her pretty head, boxing her in.

"Don't you dare kiss me." Her words are like a lash to me.

"Why do you keep provoking me?" It's like she gets off on it.

Her mouth forms an *O*, and she shakes her head, her hair brushing my bare arm.

"I'm not." Her eyes plead with me.

I lean into her neck, where her pulse spikes, and when she whimpers, it's like a bucket of water over me. She sounds like a frightened animal. I push off the wall and quickly exit her room.

No one has ever made me feel so unsure. No one has ever made me feel so animalistic. The way she looks at me sometimes.

I'm down the hall quickly, needing to put distance between Ella and me. I wasn't sure I would be able to control myself if I went back into her room. I'm consumed with an irritation I don't know how to get rid of.

The plants at the end of the hall are my destination. I move up the winding gold stairs to the attic. It's dark as I enter. I reach for the light switch, and the area lights up instantly. The space is neat—everything has a place. Nothing is left out. I want to find the small brown box, and there's no time like the present.

I want to trash the space; I hate everything about it. All the odds and ends Henry collects makes no sense, just like him. I picture him arriving in the morning to find the area destroyed. Some of my irritation leaves as I picture his face at the destruction.

I find the box stuffed behind a small Moroccan table. It's neatly tucked away. I take it out, and my stomach swirls and tightens as I push over the lid that slides open. The box wobbles in my hands, but I steady it quickly.

There isn't just one finger in the box but two. So, it is Henry. This is all I need. I bring the box over to the large lamp to get a better look. The fingers are from different people, and the second is female. Who else did he kill?

I close the box and make sure the table looks undisturbed as I leave the attic. The hallway is still empty, as it's three in the morning so no one is awake. I had been in bed, but after I heard that Ella was attacked, from Mark, I had wanted to make sure she was okay. It was an odd feeling for me, but I couldn't settle until I saw her.

I pass her bedroom and slow down. I terrified her, but I refuse to apologize, and if I enter the room I'm not sure what will happen. She'll provoke me again, and a part of me doesn't want to hurt her.

I return to my own room. Sitting on the unmade bed, I flick on the lamp and examine the finger again. I notice how neatly it was sliced off. It almost doesn't look real.

My mind snaps to the man I beat. I don't even know if he's still alive. There was so much blood covering my hands and his body, most of it from my fists.

*It's only a lump of meat*, I tell myself as I pick up the finger. It is real.

I have to bring this to my father. But now I'm presenting multiple problems. I place the finger back into the box before taking out the second one. It is smaller, definitely female. I drop the female finger into the glass of water on my bedside table. My father doesn't need to know about it yet.

I grab the glass and take it into my bathroom and hide it at the back of the cupboard.

I'll hand over the box tomorrow, but until a female body appears with a missing finger, I'll keep that one to myself.

\*\*\*

After sleeping on it, I decide that I won't go to my father. I want to confront Henry first. Let him know that I'm the one who discovered the finger. That I'm the one who finally caught him.

The house is busy this morning. I hate the noise they make as they shuffle around, always giggling, always chatting. It doesn't stop me from trying to seek out Ella. In the sea of faces, I don't see hers.

I'm not sure how I feel about looking for her. She infuriated me, defied me at every step. Refused to refer to me as Master Lucas. The times she did use my name, it sounded different on her lips.

I liked it.

Henry is already in the attic. He's frantically pulling out furniture.

"Did you lose something?" I ask as I take the final step into the attic. He swings around and nearly loses his balance. I've never seen him so white. He pushes his glasses up on his nose.

"I knew you were all kinds of fucked up, but this..." I remove the box from behind my back, his eyes zapping to it. "This is sick."

He shakes his head before dipping it.

I step further into the room. "You like to keep a token from your victims?"

He looks at me from under his glasses, his shoulders hunching forward.

"You jerk off looking at it?"

His spine snaps straight, and suddenly he's someone different. "You're so crude." He blinks rapidly.

I sneer. "You're a fucking freak. Do you know the sentence for killing?"

He's back to shaking his head again. "I didn't do it."

"Right, how did this get here?" I wave the box at him, and I swear he pales further.

"I found it."

"You know you'll have to do better than that Henry. I found it just isn't going to cut it when I present this to the committee."

His head snaps up again. He stands to his full height and pushes his glasses up on his face.

"I'm your brother. I would be hung for it."

My stomach twists at the image of him swinging from a tree. He doesn't know I have the power to choose his punishment. I wouldn't have him killed, but he would be punished. I didn't care for Declan. I just want to know why he did it.

"Was Declan touching you?" I ask.

"You're vulgar. I had no dealings with Declan."

I don't like this, us going around in circles. "Okay, you little shit, then tell me why you killed him."

"I didn't. That box was sitting in the middle of my floor. The day you arrived, I had just found it."

I scrub my face with my free hand. I have no clue if he's lying. He is very good at pretending.

"So what is your theory?" I quiz.

"Someone is framing me."

If I were to frame someone, it would be Henry. To me, he fits the profile.

But I'm still not buying into his lie. "So, who do you think framed you?" I ask.

He shrugs while tilting his head. Jutting out his chin, he narrows his eyes. "You."

"I framed you and then confronted you for being a killer and asked you who framed you?"

"I don't know, Lucas," he barks, and the anger he's struggling to keep in check is growing. His hands tighten into fists. Three black dots on his right thumb catch my eye.

"New tattoo?"

He curls his fists, and the tattoo disappears. "I just drew it on." He looks at the floor. "I didn't hurt anyone."

"Where's Alex?"

His face grows red, and his hands return to fists. "Leave him alone."

"No."

Alex is a trigger for him, his only friend.

"He doesn't even know about the box."

"I know you're lying, Henry, and I know Alex has something to do with all this."

Henry laughs, but it isn't humorous. "Do you hear yourself? You just hate me so much that you need to pin this on me." He's shouting, his temper getting the better of him. I hope it does. I hope he says something he regrets.

"No, you two are weird, and tell him to keep away from Ella. He's sniffing around her like a dog."

"You're lying." There's a tremble in his voice, and the uncertainty in his eyes has me looking at him again.

"Ask him what happened in the garden."

Henry shakes his head. "What are you talking about?"

"He was caught in the garden with Ella, and later at the ball."

His eyes fill with despair and something else that makes my skin itchy.

"Jesus Christ." Laughter bubbles up my throat. "Wow."

"Stop it." He grits his teeth.

"Does Father know?" If he did, he would string him up.

"Shut your mouth." His anger is feeding into my own. I want him to keep feeding my violence so I can release it upon him.

"You're gay." I say it like it's the funniest thing in the world.

Henry's shaking his head violently.

I'm bloodthirsty right now, and I want him to attack. "Does Alex know?" I tease, and it's enough for him to snap and charge.

Henry surprises me by throwing the first punch. I pause as I wipe blood from my nose before I grin and unleash my anger on him.

# CHAPTER ELEVEN

## ELLA

B REAKFAST IS QUIET. I can't stop staring at Vicky's empty chair. She must have slept in. There's no way he actually her sent home. I glance at all the other girls; they're all subdued. My stomach tightens when Hannah focuses on her toast and tea. She won't meet my eye. Do they all know what happened with Vicky?

I chew the inside of my mouth until it's raw. "Has anyone seen Vicky?" I ask innocently. All eyes are now on me and I swallow. This isn't good.

Hannah's wide blue eyes flicker to the left before she looks at me again. She's out of her chair and gripping my hand. "Come on."

"Hannah, don't be foolish. She isn't your friend." Jessie speaks up and I frown at her. What is going on?

Hannah ignores her and takes me out of the room.

"What's happening?" I half whisper, half shout. My nerves are already shattered after having Lucas in my room last night. He nearly kissed me. The worst part is I wanted him to. My body responded to him.

Last night, I was drowning while I stood in front of him, waiting to see what he would do. He terrified me, and some sick part of me got off on that fear. I have no idea why.

Hannah doesn't stop until we're in the drawing room, which is empty. She releases my hand and creeps back over to the door before closing it gently.

"Okay, Hannah, you have to tell me what's happening."

She nods and moves away from the door. The white cone-shaped skirt whooshes as she walks quickly to me.

"We all got a warning about keeping our hands to ourselves."

Dread starts to weave its way along the base of my spine.

"Everyone knows that Vicky hurt you and now she's gone." Tears blur Hannah's eyes.

I feel terrible "It's okay. I'm sure she'll still find someone."

Hannah shakes her head, a few red curls coming loose. "It's not that. She'll be punished."

Ice enters my veins and grips my breath. "Punished?" I whisper. I don't want to know, but I also *need* to know. Look what he did to me when I spoke to Alex. What would he do to Vicky? My legs feel weak, and I reach behind me, seeking out a chair and slowly sitting down.

"Yes, they said she was being punished. What if they kill her?"

A laugh bubbles up my throat. "Okay, now your imagination has gone wild." I'm standing, shaking my head. "I'll find out."

Hannah grips my arm. "No! Please, I don't want to see you hurt." The fear in her eyes is real, and my heart starts to pick up pace.

"You're talking about murder?"

"I know it sounds insane."

"It really does, Hannah." I'm finding this conversation is growing wings and flying away with itself. I need to find out what happened to Vicky.

"Do you know something?" The fear in her eyes is growing, expanding and passing onto me.

"No. It's just... some of the girls think Lucas might have killed her."

Now I'm laughing, but Hannah continues to stare at me.

Is Lucas capable of murder? He wouldn't hurt her over a slap. This doesn't make sense.

I walk away from Hannah even as she calls me back. But I need to know. It's a fire that's started to spark inside me, and I don't want it to rage. I need the truth, but I need to be careful too.

Mark walks out of the dining room. His eyes meet mine, and I force a half smile.

"I'm looking for Master Lucas."

One eyebrow rises slightly, but the surprise is short-lived. "He's in his study."

I shrug. "Where is that?"

Mark continues to stare at me. I don't know what he's thinking, maybe debating whether to take me or not, but he makes his mind up. "Follow me, Miss O'Leary."

Mark takes me toward the back of the house. The noise grows further away, and I twist my hands nervously.

When Mark stops, I nearly walk into his back, stopping myself at the last second. He glances at me over his shoulder before he knocks three times in quick succession on the door.

"What?" A growl from Lucas has me shuffling.

This is a bad idea.

"Maybe this isn't the best time," I say to Mark, just as the door opens.

Lucas glares at Mark before his eyes pin me to the floor.

"Maybe this isn't a good time," I say. He's holding a cloth to his bloody nose. His black clothes look like he's just been in a scuffle. He looks brooding and dark as he fills the doorframe. I just want to run.

"You have already disturbed me, so come in." He opens the door fully.

Mark steps aside to let me into the lion's cage. I inhale a deep breath, asking God to give me the courage as I step into Lucas's study.

I'm waiting for the door to slam, but he closes it surprisingly gently behind me. The room shrinks, and my hands grow damp as he walks past me and sits down in a large leather chair behind a mahogany desk.

"I can come back another time," I stutter.

He takes the rag away from his face, blood still leaking from his nose. "Just spit it out, Ella."

He's angry. I got him at a really bad time. He's staring at me like if I don't speak soon he'll get up and shake it out of me.

I force myself to stand tall. "Where is Vicky?" I hold my hands in front of me now, hoping I look confident and calm and not like I'm ready to run from the room.

"That's why you're here?" He pushes the rag back up to his nose to catch some more blood.

My mind scatters, and I feel like I'm on the ground trying to pick it up. "What other reason would I be here?"

"I thought maybe you came to apologize." He removes the rag and allows me to see his lips curling into a smirk.

I fold my arms across my chest. "Apologize for what?"

He places the rag on the table and stands.

My stomach dips.

"For being so rude last night."

Heat travels up my neck. The kiss. The *almost* kiss. My heart rate skyrockets. Was he talking about that? Did he even care? Was this just a mind game?

"I don't think I was rude." I have so much more to add, but I'm still treading carefully. He's like a bomb ready to explode, and I don't want to be the one to set him off.

"Yes, you were," he says it so matter-of-factly.

I bite my tongue.

He walks around the table with a grin. "I see your struggle. You can't help yourself. You always have something to say back."

I unfold my arms from my chest, not knowing what to do with my hands as he continues to walk toward me. Fresh blood gathers under his nose. I can't look away from the scarlet liquid.

"What happened to your nose?" I ask without thinking.

He touches it, and his fingers come away with blood on them. His eyes flicker to his fingers. I inhale sharply as he puts them into his mouth and sucks off the blood.

His smile widens at my reaction. There's blood on his lips.

"Did Vicky do that?" I ask, thinking maybe she fought back.

"You think I fought with Vicky?"

"I don't know, did you?" I swallow around the lump in my throat as Lucas eradicates the distance between us. I can't look away from his bloodstained lips.

"You still have to be punished for speaking to Alex."

My eyes skip to his. There are specks of brown floating amongst the mass of ink. They're barely surviving in the pool of black. But they are there.

His eyes snap to my lips, and my tongue flicks out and wets them. I'm frozen as he lowers his head to me. He's so much taller, so much bigger, and I'm just consumed with Lucas. His soft, full lips touch mine, and it's a bolt of lightning through my system. My hands automatically go to his chest, and I have no idea if I want to pull him closer or push him away.

He pauses, his lips on mine, giving me the opportunity to stop this. I know I should, but my body leans toward him instead. With every ounce of strength I possess, I move my face away from his. My heart beats wildly in my chest, and I have no doubt he hears it.

I release his shoulders and take a step back while his eyes bore into mine.

My nerves are jangled. "Are we even now?"

The brown in his eyes has no chance as the darkness closes around them and extinguishes the small amount of light. Once again, I want to reach for my words, take them back, and shove them down my throat.

"Not even close." His words are filled with a menace that has me stepping back.

Lucas looks away from me and focuses on the wall, like he's heard something. I'm following his gaze.

"You can go now." He dismisses me without even looking at me, and I know I've messed up.

"Lucas."

His head swings toward me at the mention of his name, but there isn't the same person there. This one is angry and dark.

"It's Master Lucas, and I said get out."

His words hurt, but they really shouldn't. I curtsy. "Master Lucas."

I'm walking around trying to keep it together, but I don't know if I want to cry or scream. How can anyone make me feel so much?

"Are you okay?"

I grip my chest as Hannah, who's dragging Jessie with her, ambushes me in the hall.

"Of course I'm okay." I'm breathless, flustered.

Hannah's blue eyes widen as she stares at my lips. Heat splashes across my cheeks. She couldn't know he kissed me.

"What's wrong?" I ask.

"There's blood on your lips. Did he hurt you?"

I suck in my bottom lip and taste Lucas's blood. I release my swollen lip. "No, I must have bitten it," I lie. My stomach tightens as his blood sits on my tongue. There's something powerful about tasting his blood.

Oh God. There's something so terribly wrong with me. This place is doing something to me.

"So did you find out about Vicky?" Jessie asks, keeping her voice low.

I shrug, knowing I failed to find out about her. My mind is consumed with a kiss when it shouldn't be. "I'm sorry."

Disappointment drapes both their shoulders.

"I don't think she's hurt. I think she was just sent home."

"But you don't know that for sure," Hannah says quietly.

She's right, I don't. Jessie's soft brown eyes are filled with worry. It isn't meant to be like this for us girls. None of us deserve to be worrying or upset or even afraid. This is meant to be a time of love and laughter.

"I think that's why we should find out."

Hannah perks up. "How?"

I grin. "We snoop."

Hannah's smile is instant. "I knew you were trouble the moment I saw you."

Her words have me laughing. "Me? Trouble?" I quiz and she nods. I don't consider myself trouble, but since arriving here, I've seemed to be in the middle of it all.

It doesn't matter, though. What matters right now is finding out what happened to Vicky, and I will find out, even if that means playing nice with Master Lucas.

# CHAPTER TWELVE

## LUCAS

MY HEART POUNDS AS my father enters the study. I hold the rag to my nose, hoping he doesn't see the uncertainty on my face.

"You had company?" He closes the panel, and while his back is to me, I try to switch off my emotions.

"It was nobody," I answer. I don't sit down in my seat, in case he wants to.

"It was definitely someone. Female. A gentle voice. She's familiar with you. She didn't call you Master Lucas." Calculating eyes focus on me.

"One of the ladies. Yes, but it's unimportant."

I decide to sit, to give myself something to do as he scrutinizes me.

"I hope she isn't responsible for this." He waves his hand in the direction of my face. There's a tug of his lips. "I could have her hands for that."

Blood pools in my shoes as I imagine Ella being hurt. "No. It was Henry. You can take his hands."

My father narrows his eyes in warning. "What were you fighting about, a girl? Is that why one of them was sent home?"

Nothing gets past him. But the irony that he thought we were fighting over a girl isn't lost on me. I wonder what he would do to Henry if he found out that he is gay. It would most certainly have Henry out of his favor. The thought of telling him is enticing.

"No, it was about Alex." I stick as close to the truth as possible. He's bound to have heard about Ella being retested. Nothing gets past my father, so I can use that to my advantage. "I caught him with one of the ladies who I had retested. I just wanted to extend the warning to Henry. But, you know Henry. He doesn't like to be told what to do."

My father's cunning eye never leaves my face, and my heart rate picks up. Can he detect the half-truths?

There's a deafening silence. I steal the moment by placing the rag to my nose, which feels like it's stopped bleeding.

My father releases me from his stare. "Declan's wake is today, so I will return officially then. I'm looking forward to meeting all these ladies. They seem to be causing quite the stir." The last part is said with a smile. I don't want my father to meet them. I don't want him to meet Ella.

"It will be their pleasure, Father. They might find you more enticing than me." I throw the rag into the bin.

"You have your father's charm. I think it's time you turned it on." He walks to the panel. "I'll see you at the wake." My father disappears, and I sit for a few moments staring at the wall.

Declan's wake might be an opportunity to see if someone doesn't arrive. Maybe see if there's a bad feeling amongst people, but first I need to do something.

I ring the lab we have on our payroll. I've never used them before—I've never had to—and I hope whoever I speak to doesn't tell my father. But it's a risk I'll take.

"Yellow Grange Laboratory."

"Master Lucas Andrew O'Faolain the third speaking." I ramble my title and can hear the shuffle of the phone.

"Master Lucas, one moment."

I hate being put on hold.

Within moments, a male voice speaks into the phone. "Master Lucas, what a pleasure to be of service to you."

"I have a finger I would like analyzed. Can I send it today?" I keep it short.

"Of course. Is it just the finger?" He sounds a little unsteady now.

"Isn't that what I just said?"

"Of course, Master Lucas. I will personally wait for the delivery."

"Good. One final thing. This stays between us."

"Yes, Master Lucas."

We'll see how loyal he is. I hang up feeling pretty certain he'll run back to my father. I just hope I have some time to figure out who the finger belonged to before he did that.

I leave the study and go straight to my bedroom. There are no giggling ladies in the hallway for once. I kick the door closed and start to strip as I make my way to the shower.

The cold water has my body taut as it hits my back. It's freezing and I keep the cold water pounding onto my body until it nearly becomes unbearable.

Switching over to hot, I tremble and shake. I stay in the one spot until it subsides. The warmth replaces the chill in my bones.

Blood from my face swirls at my feet before disappearing down the drain.

A grin grows on my face as I picture Ella watching me when I sucked my fingers. She was shocked but turned on too. My body hums when I think of the kiss. It wasn't much of a kiss, yet I felt it. My shaft grows and thickens as I fantasize about her, wanting me and touching me. I picture her as I take my cock in my hand and start to pump slowly. My free hand shoots to the shower tiles as I hold myself up.

I pump harder and faster, picturing myself inside Ella. She would be so tight and sweet around my cock. Her whimpers and moans have me jerking faster until I release across the tiles of the shower. Coming down slowly off the tips of my toes, I give my cock a few final jerks, emptying it before finishing my shower.

***

Declan's estate sits on the outskirts of Brownstown. My stomach churns as I enter the property. This isn't just about the wake. My father will arrive, and with him, I will return to just Lucas. Brendan will make sure to rub it in. I tighten my hands on the steering wheel as I follow the direction of two men who wave me to my parking spot.

Two large greyhounds roam near the front door. Declan is a betting man and had his own greyhounds in the races. They were such an ugly dog. They always looked half fed. They don't come near me as I make my way up the four steps and push open the red front door that's been left slightly ajar.

After signing my name in the book of condolences, I follow the soft chatter into a large sitting room. The décor is what you would expect for an estate house. It's a smaller scale than our own, but just as expensively decorated.

Debbie is the first to see me. Her blonde hair is pinned into a tight bun on top of her head. The black dress she wears is fitting. Her neck is decorated in pearls.

"Mr. O'Faolain." She takes my hand.

I smile at her. "Please, Debbie. Call me Lucas."

Her smile grows. "Thank you for coming, Lucas."

"Declan was a good man."

She nods, and I notice her flawless makeup. Money kept her here, not Declan. Money kept us all in our places. No one is going to marry me for anything other than power, a position. That's how it goes.

Debbie still hasn't released my hand. "He's over here." She brings me to the coffin like I might not have noticed it or known where Declan was.

I want my hand back, but I also want information. Leaning in, my eyes go straight to his hands. One is placed over the other, hiding the missing finger.

"I'm sorry about his finger," I whisper but glance at Debbie.

Her nose curls. "Would you notice it missing? I had them re-arrange his hands three times." She sounds annoyed.

"No, you wouldn't notice at all. You did a fantastic job."

She beams. "Thank you, Lucas." She says my name slowly, and I carefully detangle her from me. Someone else arrives, taking her attention off me. I turn to see Brendan, Aine, and Sean seated against the wall on high-back gold chairs, like they were the most important people in the room.

"Master Lucas," Aine greets me. My father must not have reappeared yet. He would use a wake to make his return loud.

"Aine, Brendan, Sean."

Brendan barely says Master Lucas, but he manages to get it out. The only others in the room are some younger people on their phones, settled on a large couch near the double windows. Most people are in the kitchen. Where there's food, there are people.

I return to Declan and brush a palm over his forehead. My eyes snap to his hands again. They really did cover up his missing finger. I can see the tiny gap, but that's only because I know what to look for.

Peeking out of the sleeve of his jacket is a small black dot. Glancing around the room, I make sure no one is watching. Of course Brendan is. While Debbie is greeting a lady, I make it quick, moving the white sleeve. Three black dots are tattooed on his outer thumb. Just like Henry's.

The air in the room changes, and I step back from the coffin.

"Master Andrew."

My father has arrived.


The wake turned up nothing. No one spoke ill of the dead. So if he had enemies, they sang his praises. I need to approach this from a different angle, starting with the tattoo. Why would Declan and Henry have the same tattoo?

I arrive back at the house, and as I step into the foyer, I find Ella alone and pacing. When she notices me, I can't figure out what passes her features.

*Fear?*

"I'm sorry for your loss." She steps forward, hands held tightly in front of her. She's wearing a white summer dress. It doesn't hug her curves, but she looks angelic. Black hair falls into her face, and she pushes it back behind her ear.

"Thank you."

Her eyes widen in surprise, like she isn't expecting me to respond.

She forces a smile, but it looks just that, forced. She's up to something. I decide to let this play out.

"I need a drink." I step away from Ella, but she doesn't follow. Let's see how eager she is.

"Are you coming?" I ask but don't turn around. I smirk when I hear her soft footsteps behind me. She is definitely up to something.

She looks awkward as I step behind the bar and take down a bottle of Scotch.

I pour out two glasses. She's standing a few feet away from the bar, looking around the room. I place her drink onto the counter.

"I won't bite," I say.

She gives me a questionable look. She looks ready to run. But she straightens and walks to the bar with her head high. Picking up the glass, she stares at it, and I watch her as I sip my own drink. She raises the glass to her lips, her eyes shooting to me, and my trousers tighten. What she can do with one look...

She pulls a face, and I grin at her. "That's disgusting."

I nod, walking around to her. "I agree, but it's a taste you get used to."

She has that deer in headlights look as I walk around to her. She places the glass onto the bar and puts her hands behind her back, but I see the tremble she's trying to hide.

*What is Ella up to?*

I lean against a stool, not fully sitting on it. "Do you want to tell me why you were waiting in the foyer?" I ask before removing my black suit jacket.

Her eyes roam across me, and I let her take me in. When her eyes travel up to mine, a splash of pink coats her cheeks, and I want to kiss her.

"I wasn't. I was actually about to take a walk in the gardens." She lies and tries to cover it up by taking another drink of Scotch. Her face twists in disgust, and I smile again at her small turned-up nose.

"Really?"

She bites her lip, and I think she's trying to stop a smile.

"I hope you aren't keeping secrets from me, Ella."

Her face flames. It's too easy. "No. I was only going for a walk."

I finish my drink. "Are you sure you weren't meeting Alex?" My temper flares like a match striking a box. I don't know why the feeling erupts, but she flinches.

"No." Her bark is loud, and she curls her little fists tightly at her side.

This is my fault. I started this, but I feed off her fear, and I can't seem to help myself.

"If I find out you are, I will punish you."

Instantly, her eyes flicker to my lips. I grin. "I think you like when I punish you."

She looks ready to lash out, but at the last second, something changes. She takes a step closer to me, and her eyes flicker up to mine. I don't move as I wait to see what she's going to do. A hand that I can feel tremble through my shirt touches my chest. The heat of her hand worms its way beneath my skin.

Her pulse flickers wildly in her neck as she reaches up onto the tip of her toes and presses a soft kiss to my mouth. Her lips are soft and warm. I grip her waist and she leans out, green eyes focus on me, and she's swimming in lust. I'm strong, but right now, she's weakened me.

I take her face in my hand and kiss her. It isn't soft. It's urgent and harsh. Ella surprises me when she meets my kiss with her own harshness to match mine.

The soft groan from her lips has my cock twitching painfully. My tongue enters her mouth. The taste of Scotch mixed with mint fills my own. She's perfect.

A knock on the door has me breaking away. When I look at Ella, she's dazed, her eyes overcast like she's drunk. I release her face as George steps in. He saw us kiss—I can tell from the light in his eyes.

"Sorry for disturbing you, Master Lucas, but your father requests your company."

"I'll be with him in a moment."

George gives Ella a quick glance before leaving. I turn to her now. She looks more put together but still a little flustered.

"I have to go, but maybe later you might decide to tell me the truth." I speak while putting on my jacket.

"The truth?" She sounds confused, like her mind isn't focused.

"Yes, Ella, the truth. I told you before, your eyes give you away."

I pause in front of her. "You were waiting for a reason." I touch her swollen lips with my thumb. "Maybe you could tell me tonight at dinner."

"Dinner?" Her chest rises quickly, and I think of her breasts in my hands. I release her face.

"Dinner," I confirm, and step away. I need to meet my father. "Oh." I pause at the door. "Wear something tight." I wink and her temper flares.

The spitfire I'm used to seeing returns, and I laugh as I leave the room. Tonight should be fun.

For the first time in a long time, I have something to look forward to.

# CHAPTER THIRTEEN

## ELLA

I'M ANGRY WITH MYSELF for getting so sucked in with Lucas. It isn't like he's charming—no, he's disarming. That's how I feel when he's around me, like everything logically flees and all I'm left with is a jumble of emotions. I pull my lip between my teeth. *That kiss.* I catch myself smiling and scold myself as I leave the bar with a taste of Scotch and Lucas on my tongue. I liked both.

*Wear something tight.* The way he said it had my body flaming. His kiss got under my skin, and I felt it in every cell of my body. What would having him touch me do? I sigh and catch myself smiling again as I make my way back to my room, where no doubt Hannah and Jessie are waiting on a report of my findings.

They knew I was going to wait for him. Guilt swirls in my stomach. I have nothing for them. But tonight at dinner will be a great opportunity. *I'm only going to the meal for Vicky*, I tell myself. The lie scorches into my cheeks.

"What happened?" For the second time, Hannah and Jessie scare the life out of me.

"I thought we discussed you waiting in the room," I say as I hold a hand over my racing heart.

Hannah looks sheepish. "Sorry, we were just worried." She chews her lip.

"Is that Scotch I smell?" Jessie leans in and sniffs me.

I swat her away and glance around the hallway. "Anyone could be listening."

"Are you drunk?" Jessie fires out another question as we start to walk.

"No. I had one drink."

Hannah's face lights up and she squeals. "You had a drink with Lucas?"

Jessie scoffs. "He's the enemy, Hannah. He killed Vicky."

I want to clamp my hand over Jessie's mouth. "We don't know that," I whisper as we walk up the stairs.

We all pause. Sandra is standing on the landing, hands on her hips, eyes trained on us.

I continue up the stairs. "Sandra," I greet her.

Her blonde hair is loose and falls in those perfect curls that are fit for a commercial.

"Where were you?" she asks.

Hannah and Jessie join me on the landing.

"Out for a walk," I say.

"Having a drink," Jessie replies at the same time as me, and Sandra raises a brow.

"We are allowed around the house."

"Only the designated areas, ladies." She has an authority in her voice I haven't heard before.

I frown. "We did," I respond.

She forces a smile. "Good. I just wanted to give a friendly reminder."

She moves past us and down the stairs. We say nothing until we're in my room.

"What was that about?" Hannah asks what I'm thinking.

"I don't know. Is she normally like that?"

"Up in herself? Yes," Jessie answers, sitting on my bed.

"What happened?" Hannah can barely contain herself as she sits down beside Jessie. I join them, kicking off my shoes.

I start with the bad news. "I found out nothing."

"Explain the drinking." Hannah has that same excitement in her blue eyes that I saw earlier.

"He was just back from the wake, and he needed a drink, so we talked at the bar."

"So you did talk?" Jessie raises a perfectly arched brown eyebrow.

"It was more that he was rude. I was trying to get something out of him, but it wasn't a good time."

Hannah nods and tilts her head. Jessie doesn't look convinced.

"So we have nothing. Again." Jessie slides off my bed.

"He's taking me to dinner tonight, so I have another opportunity to quiz him."

Hannah's eyes grow so big, and she claps her hands. I sometimes think she forgets this is a competition—her joy is real.

"A date?"

"No. Dinner," I respond quickly while grabbing her hands to stop her from clapping. She's making me nervous. "It means nothing," I add quickly.

"It's an opportunity. You have to use this time." Jessie's cool voice is a douse of water on Hannah's excitement.

"I will. But I don't have anything to wear."

Jessie, without my permission, walks over to my double-door walk-in closet I know is filled with gowns and dresses. She spreads out both her hands.

"You have loads."

*Wear something tight.*

"I was thinking of something a little more distracting," I say and my cheeks heat.

Jessie smiles. "Oh, I like how you think."

I'm racked with guilt because I'm not sure if I'm wearing it to distract him or to seek his approval.

"Like seduce him." Hannah wiggles her eyebrows.

"No, just have his mind wandering." I feel cheap as I say it out loud.

"Let me see what I have." Jessie leaves the room, and Hannah doesn't hold back on her excitement.

"You have great boobs, maybe have something low cut." She's nodding and smiling like it's a great idea.

The idea of having my boobs hanging out in front of Lucas has me laughing. "No way. I just meant something a little more fitted."

"What's he like?" Hannah's voice is soft, and I can see myself in her now. Waiting to hear the fairy tale. Picturing him all charming behind closed doors.

"He's... intense. Very handsome up close. That's when he's not been completely rude and arrogant. But sometimes he's soft and ..."

Hannah sighs, all dreamy.

"Intense," I finish on.

She's smiling. Guilt swirls in my chest. She deserves her prince, and that isn't Lucas. I'm not sure what he is. The only thing I know is that he's emptying me of all my previous notions and refilling it with him.

"Okay, I found three that I think will blow his mind."

Jessie arrives and Hannah claps her hands in excitement.

After what feels like hours in my room discussing makeup and the 'date,' my head is ready to explode. I've settled on a black fitted dress. It hugs my body and touches the floor. No skin is showing, yet everything is. I've decided to pin my hair up and paint my lips in red.

"He will be tripping over his words." Hannah's jaw has to be sore from all the smiling. Now, even Jessie is smiling as she nods.

"He'll tell you his password to his safe if you ask him," Jessie says.

We giggle and laugh for a while until we're called to the drawing room for some TV time. Some crime show is on, but I can't focus for even one second. My head is pounding with all that's swirling around it. Everyone is transfixed on the TV, and I use the opportunity to leave the room. I need air.

The gardens offer me the time I need. I keep my wits about me, making sure I avoid speaking to anyone. I do see a man pruning the roses and make sure I give him a wide berth. My mind won't leave Lucas. I thought I could clear it out here, but I'm still thinking of the kiss.

I shake out my hands. I need to pull it together. The question is, do I really think he hurt Vicky, never mind kill her? And the honest answer is no. He has a temper, but would he hurt one of us? No. His bark is definitely worse than his bite. Under it all, I can see a flicker of something good. But it's a flicker that can disappear as quickly as it arrives.

I find myself close to the maze. Alex brought me here that first day. It feels like such a long time ago, yet it was only days. I step into the maze, and I love that I have to focus on where I'm going. It makes my head stop spinning to just focus on this one task at hand.

The maze is bigger than I expected, and I soon realize after trying to exit it several times that I'm lost.

"Hello," I shout, hoping I'm near to the front and that maybe the gardener I saw earlier hears me. I listen, but only the rustle of the wind reaches my ears. Great.

I try again and hit three more dead ends. I'm not sure which direction I'm going in. "Hello," I shout louder.

A panic has my heart racing, and I smile to try to calm it. I'm not going to be stuck here forever. I just need to relax and start again. The worst-case scenario is I don't return, but I'm sure the girls will look for me. Someone had to have seen me come out here. My stomach twists. I tried to avoid being seen. Panic rushes into my veins again, and I take a breath. I need to keep it together.

"Hello." I keep calling every three steps I take. That's what I focus on. Three steps and call hello. I repeat this for I don't know how long, until I'm so close to giving up.

"Hello," a male voice calls back.

"Ah, can you help me?" Someone has finally heard me. Relief banishes all my earlier fears. "I'm stuck in the maze. I don't know how to get out." I shout into the bushes, unsure what direction the voice came from.

"Keep talking."

I jump at the closeness of the voice. "I'm here. Here. Here," I keep repeating until the man who looks just like Lucas appears in front of me.

My heart leaps. He has a black eye behind a pair of glasses.

"Thank you. I was so foolish to come in here," I say as he continues to stare at me. My skin starts to crawl with how he assesses me.

"You were foolish and very lucky I was here."

He hunches like a wounded animal as he speaks. He looks up at me from the corner of his eye and I shiver. The air has grown cool. Night is close. I've been out here for a while.

"Can you lead me out?" I ask as he stares at me.

He straightens to his full height and smiles. "Of course." I wonder if he's even aware of how he hunches when he speaks. It's creepy.

"Thank you." Now I just want to get away from him and the maze.

"I'm Henry." He reaches out a hand. He looks normal now, even attractive. Lines crinkle at the corner of his eyes. He's older than Lucas.

"Ella," I say, taking his hand. He stares at me until I shift under his gaze.

"I really need to get back before they send out a search party." I half laugh, but it falls flat.

"Ella," he repeats my name.

I nod. "Yes."

There's an awkwardness as we stand close to each other. "Are you Lucas's brother?" I ask to break the tension.

It does. "Yes. Has he spoken of me?" His question is delivered with a sneer that borders on deranged.

*No. Never.* "You just look so alike," I say instead. They do, but the longer I'm around Henry, the quicker that similarity vanishes.

"So he hasn't spoken of me?" He stands tall again. I wonder if he's aware of how he alters his posture.

"I really haven't spoken to Lucas."

He smiles. "Lucas. You are very familiar with my brother."

My cheeks heat. "No. I apologize, Master Lucas. I forget my manners sometimes." My skin starts to crawl again, and I scratch my neck. "I really should be getting back."

He starts to walk and I follow. Every few seconds, he glances over his shoulder at me. Each time, my heart thuds. He's making me feel unsettled.

"Have you met Alex?" He tries to sound casual, but his words are heavy.

"Yes," I answer honestly since he already knows.

"He is charming," he says, and this time it sounds like he's smiling, like he's fond of him.

"Very much so, but our meeting was brief."

He glances at me again. "You will keep it that way." He stops walking as he turns to me.

I don't respond as my heart rate skyrockets.

"What would happen if I said that you had seduced me?"

My stomach plummets. "But I haven't."

He nods and smirks. "Stay away from Alex, or this day will come back to haunt you."

I tighten my fists. What's wrong with him? "I have done nothing wrong," I repeat. It isn't fair.

"I can leave you here to find your own way out. I did, after all, create this maze, so I know you won't get out without me."

He's all kinds of crazy. It isn't even his words. His eyes dance with madness.

"You think if I don't return that Lucas won't come looking?" I try to show I'm not afraid.

He laughs and it sends waves skittering down my back. "Lucas won't come in here. He becomes a child when he sees the maze." He sounds so happy about what he's saying.

And I want to know more about Lucas as a boy. "Why, what happened?"

Henry's smile dissolves. "I've warned you now." He stands taller. "You better listen."

My heart starts to race again. I'm faced with his back as he starts walking again, and we step out onto the lawn. I was so close to the entrance.

"Nice meeting you, Ella." Henry walks off, leaving me shaken to the core.

# CHAPTER FOURTEEN

## LUCAS-BEFORE

I'M NOT SURE WHEN it happened, but Ella has managed to get under my skin. Her minty taste still lingers on my lips. My shaft grows hard just thinking about her. She has no idea how she transforms when she gets angry; it turns me on, but it shouldn't.

George nods at me from down the hall. I hate how he's aging. It's a reminder of time and the things we lose along the way.

"They're all waiting," George informs me, with a softness in his eyes I know is only reserved for me.

"Thank you, George." His brows rise, assumingly at my manners, but he schools his features quickly. I leave a surprised George behind me, the amusement fleeing as I descend into the basement. I hear them before I can even see them.

Aine's voice is the loudest.

"She is lovely." Her voice is full of excitement, and when I step into the space, they're all focused on a large screen that's projected from the back of the room.

"I recognize the face on the screen but don't know her name."

"Lucas." Aine is the first to notice me and greets me. I'm aware of the lack of Master.

My father sits back in his chair, which I had occupied so briefly. Brendan looks smug as I take my seat beside him. Sean and Cathal greet me, also with just the title Lucas.

"Isn't this exciting?" Aine says. Before I can ask her what's exciting, she's facing the screen again.

Father clicks a small device in his hand, and the image changes. I remember this girl's name—Hannah—only because she's Ella's friend.

"Oh, she's very pretty." Aine leans back, legs crossed as she taps her fingers to her chin. The men aren't commenting as Father goes through the slides of the girls. When Ella appears, my heart thuds, but I keep my features schooled as my father takes a quick glance at me at each slide.

Ella's green eyes fill the screen. That's all I see, and I'm so tempted to smile. She looks so naïve and innocent, so easy to break, but that's not true. She's the strongest of them all. Push her and she will push back twice as hard.

Ella disappears and Father clicks the next slide, and a blonde-haired girl fills the screen. I don't like how my father turns back to us with a smile in his eyes. My stomach twists.

"This will be the future Mrs O'Falaoin."

I've always known I'd have no say. I had been raised knowing I could never choose. That the choice would be with the members, and my father would have the final say. We have to marry for status, power, and money. I was okay with that—I always have been—but right now, my stomach tightens.

"She's a Crowley," my father adds.

"I second this choice." Brendan speaks up, and I want to smash his face in.

"Her parents have been married for thirty years. I'm not sure if I can say happily," my father adds like it's a joke, and Aine laughs into her hand.

"Her father is worth one point one billion and assures a large stake will be given to us. They have read all the rules and have signed off on them."

My heart beats wildly. He already made the deal.

"I agree with this choice." Cathal gives his approval.

"They've asked for a small favor. The first heir to be named from their side."

"I don't think that's wise, Master Andrew. Tradition would be spoiled," Brendan says, and I sink further into the chair like this isn't about me.

"I have agreed that if it's a girl, they can call her what they want. But the boy will carry on the name Lucas and Andrew."

I glance at Brendan, and he nods his bald head. For the first time, my father's eyes land on me.

"What do you think, son?"

*I have no choice, so why ask me?*

"You know best, Father," I answer and something flashes across his face.

Aine and Sean still haven't voted, but my father will get their votes one way or another.

"I agree with this choice," Sean says, and I try not to shift. It doesn't matter, I know that, but each time they vote, it feels like a nail in my coffin.

Aine smiles at me like we're voting on where to go on fucking holiday and not my entire future.

"Your children will be stunning." She casts her vote, and the projector switches off, the lighting in the room dimming. I look up to meet my father's eyes.

"We have your wife." He smiles.

I nod, unable to find the words. No one notices the turmoil inside me, and I know I should switch off my emotions, but they're swirling too quickly for me to grab them. The conversation switches to Declan, but we're no further on to understanding what happened to him, and Debbie isn't pushing for answers, so it takes the pressure off us.

The meeting ends and I feel like I've coasted through it. I get up to leave with the rest.

"Lucas." My father calls me back in, and I grit my teeth.

"I have a car in the shed that needs attention. You will meet me there." I'm glaring at him, thinking of what that means.

He has someone else tied up. Someone is going to die at my hands. I swing away from him before he can see the turmoil in my eyes.

Outside, the air is cool on my clammy skin as I walk to the shed. I don't enter. I don't even check the door to see if it's open. To me, it's still a forbidden place. I wait for my father to arrive.

The man hanging from the ceiling by his arms is older than the last. He's fresh; there isn't a mark on his body. He isn't crying as we step into the room. He watches us. I also notice he isn't wearing a gag, yet he doesn't shout out.

"This is a problem that you refused to take care of." My father moves to the small table that hold his leather gloves. He doesn't put them on, only picks them up.

"This is Dave. He likes to hurt women."

I glance at Dave. He's tall; his feet touch the floor, though the pull on his arms isn't as severe as the last man. Dave clenches his jaw, but he doesn't correct my father.

"This was brought to your attention," Father adds.

"Yes, I was dealing with it."

He flashes me a warning at my disrespectful tone. "You didn't, because now I'm dealing with it. The only thing I can agree with is that the electric chair is not fitting for him." My father walks around now so he's facing Dave.

"What do you think your punishment should be?"

For the first time, Dave's eyes glow with fear as they jump from me to my father. Without looking at me, my father reaches me and hands me the leather gloves, which I take.

So it doesn't matter what Dave thinks his punishment should be. My father has already decided what I'm going to do.

"I don't know, Master Andrew. I won't put my hands on her again." Dave's words are pleading, and I don't look up as I push my hands into the gloves, silently questioning how much blood they've spilt.

"You won't, because this time we're going to hurt you."

For the first time, Dave whimpers, but he doesn't protest.

"The next time, I will cut off your hands."

As my father threatens Dave, I picture all my emotions. The redness inside me has grown; it's always growing. I grab it and the blackness, taking everything else, just like my father taught me, and pushing it into the box.

I don't know what my father sees in me when I look up, but he smiles and gives me an approving nod.

"Don't hold back," he instructs and I don't.

I hit Dave's body with so much force that I hear a rib crack on the first punch. His roar fuels me. His screams become my music, his body my punching bag. I don't stop until my arms tremble and my body is coated in sweat. I'm breathing heavily, my eyes trained on the blood on the concrete floor. I don't fully look up at Dave, but I know his head rests on his chest.

"Discipline will keep them all in line. It's not easy, my son, but necessary." My father pats my shoulder, and I don't linger in the room with my destruction. I take off the leather gloves to find my hands a bloody mess. All my previous wounds have reopened.

When I leave the room, my father's gaze flickers to my hands. Annoyance fills his face. "You will have to wear gloves tonight."

*Tonight?*

"I've set up a dinner for all the ladies to finally meet me."

My stomach twists as I think of Ella. We had dinner planned. I push down the emotion. I can't let my father see anything, so I nod.

"Good." He stops before climbing the stairs back up to the shed. "Sandra will strengthen this family again. We'll become the family we once were."

It's like a punch in the stomach, or seeing a face you haven't seen in years. He mentioned it; he mentioned the past. He must see it on my face. I want to ask about her. This is the perfect opportunity. I've never been given one before, and as a kid, if I asked about my mother, I was shot down.

My heart is pounding a mile a minute. "Is she…" I trail off when his eyes flash in warning.

"She's fine. Now, you need to get ready for this dinner." He climbs the steps, and each one I take, I try to piece myself back together and not think of my mother locked away in a madhouse.

I don't shower when I return to my room. I change my clothes and find a pair of gloves to cover my battered hands. I try not to run to Ella's room. When I reach the landing, no one is in sight. My stomach twists painfully, and I clamp down on the emotion and knock on Ella's door. She doesn't answer. I turn the handle, knowing it won't be locked. Her room is empty. Stepping in, I take in the chaos of her room. I wouldn't have thought it'd be like this. Dresses are thrown across the bed, and I nearly trip over shoes on the floor. Her vanity table is littered with makeup. There's a table drowning in books. I pick one up —Jane Austen's *Pride and Prejudice*. A small silver bookmark is placed in the center. I put the book back down.

The room smells like Ella—soap and something so feminine that, even with so much on my mind, my shaft grows hard.

"Hello." A soft female voice lingers at the doorway. Sandra Crowley, my future wife, smiles at me.

"Have you seen Ella?" I ask her.

She frowns like she's thinking. "I can't say that I have, Master Lucas. Can I give her a message?"

A pencil and a pad sit on the bedside table. I pick them up. I'm not sure what to write. She would already know that I won't be having dinner with her since everyone else was.

My hand hovers over the notepad. This is dangerous. It's leading to a dead end. I glance up at Sandra, who still stands in the doorway waiting for my answer.

We will reschedule dinner.

Lucas

I hesitate with handing it to Sandra. "No. There is no need." I turn to Ella's bed and place the piece of paper on her pillow. Sandra watches my every move, and when my eyes meet hers, she smiles. She knows she'll be picked. No doubt my father has already had a conversation with her.

I step out of Ella's room, forcing Sandra back and closing the door.

"See you tonight, Master Lucas," she sings sweetly after me as I pass her without a word. Blood is refilling my gloves as I clench my fists and leave to get ready for the charade tonight.

# CHAPTER FIFTEEN

## ELLA

T HE SKY HAS DIMMED as I walk back to the house. I keep looking over my shoulder, expecting Henry to be behind me. Another shiver assaults me, and it has nothing to do with the weather. The house is quiet as I enter the foyer and make my way up the stairs.

My skin crawls again when I think of Henry. He really left me with an unsettled feeling. I want to scrub my skin and wash him off. Even though he didn't touch me, it feels like he did.

My room is still messy, and the surroundings that were becoming familiar make me settle a bit. The dresses are still thrown across my bed, the tight black one sitting on top of the pile. My stomach squeezes.

I need to shower and get ready. A small square piece of paper sits on my pillow. I unfold it and my heart instantly pounds when I see Lucas's name at the bottom.

**Meet me at eight in the main dining room.**

**Can't wait.**

**Lucas x**

I'm staring at the *x*. His handwriting is neat and precise. I read it again and smile.

*I'm doing this for Vicky*, I tell myself while stripping off my clothes to get into the shower.

My mind flickers from Henry to Lucas, and when I get out of the shower, I feel dizzy with my thoughts. I try to push them all aside as I start to get ready. My stomach flips when I stare in the mirror. The dress is tight. My mother would drown me in holy water if she saw me now.

I shift, thinking maybe I should change and go for something ladylike. Something she would approve of.

*Wear something tight.*

Lucas's words have me applying makeup. When I brush the red across my lips and smack them together, I meet my eyes in the mirror. I look so different, older. I grin. Sexy. Very sexy.

I keep second-guessing myself. I want to be late, but not to the point he thinks he's been stood up. After slipping my feet into high heels, I take one final look in the mirror before leaving my room.

I'm aware of how quiet it is. I thought Hannah and Jessie would be waiting in my room. Maybe they were watching TV in the drawing room. I was passing it so I would pop my head in and see if they were there.

I'm nervous.

So nervous.

I've decided I will tell Lucas about Henry so it won't be something that can come back and haunt me.

The drawing room is empty. I don't have time to look for them. I'm sure they'll pounce on me the moment the dinner is over. My stomach churns, and I push my hand against it, asking it to settle.

*This isn't a date*, I repeat, trying to settle my nerves. The main dining room doors are closed. They're normally open, and I'm surprised to see George standing at the door. His eyes widen when he sees me, and he reaches for the door to open it. There's something in his eyes that passes quickly before he pulls the door open fully. I keep my head bowed as I step into the dining room.

My head spins when I focus on the table, and everyone is focused on me. The blood in my veins turns cold, and I stumble in my heels. Sniggers ring out. A chair screeches. I hear every noise as I find my balance. My face flames. All the ladies are here, and everyone is staring at me. Lucas's dark eyes are empty as they meet mine. He'd set me up.

I continue walking and focus on the empty chair between Hannah and Jessie. They must have saved it for me. All the ladies are in stunning ball gowns, and my tight dress makes me look cheap.

A man sitting beside Lucas never takes his eyes off me. I stand taller and hold my head high as I walk to my chair, trying not to throw up. With the pounding in my ears, I can't hear Hannah as she greets me.

I know I need to calm down. Digging my nails into my palms helps me focus. The pain shoots up my arms, and I look up to find Lucas's father staring at me. There's no mistake about who he is. His lips tug up into a half grin. The way he looks at me makes me feel small.

*What's going on?*

I want to look at Lucas for an answer, but I'm afraid I'll leap across the table at him. He tricked me.

"I always think a lady should be fashionably late, but you, my dear, have sure made your entrance boldly." He's speaking to me, waiting for an answer, and I'm all tongue-tied.

"Sorry," I bite out quickly, and I swear I hear a few people gasp.

"I will excuse your manners since you missed my introduction. I'm Master Andrew, Lucas's father."

My throat tightens and squeezes with pure embarrassment. I glance at Lucas. I shouldn't, I know that, but I'm seeking out help. He's drinking from a tall-stemmed glass, his eyes distant, like I'm boring him to tears.

"I do apologize, Master Andrew." I dig my nails into my hands as I speak.

Hannah's small hand touches my leg, and I know she's telling me she's here. I feel like crying. Sweat gathers on my brows. Using the cloth napkin, I dab it carefully and slowly, trying not to draw attention to myself. But Lucas's father glances at me from the corner of his eye, freezing me to the spot. I drop the napkin onto my plate. It looks like everyone has eaten; their plates are already gone.

The door opens, and three ladies step in. They don't approach us, but Master Andrew waves them over. Within seconds, they've removed all unnecessary cutlery. One of the ladies stops at my plate.

"You can take it," I whisper to her, trying to force a smile. It's shaky, and I'm sure it looks pained.

"I'm sorry, Ella, but you will have to skip straight to dessert," Master Andrew addresses me again.

I swallow around the dryness in my throat. "Of course, Master Andrew." I reach for the water to quench my dry throat. The tremble of my hand is so obvious. I pull back to hide my hands and hit the glass of water, knocking it across the table. It's like a stampede of elephants as everyone jumps away from the table.

Master Andrew tuts, and over the noise, it reaches my ears as I mop up the water with my napkin.

"Leave it," Lucas barks at me as the room falls silent.

I meet his angry eyes—the depths are endless and dangerous. He works his jaw as he stares at me, and I've never wanted to slap someone like I want to slap him right now. My hand tightens around the napkin, and his eyes trail to it before snapping back up to me.

"Clean up this mess," Lucas's father calls, and the servants start to dry up my mess. The girls are looking at me like I've lost my mind. Everyone's dresses are fine, and once again, I die at all the stunning gowns.

Hannah's strong presence is beside me. It's awkward as we wait for the table to be reset. I can feel Lucas's eyes on me, but I don't dare look up. Right now, I'm just trying not to cry. Why did he do this to me? Was this punishment for Alex?

Once everyone is reseated, dessert arrives and the chatter commences. I pick at my apple pie and cream; it lodges in my throat, and when I swallow it feels like dry sand. I spend the rest of the time swirling it around the bowl as Master Andrew boasts about Lucas. What a perfect son he is, how fantastic he is at sports, what a pleasure he was growing up...

There are giggles and even Lucas speaks, gripping my attention. He sounds normal. No barking or anger. His father smiles fondly at him.

"I will, of course, be taking each lady out on a date." There's an excitement in the air. Lucas smiles at us all, and when his eyes clash with mine, they flash with something before he skips me quickly. Pain sears my stomach.

"I'm very excited to get to spend that quality time with you ladies."

I want to call him out on his blatant lies. I don't drink wine, but a glass in front of me tempts me with the promise of numbness. I manage to reach it, pick it up, and even drink down half the glass without spilling a drop. The alcohol warms my blood. As I place it back onto the table, Master Andrew is watching me. I can see the disapproval in his eyes before he paints on a fake smile and faces all the ladies again.

"I'm not going to lie. But the dates were my idea." He glances at Lucas, and it's like I'm watching the worst play ever. Lucas is acting like a puppet; he's smiling at his father like he cracked a joke. But why is everyone drinking up the lies?

"I have noticed"—Master Andrew exhales like his next words pain him—"that my son has started to favor one of you over all the others."

I can feel a few glances my way. My heart pounds and when I peek at Lucas, he won't meet my eye, but he knows I'm staring at him.

"Sandra, my darling, you are stunning, but all the other ladies deserve their chance too."

My mouth fills with saliva.

*Sandra? Sandra?*

Sandra raises her glass, a smug smile on her face, and her eyes shoot to me before returning to Master Andrew. "I will be a lady and allow everyone their opportunity to win Lucas's heart." She sounds so smug.

What's going on? I empty the wineglass, looking at everyone, trying to figure out what I missed. My mind is a mess.

"Why don't we all retire to the drawing room for a nightcap?" Master Andrew suggests.

Everyone is smiling, standing, but I don't move as pain continues to rip through me.

"Come on," Hannah whispers, reaching for me.

I don't dare meet her eyes. I know how kind Hannah is, and I know her eyes must be filled with pity. Different colored gowns all swish across the floor, and I've never felt so out of place. If this was punishment, Lucas made his point.

I take another glass of wine the moment I enter the drawing room. Everyone is talking about the upcoming dates. The excitement in the room has my skin itchy.

I have to sit as Lucas and his father continue praising the ladies and then praising themselves. I'm not unaware of how I'm skipped each time. His point has been driven home. He made a fool of me and I'm listening. The glass is empty, and I need another one. It's making me feel warm and settles my panic. I want to laugh and call Lucas out on his fraud as he talks about how he played football in college. He's acting... normal.

I'm glancing at the girls who are eating this up. My eyes clash with Lucas, and my heart pounds. You won. I hope he can see it in my eyes, which he says he can read so well.

I stand up and a few others glance at me. "May I be excused, Master Andrew?" I can't sit here any longer, tears burning my throat.

He nods at me and turns back to the other ladies, my dismissal quick. Like I'm an annoyance. My heart pounds at each step to the door. It's freedom from this charade, but once I step outside that door, I know I'm going to be alone and devastated with what's just happened.

# CHAPTER SIXTEEN

## LUCAS

ELLA LEAVES AND I want to race after her. I have never seen her fall apart like that. I tighten my hand into a fist. The squeak of the leather gloves has me relaxing my hands as my father gives me a sideward glance. He diverts his attention back to his audience, who he's captured beautifully. My stomach twists every time I think of the hurt on Ella's face.

My eyes snap to Sandra, who's watching me, and I can see the smile in her eyes. She must have removed my note. Each time Ella stumbled over her words or knocked over the water, Sandra's joy emanated from her. I wanted to hurt her. I glance at Hannah as she chews on her lip, and her eyes keep snapping to the door that Ella left through. Her worry is making my own grow.

"Excuse me, ladies." I stand up and speak. I can feel the waves of disapproval from my father. "I'm sure my charming father can keep you all entertained for a moment." I force a smile their way, and they giggle like a bunch of hyenas.

My stomach dips as I turn to my father. "Master Andrew."

He pulls his mask back into place. "I would be honored to entertain these stunning ladies."

More giggles. I don't linger but leave the room. I know I don't have much time. I just need to find her. I take the steps upstairs two at a time and pray she's in her room. Her door is closed. I knock, but I don't give her a chance to answer. Pushing open the door, my heart thuds. The room is empty.

I'm about to leave, when she stomps out of the bathroom. Her hair, which had been pinned up, is free, falling around her shoulders. Her eyes are on fire. I don't think I've ever seen anything so beautiful. I want her. I want every single part of her.

"Get out!" She's loud, too loud.

I kick the door closed behind me and immediately advance on her. "Keep your voice down."

Her eyes flash, and I grip her arms, stopping whatever she wants to say. I wish I wasn't wearing gloves so I could feel her skin.

"I left you a note," I say quickly, hoping to douse the flames that will consume us both.

She pulls away, and I'm shocked when she slams her hands into my chest. Not the reaction I was expecting.

"Get out." Her chest rises and falls rapidly, and behind her rage, I see it—her pain. I've hurt her.

"Ella." I push a warning into my voice.

Her eyes blur with unshed tears. "What, Lucas? You'll punish me?"

I get over my shock of her putting her hands on me and take a step toward her. She doesn't back away from me.

"Is that what you want? You want me to punish you?" I want to kiss her so badly. Her red lips are full and moving again.

"Haven't you already? Why?" Her face is crestfallen. "Why would you humiliate me like that? I thought I was already punished for talking to Alex." Her brows pull down, and she shakes her head.

My treacherous heart beats wildly. "I left you a note," I defend myself.

She laughs bitterly. "I got the note."

That surprises me. She turns on her heel, and I'm ready to reach her and pull her back, but she doesn't go far. She picks up the piece of paper off her bedside table and hands it to me.

"I told you we would reschedule," I say while opening it.

I can't help the smile that grows on my face; for the first time it's real. I didn't cause this. I glance up at Ella, and her eyes grow wider as she stares at me.

"This isn't my handwriting. That's not my note." I try not to sound so smug. Ella looks ready to explode. She snaps the note back, looks at it, then at me. "You're lying." Her voice is whispered.

I don't think I would know what she's saying if I wasn't watching her lips.

"Don't call me a liar," I warn and eradicate the space between us.

I see her conflict. I see her confusion. I've held back and my resolve snaps.

A squeal leaves her lips as I take her face in my hands and don't wait for her permission to kiss her. Her lips are frozen under my touch, but they soon mimic my movements, and Ella melts into me. Her body is warm against mine. My shaft grows quickly—I want her so bad. When she stepped into the dining room, I couldn't take my eyes off her.

She was stunning. All I wanted at that moment was to have Ella bent over the table, where I could take her over and over again.

A moan leaves her lips. Her hands are flush with my chest, and I can feel the slight push she gives me. There isn't much force behind it, but her internal struggle is leaking out. She pulls her lips away from mine, breathing heavily.

"Lucas." My name on her lips has my cock twitching. She sounds tortured.

I know I shouldn't be doing this. How would all this end? Ella stares up into my eyes.

"I didn't write that note." I know who did, but that wouldn't change this situation. It was foolish of me to think that Sandra wouldn't remove my note. I didn't think she would deceive Ella by writing her own.

"I'm sorry." My heart means it, and Ella's eyebrows shot up in surprise.

"I wish I could change things." There, I said it out loud.

Ella drops her eyes, cutting me off from her soul. It's an instant loss I refuse to accept. I tip her head back by holding her chin.

"Say something." Where is that fire?

"I want you to leave." She blinks and a tear falls.

Her words are like a lash to my back. I tighten my hold on her chin. She flinches and I want to take back control. She can't tell me to leave. She can't want me to leave, but she does.

"I told you, I didn't write that note," I repeat and when Ella stands taller and pulls her chin from my hand, I know I've lost this battle.

"I believe you. But it doesn't change anything."

I don't reach for her again. Maybe it's better this way. We'll both get hurt. She's already penetrated my skin and slid so silently into my bloodstream. I hadn't noticed until today how much I wanted her. How easily I could enjoy her company.

She swallows as she stares up at me. Her wide green eyes are still brimming with pain—pain I caused. My father had humiliated her, and I sat stiff and shut off all my emotions. I couldn't have interjected. If he knew how I felt about her, what would he do? I couldn't have Ella hurt. So I needed to make the pain a bit less for her.

I close the distance and place a kiss on her forehead. I linger longer than I should. It's on my lips to apologize again, but I don't. I don't look at her as I leave her room.

George is at the bottom of the stairs, and I hesitate. "Your father wants you to return." George's eyes hold pity.

"Thank you, George." Once again, he looks surprised at my manners. Before I enter the room, his old hand touches my shoulder. He doesn't say anything, and when I look at him, he releases me and walks away.

The room is erupting in giggles as I join my father. He gives me a moment's attention. I can't read the look, so I sit down and try to shut everything down. I can feel Hannah's eyes heavy on me, so I look at her and give her the briefest nod. She bites her lip as she sees it.

After that, I keep my feelings in check. Laugh when I should smile and lie about growing up in a happy household.

When my father calls it a night, we both give each lady a kiss on the cheek. Sandra is the last. No doubt she did that on purpose. She curtsies while smiling up at my father, who takes her hand and kisses it. She turns to me, and it might be small, it might not matter, but I refuse to kiss her.

"Good night, Miss Crowley."

Her smile falls, but she replaces it quickly. "Master Lucas."

I turn away from her before I hurt her. When the door closes, it's me and my father.

"That went well," he starts with, and I just want him to say what he needs to about Ella so I can leave.

"Good night, son." I raise my head to look at my father. His smile is cruel as he holds the door handle.

"Sleep well." He closes the door, leaving me alone with a new fear. Is he going to hurt Ella? Why didn't he mention it?

A knock on the door has me looking up. George is there, and I'm holding my breath, though I don't know why.

"A phone call, Master Lucas."

"Take a message." I know being gruff with George isn't right, but I'm filling up with an uneasy feeling.

"I did offer to take a message, but it's from Yellow Grange Laboratory. They said they'll only talk to you."

I run a hand across my face. "Of course. I'll take it in the study."

I try to push my troubles aside as I sit down in my office chair. Picking up the phone, I take the information that surprises me.

"The interesting part was that the finger was embalmed, preserving it all these years."

Thirty years ago. The finger is thirty years old.

"We do have a match. A Sorcha Newtown." The name means nothing to me.

"Anything else?"

"It's her wedding finger."

I don't know what any of this means, but it gives me somewhere to start digging for an answer. I need to find out who Sorcha Newtown was.

I end the call with instructions on delivering the finger back to me. I repeat my earlier warning about not telling anyone, which will buy me some time. No doubt, my father will be informed. Fear makes them responsive to him. After placing the receiver in its holder, I think about my father's earlier response to Ella, or his lack of one.

A part of me wants to have her sent home so she'll be safe, but the more selfish part of me wants to keep her here.

I'll have Mark watch over her when I can't. Keeping my distance would be the right thing to do for both me and Ella. I just don't think I'm that strong.

# CHAPTER SEVENTEEN

## ELLA

L UCAS HAS INVADED EVERY space inside me. I still feel the burn of his kiss on my forehead. It was heavy with goodbye. It was heavy with his apology. It was heavy with regret.

I swallow around the lump in my throat. Too much swirls around me. Sucking in my lip, I bite it hard and try to stop the tears that want to flow. I don't know how long I stand like that in a tornado of humiliation, fear, and longing when the door opens.

Hannah's there, and it's like the wind stops howling and an eerie silence takes over. She breaks it when she rushes to me with tears brimming in her eyes.

"Oh, Ella."

I'm in her arms, and I can't stop it. I can't control the tears that rip free from me. I cry for the girl who was sold a fairy tale. I cry for the child that danced on her bed in a small yellow dress thinking she was just like Belle. I cry for today. I cry for now. I cry for wanting him.

"It's okay." Hannah runs her hands up and down my back. I step away from her and try to stop the flow of tears, but looking into her eyes is like looking into flames that ignite my pain.

"I've dreamt of this my whole life," I tell her and she's nodding. I know she would have dreamt about it too, but I just need to get it out of me. I need to make sense of my pain.

"I'm here. I made it." My throat burns as a fresh wash of tears erupt. I can't even finish my sentence or train of thought, but Hannah stands patiently.

I shrug while tapping my chest. "I just feel it in here." I have no other way to explain how this all feels.

"You'll be okay." Hannah brushes hair back from my face, her smile wide and sad. "You're the strongest of them all."

I half laugh, half cry at her words before sniffling. "I don't feel very strong."

"You are," she reassures me.

"I know you must have dreamt of this moment too. I wasn't trying to be insensitive."

Her eyes grow lighter as she shakes her head. "I didn't ever believe I would be picked from seven other girls. So I've already applied for college."

That surprises me. "Why would you not be picked?"

I think she's the most beautiful of us all.

She shrugs. "I don't know. I just didn't think I would, so I'm okay with it."

I wish I was like her. I wish I hadn't set my whole life on this, but from as far back as I can remember, everything I did was about this moment. It was all building up to it.

"College sounds nice. I think I'll have to apply." I can't stop the quiver in my voice.

Hannah shocks me by laughing. "No, you won't." Her laugh melts into a smile. "You will marry Lucas."

She has no idea what she's saying.

The door opens and my heart thunders. Jessie steps in, looking unsure. "Is it okay to come in?"

I swallow down my upset and smile at her. "Of course."

She closes the door behind her and gives me a brief hug, but it means so much to me. Having Hannah and Jessie will ease the ache I'm feeling.

The girls are good to me. Over the next few days, they try to keep me occupied. We spend the time watching too many criminal investigation programs. On one of the episodes, it's about a staged suicide. I shift uncomfortably. I hate the feelings it drags up in me, ones I never really faced before.

"I'm going for a walk." I get off the couch, and Hannah stands too, stretching.

She's been stuck to me since the whole Lucas thing happened. I haven't seen him in days; he had just disappeared. I've found myself looking around me for him as I walk through the house, but each time, I only come eye to eye with Mark, who's starting to creep me out.

"I'm coming too."

I wave her off. "Stay and watch your program. I promise I won't be long." I just want the time to myself. Jessie pulls Hannah back down onto the couch.

"She's fine," she tells her, and I leave the girls watching TV.

It's cool outside, and immediately, I regret not wearing something warmer. My long skirt and light shirt were fine in the house, but outside, a wind that carries a coldness blows.

Inhaling the fresh air, I try to rid my thoughts like they're pebbles, leaving each one in the flower beds as I pass. As I mentally do this, I collect an actual flower in its place. It's therapeutic.

I want to find that happiness I always felt with life. The wonder, the mystery. The possibilities, to me, were always endless. Like an adventure was just around the corner, one that would shape me into a strong person.

I never expected this place. I never expected Alex to leave me that first day. I drop a mental pebble and pick a flower. It's a yellow buttercup, the color vibrant and fresh.

My hands tighten and I try not to crush the flower as I think of my punishment for speaking to Alex. It also makes me think of the handshake I had endured with Lucas. I frown when I think of every insult, every hurtful tactic of his, yet I saw past all that to the man behind the mask. The man who seared me with a kiss. I'd never felt so off balance with someone before. Like the ground was shifting under my feet. I look up as I pass several flower beds.

I stop to try to sort it out. I just feel lost. I have no idea what's going to happen or where this will end.

I walk as far as the maze but don't enter it. I don't want to be in Henry's company again. The thought of him makes me wrap my arms around my waist and return to the house.

I arrive just as supper is being served. We've all fallen into a routine over the last couple of days. It's like since Lucas disappeared, we've just learned how to fill our days.

The soup warms me, and I'm aware of how quiet Hannah is. "What's wrong?" I ask her and she looks at Jessie.

"Jessie." I raise a brow, knowing whatever it is, Jessie will spit it out. Hannah has a tendency to go around things, though I know she's just trying to spare my feelings.

"The dates started the other day."

I try not to react. My stomach hollows, and the soup hits the pit of it heavily. I bob my head while Hannah chews on her lip. "We all knew they were happening."

I want to ask who went and where. I don't think I can eat. After placing my spoon into my bowl, I butter a small roll to give myself something to do.

"Bernie and Mary had their dates," Hannah whispers to me. The other girls are so loud that they can't hear us.

"Where did they go?" When I ask, Jessie and Hannah smile. "What?" I question.

Hannah tries to look innocent. "I just thought you didn't care."

"I don't."

Jessie snickers.

I force a spoon of soup into my mouth and decide I should forget about it. It doesn't matter.

"Both of their dates were in the garden."

I incline my head while taking another spoon of soup. I know Jessie is still smiling so I refuse to look at her.

"They said he was charming."

I can't stop myself from looking at Jessie, and she bursts out laughing.

"Stop teasing," Hannah warns, and the tension in my body has me stiffening.

"I'm only messing," Jessie says.

I need to relax. They were so good to me the last few days. "I know. I'm too uptight," I say with a smile.

"Yeah, I do think you need to loosen up a bit." Sandra's voice is like nails on a chalkboard.

"Private conversation," Hannah informs her and I grin. Hannah is always nice, so to see her with a raised brow and attitude is funny.

"I just think Ella needs to lighten up. No one died."

I glance at Sandra with her smug smile. Does she know? Was that a direct jab at me? My heart pounds wildly. She couldn't know. Unless Lucas somehow knows and told her. My hands grow slick with sweat.

I force a wobbly smile. "You're right, Sandra. No one has died, yet."

Mary and Bernie sit on either side of her and inhale deeply, like what I said was scandalous.

"Did you just threaten me?" Sandra doesn't sound put out. In fact, she sounds smug.

"I don't want to report you to Master Andrew. I'm sure threatening my life would have you sent home. I mean, Vicky was sent home over a slap, and since I'm the favorite and about to have a ring on my finger…" She spreads her fingers and looks at her imaginary ring.

I feel sick.

"Maybe it's time you went home so we don't all have to look at your pitiful face." Flicking her long blonde hair across her shoulder, she glares at me.

Hannah leans forward, but I put my hand on her arm to stop her.

"Report me," I say, and Sandra's glare dissolves. Now she just looks unsure. I push out my chair and stand.

"I will," Sandra bites back, her temper flaring.

"Do that," I say with a smile.

Her cheeks glow. "I will," she shouts.

My smile widens. "Good. I don't want to be here." I turn on my heel, and not for the first time, find someone watching me, only this time it's Master Andrew.

It's my turn to have my cheeks blaze with color. He's walking toward the table, and honestly there's a large chance I'm going home, so I continue to leave the room. I don't look at Lucas's father as I pass him. I'm ready and waiting for him to stop me, but he doesn't. My pace slows, and I glance over my shoulder at his receding back.

"Could I have a word, Master Andrew?" I can hear Sandra say.

"In a moment," he tells her.

I'm out the door with a pounding heart and sweaty palms.

Why didn't he say anything about what he overheard? Was there a chance he hadn't heard us fighting?

Does it really matter?

I go to my room and consider packing so I'm ready. But I'm not ready. Instead, I take a shower and change into my nightdress. I'm pacing, staring at my door, but no one enters. No one comes to send me home, and that in itself is far more disturbing.

I'm waiting and waiting—for what, I'm not sure—but I finally get into bed and close my eyes.

Sleep is hard to find, but it finally sends me down a dark path, one filled with memories of my father. Against my will, he haunts me with his songs and smiles. I can see the vodka bottle lying on the wooden floor, his feet floating in the air. Hands cover my eyes, and I'm surrounded by my mother's perfume and tears.

I wake with a pounding heart. I'm not overwhelmed with sadness, but I was only six when my dad died.

I was only six when he took his life.

I was only six when I found him hanging from the fan ceiling.

# CHAPTER EIGHTEEN

## ELLA

Pushing back the quilts, I hope to also push aside the doom I'm feeling as I step out onto lush carpet. I focus on the feel of it under my feet and the feel of the soft sheets under my palms. I focus on the here and now.

Glancing around my room, I notice it's as messy as my mind, so I start to clean. I clean until the sun breaks through the crack in my curtains. I do as my mother always told me. You must touch each item in a room to effectively have the room cleaned. So that's what I do. Every item, every garment, moves through my hands. I focus on textures, colors, and the smell. Once I have that done, I take a shower and get dressed for the day.

I'm sitting on the side of my bed, ready for breakfast. The door creaks open, and I'm expecting Jessie and Hannah since I didn't see them after my fight with Sandra.

Blood pools into my shoes as Master Andrew steps into my room, a crooked smile on his face he gently closes the door behind him. I swallow as I focus on his leather-gloved hands.

My mind flashes to all the murders we saw on the criminal show. I shush the overdramatic voice in my head and get off my bed.

"You are a very hard woman to get by herself." His words are delivered with a smile that chases a shiver down my spine. "Your friends are very loyal," he continues as he steps into the room and looks around him. "I had to send them all for breakfast early, along with Mark, who seems to be hovering over you."

That snippet of information surprises me, but I don't allow him to see it. I hope I have my emotions hidden.

"You didn't know you were being watched?" He sounds amused.

I mentally kick myself. I'm so easy to read. I need to focus on the floor or something so he can't see my eyes.

"No," I answer him as he stands, staring at me. The depths of blackness in his eyes are endless.

Lucas's father removes his gloves, and my shoulders loosen. "We have rules in my home. We have rules in my community." His smile sends another shiver racing down my spine. I tighten my hands in front of me.

"Why do you think we have rules, Ella?"

I hate my name on his lips. I can see the intimidating part of Lucas in this man, but that's as far as the similarities go.

Before I can answer him, he raises his hand. "To keep people in line. Otherwise, chaos would descend, and with chaos comes a collapse of the community. It's like a vicious dog. You must keep a tight hold on the leash. Only let him go so far. Hold it tight but never release him."

*Is he comparing us young girls to vicious dogs?* I don't comment. I don't think he wants me to anyway. He continues his lecture that is surely going to lead back to me fighting with Sandra. My stomach hollows with the thought of leaving.

"During this race for my son's hand, there are rules." He pauses and I nod.

He smiles. "If you put your hand on someone, you are disqualified and sent home. We have a very clear example of this with Vicky, who hurt you, and my son had her removed instantly."

My heart skyrockets.

"If you threaten someone's life, you are disqualified and sent home with no compensation package."

Compensation package? I had no idea any of us got one.

Lucas's father exhales loudly like he's been pondering, but he hasn't. This is rehearsed; he knows the end result. I just wish he'd get to it.

"So how do you plead, Ella?"

Here it is—he's offering me an out. I want to take it, but what am I going back to? My mother? I will never see Lucas again. Will I get to say goodbye?

"I threatened her," I answer honestly and look away from Lucas's father's gleeful smile.

"I know you did. I heard you. You aren't stupid enough to lie to me." His words grow harsher as he steps closer to me. "You might think you have my son's protection, but you don't."

I open my mouth to respond, ready to disagree. I never thought for one second that I had Lucas's protection.

"I'm not looking for an answer." His raised voice roots me in place. "You were also retested after being found with Alex?"

Fire flames across my chest and up my neck. Not this again. "Yes," I answer.

"The results?" He raises a brow. He knows what happened, so why is he making me say it?

"I didn't do anything." I hate the quiver in my voice.

It's only a split second, and Lucas's father is in front of me. The sting of his glove across my face has saliva pooling in my mouth. He steps back quickly, and the air catches in my lungs. He just struck me.

"You have no manners. You're like a petulant child. You must answer me with 'Yes, Master Andrew.' The fact I even have to correct you on this is annoying."

I touch my throbbing cheek as my vision blurs with tears. "Sorry, Master Andrew."

He releases a heavy sigh, and I'm questioning if he just did that. But my burning face confirms he did.

"Why were you late to the meal the night you made a mess at the table?"

My brain is scrambling. My burning face takes up too much of my thoughts. I try to push it down. "I got lost in the maze, Master Andrew."

His smile is cruel. "And I'm just to take your word for it that you weren't with Alex again?"

I tighten my fists at what he's saying. I look away from him before he sees my anger. *Focus, Ella.*

"Of course not, Master Andrew." I look up at him now. "Henry found me in the maze. He can vouch for me." Jesus, I hope he would, but he's the only other person who saw me that day.

"Henry?" He seems surprised.

"Yes," I bite out and his head snaps up to me, anger filling his eyes. A bolt of fear shoots through me. "Master Andrew," I quickly correct myself.

"What will I do with you?" He's taken a step closer to me. I can't look away from the gloves he holds in his hands. My body is tight, waiting for him to strike out.

"I'm asking you a question."

Sweat has gathered at the back of my neck, and I want to scratch it but I don't dare move. "I'll get packing, Master Andrew. I did, after all, threaten Sandra."

His laugh is harsh. "Oh, Ella. I'm not sending you home."

My confusion overflows my system, and my body grows heavy with a need to sit.

"You are the leash I need to use to keep my vicious dog in line. He favors you, I see it. Everyone does. Personally, I don't see why he would pick you."

His words have my heart lifting at the acknowledgment that Lucas favors me, but also crashing at what he's saying.

"But, alas, here we are. I will punish you for threatening Sandra and for being disrespectful on several occasions."

I want to ask what my punishment will be, but I hold still, trying to focus over the blood pounding in my ears.

He slowly places his gloves back on. "So here is my warning." He looks up and smiles softly.

"Play nice." He closes the distance, and I lock my legs so I don't instinctively step back. He's glaring at me, his eyes roaming my face like he's searching for something.

"Yes, Master Andrew." My words have the desired effect. He steps back, turns on his heel, and leaves my room.

In my bathroom mirror, my face is raw, red from the slap. I run a washcloth under cold water, my hands shaking as I try to complete the simple task without dropping it. Pushing the cold cloth against my face, the relief is almost instant. Water drops along the sleeves of my jumper, but I don't care.

I place the cloth under the cold water again before placing it back on my face. I stay at the sink and keep cooling my face down until the cold starts to pinch my skin. I refuse to meet my eyes in the mirror. I refuse to let what just happened sink in.

I don't want to give him any more power over me. This is my choice, what I do with this moment, and right now, I decide to bury it along with all my other moments.

I change my top and take my hair down, letting it cover my swollen cheek.

Everyone is at breakfast when I enter the dining room. I know it will take a lot to act normal. But he won't win. I won't hide. This is my way of standing up to him.

Talk ceases as I enter and I look up, refusing to be leashed. Sandra's cheeks redden at the sight of me. She must have thought I was gone, and I use my little moment of victory and smile at her. The pain in my cheek ignites at the movement.

"Sorry I'm late," I tell Hannah, who's staring at my face, and I shake my head and hope she can see the pleading in my eyes not to ask.

Surprisingly, she doesn't, and we get through breakfast like it's any other morning.

After breakfast, I stick close to Hannah. I don't want to be alone with my thoughts. She seems very distant today, and I wonder if she's worrying about my face. Jessie hasn't said much either, and now I wonder if something happened to them for being my friend.

"Are you okay?" I ask Hannah as we settle in the drawing room. I have no idea where Sandra, Mary, or Bernie are. I'm just glad they aren't here.

"Yes," Hannah lies.

Jessie rolls her eyes. "Dear God, just tell her, Hannah."

My stomach twists as I look at Hannah. Oh, no. Dread pools in my shoes as she looks up at me. *Please don't tell me he hurt her.*

"My date with Lucas is today."

I let out a half laugh of relief. "Stop worrying and enjoy it." I give her a real smile, and her lips tug up, her blue eyes widening.

"Thanks, Ella." She hugs me, and when I meet Jessie's eyes, she isn't smiling.

"You want to tell us about your face?"

I'm more grounded now, so I keep my smile on as I think of Hannah and Jessie being safe.

"I'm embarrassed, but since you both are my friends..." I sit down with a smile. "I tripped over a floor full of clothes." I hold up my hands.

Hannah buys it and starts laughing. Jessie smiles, but she's not completely convinced.

"I went to your room last night after the whole Sandra thing, but you were asleep," Hannah says when she stops laughing. "And it was a mess."

"Yeah, Master Andrew kept us talking until I wanted to shove a bread roll into his mouth to shut him up."

I grin at Jessie. I wouldn't mind shoving a few more into his mouth too. I'm sure they would fit.

I keep my mind focused on the here and now as we chat. I don't let it drift off to the dark corner of my mind. My smile widens as I strengthen my resolve. I am not going there. No, I'm staying here with my friends, even if it lasts only a little while.

# CHAPTER NINETEEN

## LUCAS

I'VE SPENT THE LAST few days going through the members' records. I found a Sorcha Newtown, but nothing much about her. She was married with one child. Her family donated five million to the community. But there's nothing about her death, and no details at all about a missing finger. I've locked myself away, hoping to keep my distance from Ella. Each day, it's getting harder. Having Mark giving me updates has kept me from going to her.

*She is safe.*

I pick up another old leather-bound book and flip it open. The pages are surprisingly fresh. Everything is handwritten and curvaceous, making it hard to read.

It's a list of rules. Some of them are laughable. If you're caught stealing from a member of the elite community, you lose a hand. If you steal from your own neighbor, it's a full thirty seconds in the electric chair—unless that member is from the elite community, in which case it reverts back to the first rule and you lose your hand. Put your hand on an elite, and you also lose a limb. I flicker through it, my stomach twisting. These could still be enforced if we wants.

I couldn't imagine that these specific rules are in the ladies' contracts. A reference to the rules in the smallest of prints is what I imagine. I stop turning the pages when I make out the word *finger*.

If one is found to be unfaithful to their spouse, they'll be given two minutes in the electric chair, followed by the removal of their wedding finger.

I'm rereading it, making sure I have it correctly. My mind skips back to Declan's wake. His hands had been perfectly arranged, but when I looked closely, I could see the slight gap. It was his wedding finger too.

Both Sorcha Newtown and Declan were having affairs. Both lost their ring fingers. But why are both of them dead? Why did someone see fit to kill them?

Closing the book, I stare out from the desk in the small room, where all the files, rules, and the history of our community are kept. Getting up, I take out Declan's file. There's no mention of his tattoo or how he died. I'm surprised to see they mentioned his finger, but not which one was missing.

I pause at the noise of someone outside the door. My heart palpitates and as quietly as I can, I put the file and the book back, just as the door opens. My relief is short-lived as Mark steps into the room. There's something precarious in his eyes that has my full attention.

"Master Lucas, I have word on your father."

My heart crashes against my chest. Mark's skin has whitened, and I'm tempted to grab him by the collar of his shirt.

"He visited Ella."

I don't move. I don't breathe.

Mark purses his lips. "I'm not comfortable reporting on him."

I react quickly, pushing the table aside, and I hold firm, not touching him. "Tell me everything."

"As far as I can gather, she threatened Sandra's life."

Trepidation drips slowly into my bloodstream and feeds my fear. What is the punishment for threatening another lady?

"So he had a word with her about it. I'm not sure what transpired, but he struck her."

The blood freezes in my veins.

"Master Lucas, you should..." I'm out the door, with Mark on my heels. "Think about what you're doing. This isn't wise."

I pause and I'm so close to hitting him. "Be quiet."

He's stiff as I turn to him, but he stops following me.

I can't allow any thoughts or feelings to enter my system. My goal is to get to my father. That's it. I don't see the space around me as I move. My footfalls are as quick as my heartbeat. I find him in the main library. His smile is quick when he sees me. It's not a smile you give to a son you love. It's a smile of victory, like he knows what he's done.

My steps falter and I breathe for the first time. Mark's words about this not being wise are at the forefront of my mind. I want to let him know he's right about Ella, but it would put her more in his line of sight. My hands tighten, but he struck her. He put his hands on her.

"Is there something the matter, son?" His taunting tone should be my indicator that he's toying with me, but I eliminate the space between us.

"You put your hands on her." The words are low as I try to reel in some of the darkness that floats around me. My father pauses what he's doing.

His smile is gone. The deadness in his eyes would terrify me on any given day, but today, I'm beyond the consequences.

"She's off limits." My voice remains low. If it rises, I fear I'll snap.

"You don't give me orders."

My resolve liquifies onto the floor, and I grip his neck, his eyes widening in shock.

"She's off limits," I repeat.

He removes my hand from his neck. The shock passes quickly. "I did you a favor. She should have been punished for her actions." He steps away from me, and rightfully so. "She may still be punished."

He's toying with me. I could play along to a lot of his games, but just not this one.

Not her.

"I'll marry Sandra. I'll be the leader you want me to be. But, Ella has to be left alone or I won't make this easy."

His lips quirk up. "She will have to be punished for threatening Sandra's life."

I'm already shaking my head. "No. There will be no deal. She is to be left alone."

"How will it look to the other girls?" My father doesn't really care how it will look.

"I'm sure you can think of something to say."

His smile is gone as he takes a step toward me, but he still keeps his distance. The red mark around his neck looks starker now. "Fine, she won't be punished."

I'm not satisfied. I want his blood for touching her. He must see the hunger in my eyes for violence.

"You do know—and I'm only telling you this so you can control yourself better—that her family is now bankrupt."

I take a step closer. "I don't care. She's off limits."

"I'm trying to educate you, son."

I don't respond. I don't care what he says. His words are twisted and dipped in his own personal venom.

"Her father killed himself to clear all their debts, but suicide isn't an insurable death, so her mother was left with the bills. Ella has been groomed for you, for your statue in this community, for your money."

*Her father took his life. Oh, Ella.*

His words annihilate any calm I had, and I'm fueled with a new anger. He's breaking down my walls to the darkest part of me.

"I don't care. She's to be left alone." I feel powerful for the first time when I see fear widen his eyes. He tries to bounce back. He tries to smile, but it's wobbly.

I don't hear the knock at the door. I don't know how many times George has called me, but my father stares over my shoulder.

"Master Lucas, Master Andrew." He nods to my father.

I can't speak or the anger will flow right out of me, and George isn't my target.

"Your date is ready and waiting." He bows quickly and leaves.

Date. I have a date with Hannah now. Some of my anger deflates but ignites as I glance back at my father.

I know I will be punished for my outburst today, for putting my hands on him. According to the books, I could lose my hand, but I can't stay quiet.

"She will be left alone?" I repeat.

I need to hear him say it. There's a lull I want to pack with anger, but my father turns his back on me.

"She will be left alone." He walks to his desk and sits down. When he looks up at me, his composure is back and anger swells in his dark eyes. "But you will be punished."

I nod. I accept that. "Yes, Master Andrew."

His lips curl up, and he bends his head and continues on with his paperwork like we just had a father-son chat.

\*\*\*

The picnic has been set out in the same spot as all my other dates. Only this time, I don't mind being in Hannah's company. She eats the grapes slowly as she looks around her. When her eyes land on me, she coughs, which turns into a choking noise, and she reaches for a drink and gulps it down. When I reach her, she's red in the face but breathing.

"That grape really got stuck." Her voice quivers as she glances up at me.

I sit down and try to calm all the wrong in me. "I'm glad it's unstuck."

Her smile is like a 100-watt bulb. Her eyes are wide and sky blue. She has an innocence about her that I like. Her friendship with Ella is real. She couldn't fake it, and Ella needs a friend right now. I pour myself a glass of water and refill Hannah's.

"It's a beautiful day, Master Lucas." Hannah sips her water.

I can't stop the tug at my lips. She's so nervous. "I don't bite," I say.

She gives a nervous laugh. "Well, I don't taste very good." She quickly slaps a hand over her mouth, and her face inflames. "I didn't mean it like... You said bite and..." She rolls her eyes.

I know there's nothing sexual about her reference, and I allow Hannah's temperament to ease my shoulders.

I smile. "Speak freely, Hannah."

She removes her hand from her mouth and smiles widely. Picking up a small sandwich, she starts to eat.

"I think you need to marry Ella and not Sandra."

"Why is that?" I ask.

"Ella is kind, caring, and beautiful. She's pretty funny too."

She's really trying to sell her friend. She stops to eat her sandwich, and I wait, letting her chew.

"Sandra isn't all the things that Ella is. In fact, she's the opposite." She looks up from her sandwich to see my reaction.

"You said to speak freely." Her lips tug down.

I try to relax. I'm not making this easy on her.

I bring another smile to the surface. "Yes, I would like that." It's not fair to her to spend the date talking about Ella.

"Tell me about you," I say.

She's eating again and I suppress another smile. "I like peanut butter sandwiches."

I open one of the sandwiches on the plate in front of me. "Cucumber." I never liked them.

She shrugs. "I'm an emotional eater. I eat when I'm nervous."

"Tell me something else." There's no point in telling her not to be nervous, because she will be regardless. I never make it easy for people. My presence always makes people nervous.

"I want to be a doctor."

Her admission surprises me. She's the first that has spoken of a life beyond marrying me.

"How would you marry me and be a doctor?" I ask.

She smiles. "I didn't expect to be picked, Master Lucas." She starts to eat another sandwich, her cheeks rosy red.

"Don't cut yourself short, Hannah. You are far more worthy than most of the girls."

She smiles, a piece of cucumber stuck in her teeth. "Thanks. That's really sweet." The piece of food dislodges, and she shrugs. "But I think someone else has captured your attention."

I take a drink of water so I don't smile as she swings the conversation back to Ella. Ella, who I can never have. Knowing that makes me want her more.

The piece of paper in my pocket feels like it's burning me. I reach in and take it out.

"Can you give this to her?" I ask.

Hannah is no longer smiling. Her face is serious as she reaches for the note, but I hesitate. After what Sandra did with my note, I'm apprehensive.

"If I find out you tampered with it..." I force the warning into my voice.

Hannah is like a deer waiting for the impact of an oncoming car.

I smile and her body softens, but she still seems wary.

"Just give that to Ella."

She takes the note and holds it tightly. We continue our date, and as nice as Hannah is, my mind won't leave Ella. Our date is tomorrow, and I'll finally get to see her.

# CHAPTER TWENTY

## ELLA

I KEEP PACING ACROSS the floor as I wait for Hannah to return from her date. I've left the door open so I can see out onto the landing. The noise of someone climbing the stairs has me sitting on my bed and trying to look like I'm not counting down the seconds since she left. Her smiling face appears at my door, and I try to look surprised.

"Hi."

Hannah races to the bed and lands beside me with a piece of paper in her outstretched hands.

"What's that?" I ask.

"It's for you. From Lucas."

I take the note and open it. Hannah's excitement has me smiling.

I look forward to seeing you at our date tomorrow.

Lucas

I glance up at Hannah. "My date is tomorrow."

She claps and bounces with excitement. My own is bubbling up, until she stops and gives me a soft smile.

"Are you going to tell me what really happened to your face?"

I'm surprised by her question. I really had thought she believed me. I rise and put the note that Lucas gave me into my drawer.

"Lucas's father slapped me." I return to the bed and can't help but touch my face. "With a pair of leather gloves."

Hannah shakes her head. "What? Why would he do that?"

"He said I had no manners." This knowledge is dangerous to share, and the last person I want to endanger is Hannah. I know I still have to be punished. I have no doubt that Lucas's father isn't finished with me yet.

"Oh, Ella. What a monster." She squeezes my hands.

"Hannah, you can't ever tell anyone."

She chews her lip, and I pull her hands, getting her full attention. "I'm serious. Please don't tell anyone."

She nods reluctantly. "Okay."

"Now tell me about the rest of your date." I move to calmer waters and listen as Hannah tells me every detail. I smile through most of it. She sounds hilarious.

I spend the rest of the day in a daze. I try to avoid Sandra and her narrowed eyes. She looks angry every time she sees me. She must be surprised that I'm still here and wasn't sent away. I want to tell her that I'm just as surprised as she is.

That night, I can't sleep and toss and turn until the morning bursts through my curtains telling me it's going to be a warm day. I've decided for today that I will wear a lilac spaghetti-strap summer dress for my date with Lucas. The way we parted the last time made me nervous. I'm excited to see him. I've missed seeing him, but I also have to remember that this isn't going to go any further. Sandra is his future, not me. Straight away, my heart plummets as I think of his father's words. I've been kept here to keep him in line. I need to warn him. I don't know what Lucas can do, but I need to tell him.

He never has to know about the slap—I'll leave that out. I doubt he would believe me anyway.

I arrive at the spot where we're having our picnic. George smiles at me. "Miss O'Leary." He greets me while gesturing to the rug placed on the lawn. It's surrounded by all the flower beds. It's a perfect place.

"Thank you." I sit down and take in the wicker picnic basket that's half-open. The food has already been laid out, and it's identical to what Hannah described. My stomach churns nervously, and I run my hand across my hair and fix my dress. I'm so nervous.

I'm not sure how he'll act around me. My stomach flips as I spot him across the way. He looks even more divine, and I try to calm my pounding heart. He's favored a white shirt that has three buttons open at the top, showing his tanned skin. The closer he gets, the heavier my heart beats, and I drop my gaze from his inky eyes. I can't figure out if he's happy to see me or not, but I pour myself a glass of water and instantly think of Hannah eating all this food.

I smile and it calms my heart. Lucas's legs come into view, and he squats down in front of me. I look up into eyes, and I wouldn't mind drowning in them. He reaches out a hand.

"Come for a walk with me."

George is still here, and he clears his throat. In a warning? I'm not sure how wise it is. But, this one day, this one moment, I will live it. I place my hand in his. The feel of his skin is warm, and I allow him to help me to my feet. Once I'm standing, there's a moment where we're standing so close and he still holds my hand. Against my better judgment, I look up at him. His free hand touches my cheek with a gentleness that weakens my knees. His eyes are an oasis of turmoil as he strokes his thumb across my damaged cheek.

No words are passed between us. No words are needed. He knows. He knows and he's angry. My vision blurs and I want to cling to him, but I remember George is watching. Letting my eyelashes rest on my cheeks, I release Lucas's hand and step away, causing his hand to flutter to his side.

"A walk sounds nice." My voice is more controlled. When I glance back up at Lucas, his eyes search mine for answers.

I start to walk, cutting off his nonverbal interrogation of my heart.

"I haven't seen you around much lately, Master Lucas." My delivery of his title is automatic. Maybe his father's discipline did work.

Warm fingers wrap around my wrist and over the beating of my heart. "He will never put his hands on you again."

Each strike of my heart is bending the bit of willpower I had coming to this date. "Thank you," I whisper. I have no idea what Lucas had to do or say to make that possible, but not to be in constant fear of his father means everything to me.

His eyes bore into mine until it's nearly uncomfortable to hold his stare. He's too much right now—too much anger, pain, and regret swirl in his stunning eyes.

We continue walking, both of us silent. It's not how I saw this date going. I don't know what I expected, but not this kind of pain. Each time I steal a peek at Lucas, his jaw is clenched or his shoulders are tight. He doesn't seem like he wants to be here.

Maybe that's why he wanted us to walk instead of sitting down and talking.

We walk along the hedge of the maze, and I know soon we'll come to the opening. The maze I nearly got lost in. I shiver as I think of

Henry, but the cold abates quickly as I feel Lucas move closer to me, his warmth wrapping around me like a warm blanket.

"Are you cold? I'd offer you a jacket if I had one."

I think of him taking off his shirt for me. I'd get to see what's underneath. I try to drag my mind out of the gutter. "I'm not cold," I admit as we reach the entrance of the maze. I have a thought, and my heart pounds as I take a step toward it.

"What are you doing?" Lucas doesn't follow me as I take a few steps into the maze.

Looking at him over my shoulder, I see fear in his eyes. "Come in."

He doesn't move. "Come out." He sounds irritated, and I know if I go back out to the garden, our date will end and I might not see him again. My stomach twists painfully. This is my only chance. I turn and run into the maze.

"Ella." His warning has me smiling. He's mad, but he's following me.

I don't really go far, and he catches me easily. Spinning me around, I second-guess myself when I see the fire in his eyes. His lips crash down on mine, and I react straight away like two chemicals mixing, exploding, and becoming one.

I cling to his wide shoulders as he moves us back toward the wall of greenery. Twigs and branches dig into my back, but it supports us and allows our bodies to mash together. I can feel his erection, and I grow wet instantly. Lucas's large hands graze my shoulders, pushing down the straps of my dress. His lips leave mine and follow the path that his hands just made.

Each kiss is carved into my skin, branding me. Scarring me. I pull Lucas's face back up to mine, craving his kisses. He's panting and so am I.

When he pauses, I fear he'll stop. I don't want us to think right now. All I know is that I just want him. I slam my lips against his, and he groans into my mouth before pushing his body harder against mine. His erection has me shifting.

His hands grip my face as he deepens the kiss with his tongue. He tastes of mint and lust.

I touch the bare skin at the top of his shirt and want nothing more but to have it off. The heat of his skin has my own searing.

When his hands leave my face and touch my arms, I shiver under his fingertips. My shiver turns into a tremble as he continues down and slowly lifts my dress until his hands touch my bare thighs. It's a bolt of lightning into my system, and I cling to his shoulders again to keep myself upright.

Lucas's lips leave mine as he kisses my jawline, at the same time pushing aside my panties. Automatically, I spread my legs a little more, giving him access as he dips his fingers inside me. Both of us groan.

"You're so wet," he whispers in my ear as he pushes his finger deeper before pulling it out. The loss is immediate. I groan, and he pushes back in. This time, with two fingers, stretching me.

I spread my legs further, giving him more access. His lips return to mine, and our kisses are broken with my heavy gasps and moans. Lucas continues his rhythm of plunging his fingers inside me. My body is alive. My breasts feel heavy in my bra, and my nipples brush the fabric almost painfully. A feeling in me is building, and I clamp down on Lucas's shoulder as he moves quicker.

"Lucas." I call his name as my body is overtaken with bliss.

"Come for me," he whispers against my lips, and I shatter right there on his hand.

The comedown from such a high is strange. I take in my surroundings. It's like I woke up. Lucas is watching me, and there's a look of awe in his eyes. He removes his hand. His fingers are slick with my juices, and I inhale as he sucks them.

My heart beats wildly. I'm trying to understand this want in me, because I want him again already. How is that possible? My dress has fallen back into place, and slowly, Lucas pushes my dress straps back up before placing a kiss onto my swollen lips. I can taste myself.

"You taste so sweet," he tells me and my core tightens again. His erection seems larger now, and I wonder what that would feel like inside me. My cheeks blaze.

"You're perfect. Don't be embarrassed." He steps away with a pained expression on his face and reaches back, wrapping his fingers around mine. I know this isn't one-sided. I wanted to touch him too, but I'd never touched a man before.

"What about you?" My cheeks grow hotter.

"We have time, but not right now." He tugs me with a devious grin on his face as we walk deeper into the maze, one I hope we never return from.

# CHAPTER TWENTY-ONE

## LUCAS

I TOLD ELLA WE had time, but we don't. My body still hums with a want for her. I won't allow it. It wouldn't be fair. Her hand fits perfectly in mine as we walk through the maze. Each time I look at her, my cock twitches. She's stunning. Her smile has me pausing, my heart tripping over itself. I love what she does to my system, flooding it with all of her.

"Why did you hesitate coming into the maze?"

Her question catches me off guard. Did I? I'm thinking back to when she stepped into the maze I hadn't wanted to enter. I didn't want her to come in here and feel the darkness of this place. But that isn't possible. The only thing Ella is doing is replacing the darkness with her light.

"I got lost in here when I was eight."

She nods. "I got lost in here the other day." Her eyes dart to the left. "Henry found me."

The blood turns to ice in my veins. "Did he hurt you?" What had she endured at his fucking hands?

She looks at me again. "No. He helped me find my way out. How did you get out?" She's telling the truth.

"My mother found me." The painful memory has me releasing Ella's hand. She looks hurt when I untwine our fingers.

"Henry led me into the maze and left me here." I look at the hedges now. They don't seem so scary. At eight, the maze was terrifying. As I grew up, it felt worse that he had walked me in here on purpose and left me. He was a cruel nineteen-year-old.

"It took them two days to find me. They had no idea where I was."

Ella's eyes grow impossibly wide, and she shakes her head. I start to walk because I don't like sharing, and I might find it easier to talk while I walk.

"George told me my mother couldn't be controlled when she found out that Henry did it on purpose. He was jealous of her love for me."

I glance at Ella, and she's staring directly at me. I reach back and take her hand in mine again, twining our fingers. Her smile is soft before she bites her lip.

"She beat him really bad." That day is foggy to me. I had spent two days terrified and alone. I remember my mother's beating heart as she carried me from the maze. I remember her holding me so tightly that it hurt. My father's shouts were so loud that they hurt my ears. Light was shone in my face, and it disappeared as my mother held me tighter until my father coaxed her to release me, to let the doctors make sure I was okay.

I was more traumatized than injured.

"My father stopped her." I glance at Ella again. I felt bare talking about this. "She nearly killed him."

Ella doesn't speak, but I see the horror in her eyes.

I stop again and look around the hedges. "He built this maze to trap me." I'm half smiling at his dedication to hurt me.

"That's so horrible, Lucas. I'm so sorry." Ella tightens her hold on my hand as she speaks.

"He gets credit for dedication." I try to lighten the mood. I've never shared this with anyone.

"Why does he hate you so much?" Ella asks the question I've always asked myself.

"My mother favored me." My heart pounds. I haven't thought about her in such a long time. Now every bedtime story, every teddy bear picnic, roars to life inside me.

"Your mother?"

I have to release Ella's hand again. She's poking too much, and I don't like it. I stop walking and turn to face her. I don't know what I'm ready to do, but she has this look on her face of devastation that causes my anger to deflate.

"She's locked away. I don't know where. But my father visits her. We aren't allowed. She's... not balanced."

Ella takes the two steps that separate us and wraps her arms around my waist, while leaning her head against my chest. It takes me a moment to respond to her hug before I wrap my arms around her. I can feel the dampness on my shirt before I hear her sniffle.

"Don't cry." I try to make her look at me, but she isn't letting me go. Placing a kiss on the crown of her head, I pull her closer and hold her for just a little while.

She gives another sniffle before leaning out. She's rubbing my shirt, trying to wipe away her tears. "I'm sorry."

Her body this close is taking its toll on me. "I don't mind having my shirt soaked with your tears," I say.

Her eyes dart up to mine and she smiles. "Yeah, you have a thing for body fluids."

Her words are a joke, but my body hums thinking of how sweet she tasted. Her eyes widen.

"I meant the day you tasted your blood." Her chest flames, and I'm smiling as I take her face in my hand and lower my head to hers.

"No, you didn't. You were referring to how I tasted you."

Her nostrils flare and her chest rises and falls quickly. I kiss her softly, and I know I'm prolonging the agony. Our time is running out. I don't want anyone to know we were missing. I don't want to draw attention to Ella any more than I already have. My father's word is something, but it isn't a guarantee. I can't keep her safe here.

I keep hold of her face as I lean my forehead against hers. My cock twitches as her breath fans out across my face. Her breasts are flush with my chest, and my resolve is shaking.

"I'm sending you home," I tell her.

She steps away from me, confusion etched into her pretty face.

"No." She's shaking her head as she speaks.

"Don't argue with me. You're going home." I can't keep her safe, and she's too precious. I force as much authority into my words as I can manage.

Ella looks panicked. "I'm not going home. I can't."

I feel like the parent who tells a kid there's no Santa. She looks devastated.

"This is not up for discussion." I cut her off abruptly and walk away.

Glancing back, she's still standing in the same spot.

"Ella, we have to go back."

Her eyes are floating with her pain. I tighten my fists and march back to her.

"Please, Lucas." She blinks and tears spill down her face.

"Stop doing that." I close the distance between us and wipe her tears with my thumb, but more fall. "Stop it, Ella."

I caused this. For each one I wiped away, another fell, and she isn't stopping.

"I'm trying to protect you." I grip her shoulders.

"No! You're trying to get rid of me."

My hold has grown tight on her. I can't seem to control myself, so I release her abruptly. "Do you really believe that?"

"I don't want to go home."

I'm shaking my head. She's bending me too easily, and that in itself is dangerous. "You're going home." My words don't hold as much conviction this time.

"I don't want to leave," she pleads. "I have friends for the first time in my life…"

My treacherous heart can't stay and watch her cry anymore. She's in my arms as I kiss the crown of her head.

"Why can't you just do as you're told?" I say, but I know I can't send her home. It's selfish how glad I am that she fought me on it. "We need to get back." I feel pained releasing her.

Her eyes are red from crying, but her tears have stopped.

"So, I get to stay?" Her voice is full of innocence, and I wonder if she has any idea the effect she has on me. How easily I bend to her will.

"Yes. But Ella, no fighting with the other girls."

Her lips form a straight line.

"Stay under the radar," I add and she nods while my words are stoking the ambers in her eyes. She doesn't say anything, and I'm fighting a smile that I wrestle with and then lose to.

"You look beautiful," I tell her as I take her face in my hands. She inhales quickly before I place a kiss on her swollen lips. "We need to go back," I repeat and drag myself away from her.

"Could we just get lost in here?" She bites her lip.

I give her a warning look. "Don't tempt me." I focus on leaving. Each step back to the gardens has the weight returning to my shoulders. I pause before we leave the maze completely. I can't look at her. "This thing with us has to end now."

It's not a thing; it's so much deeper. It's taken root in me, and I don't think I could ever get Ella out of my system, but what I'm doing is stupid and reckless. She's worth so much more than a fumble in a maze.

"It's over," I say as harshly as I can, before stepping out onto the lawn. I know she's behind me, and I don't look back as I pass George and walk back to the house. It's cruel and wrong to leave her, but I don't know how I can ever make this right with Ella. She's filled every space in me, and I feel like I am becoming obsessed with her. It is a deadly obsession that will get her hurt, and I can't allow that to happen.

After telling Ella about Henry, it made me hate him even more. I had buried a lot of those feelings as we just coexisted in the same house, but now I just want a row.

He's easy to find—in his attic, sitting in the chair that's suspended from the ceiling.

"I don't want you here," he says without looking at me.

"I don't want you here either. But here you are."

His head snaps up to mine. "What do you want?"

"You and Declan were lovers," I state.

He's off his chair. "I already told—"

"You already lied to me. You both have the same tattoo. His wedding finger was cut off, which means he was cheating on his wife. So with a matching tattoo, I'm assuming it's you."

"I didn't think you had a brain cell between your ears."

Henry's words irritate me more than they should, and I want to hit him. "What does the tattoo mean?"

He sneers but it falls flat. "None of your business. It's private."

"You and Declan got matching tattoos." I grin.

He hunches while looking at me. "Don't make fun of us."

So he was having an affair with Declan. "Did you kill him?"

"I want you to leave." He stands to his full height, pushing his glasses up on his face. I notice the darkness under his eyes. Did they love each other? Does it matter?

"I want answers, Henry. I still have the fingers you were getting off on having."

"Stop being so vulgar." His voice rises, the high pitch making his voice more feminine.

"Tell me and I'll leave."

"I didn't hurt him." He steps away from me, hunched, and climbs back into the chair. His movements are unnatural.

I hate being in his presence. I want to ask why he left me in the maze. Why he tried to fucking kill me.

"Why are you still here?" he asks, twirling the chair. I think about dragging him out of it and finishing what my mother started.

The thought has me leaving. At least I know who Declan was having an affair with. Someone else knew and killed Declan for it. Maybe Henry was lying and he killed him. I wasn't convinced by his answer.

George is waiting for me at the bottom of the stairs.

"The picnic has been tidied, and Lady Ella has been returned to her room, Master Lucas." He says this like he's told me about every date I've had. But this is a first. He knows I treat her differently.

"Thank you, George. I want to ask about a member who passed away."

George holds still and nods. "Of course, Master Lucas."

He was here from the start with my family. He must have seen every member pass through these doors. "A Sorcha Newtown."

Something flashes across George's face. It's gone quickly, but I see it—fear. Is he afraid of Sorcha?

"Yes. She was a member." George tries to leave, and that just raises my curiosity.

"Tell me about her."

He pauses and glances around the foyer before stepping back to me. "Master Lucas, it was such a long time ago, and this old brain is tired." He smiles.

"Just tell me what you remember." My tone drops.

"She was a member briefly. She died. I don't really recall much."

I nod. "Yeah, my father told me a member died thirty years ago. The same way Declan did."

George looks away, and it's like he's thinking. I don't want him to think. I want him to tell me what he's holding back. I know he's holding something back. He knows more.

"George, I will find the truth one way or another." I step away and his old hand touches my arm, stopping me.

His eyes are filled with a past that weighs heavily on his shoulders. "Sorcha Newtown is Alex's mother."

"Alex Bradley?" I want to add, *the freak who hangs out with Henry?*

"Yes, Master Lucas. He keeps his father's name, not his mother's."

"Anything else you can tell me?"

He shakes his old head. "No, Master Lucas."

When George leaves, I try to piece this together. Alex's mother was a member, and she died just like Declan. Her finger was removed, just like Declan. Frustration has me clenching my fists. The closer I get to this, the more questions it raises.

# CHAPTER TWENTY-TWO

## ELLA

I T'S BEEN DAYS SINCE I saw Lucas. I've hovered around the house trying to get a glimpse of him, but he's nowhere in sight. I never told him about the conversation his father had with me, or more accurately, the threat of using me to keep him on a leash.

"Please sit down, Ella. You're driving me crazy." Hannah glances up at me from a book she's reading. I fold my arms across my chest but stop pacing.

I need to find Lucas. I need to tell him. It's a half-truth. I miss him so much. I just want to see his face. I look up now at the painting on the wall, the one I had admired on the first day here. It looks nothing like the Lucas I've grown close to. The one in the picture is arrogant and cruel. Lucas is kind and sweet.

I exhale loudly. "I'm going for a walk."

"Every time you go for a walk, something bad happens. Just stay here," Hannah says and Jessie laughs at her.

"That's not true." I fold my arms across my chest.

Hannah raises a brow.

"I'll stay away from the gardens," I say and leave the room before Hannah can follow me. My anxiety at not seeing Lucas is at an all-time high. My body hasn't come down off the high he had placed it on while in the maze.

Everything about our date left a mark on me. His touch haunted me at nighttime. All I want is his hands on me again. I've been waking up in hot sweats, something that's never happened to me before.

His story has also haunted me, and it made me really see how damaged Henry is, to hurt Lucas like that. I had so many questions that I didn't ask. Lucas looked so vulnerable one moment as he spoke, and the next, I feared him. I wasn't sure if he would snap. I didn't believe he would ever hurt me, maybe not intentionally anyway.

He's volatile.

Yet, here I am still searching for him.

The yard I step out onto is empty. I haven't been around the back of the house. There isn't much out here, only sheds and a decked-out area that circles around half of the back of the house. I follow it and can see into the dining room. It reminds me of the day Alex was out here.

Noise of a shed door opening grabs my attention. I freeze as Lucas's father steps out onto the gravel. He's dressed in a suit. He doesn't see me as he walks back to the house. What was he doing in the shed dressed like that?

*Go inside, Ella*, I tell myself while my feet move toward the shed. I glance over my shoulder to make sure no one sees me. The creak of the shed door has me stopping abruptly.

"Lucas." I say his name out loud, though I hadn't intended to.

He swings around and faces me, and there's a wild look in his inky eyes. Sweat coats his black T-shirt, which sticks to his hard chest, but it's his hands that have my heart stalling in my chest.

"What happened?" I'm trying not to cry. His hands are torn open, and blood is oozing out of too many wounds to count.

He hasn't answered me, and I look up at him. I can't decipher what I see on his face. He's staring at me, and I want to take a step away from him.

"Lucas," I say quietly.

"Go inside, Ella." He turns away from me.

I'm chasing after him. "What happened? Talk to me."

He snaps around, and fear wraps tightly around my throat, but I stand my ground. "Please," I beg and hold my breath.

He takes my hand in his and hisses. The action causes more blood to flow. His touch is surprisingly gentle as he leads me around the back of the house.

"Are you going to tell me what happened?" He won't speak to me, and that's making me more afraid. He's angry. Is he going to punish me?

I don't pull my hand from his damaged one so I don't hurt his wounded hands. He circles around a hot tub and toward a set of double doors, which he opens before dragging me inside. I don't have a second before he releases me and closes the door. Drawing heavy dark drapes, he plunges the room into darkness. My heart threatens to rip free from my chest. He's breathing so heavily I can hear him.

I call his name again, and his steps move away from me. The room is flooded with light. Lucas is on the far side, blocking the main door.

I glance around and take in the bedroom. My eyes dart to the black bedding. Is this his room?

Lucas glares at me. I remain still as I take in every inch of his room. My eyes keep returning to the bed. I feel giddy, which is such a wrong feeling to have right now. Lucas opens another set of double doors, which lead into a huge bathroom.

He disappears and I can hear water running. I follow him, not wanting to let him out of my sight. I hover at the door. His wide back is bent over the sink as he washes his damaged hands. I glance at the mirror above his head, and my heart pounds as my eyes meet his. I've never seen his eyes look so black. So raw. So violent.

"What happened?" I ask, my voice sounding strangled as I step into his bathroom. He drops my gaze, and I focus on his hands. The blood keeps flowing.

"You need stitches," I tell him.

"You shouldn't be here." He says each word through gritted teeth, and my heart skyrockets.

I swallow and get a towel. "I think we should put pressure on the wounds to stop the bleeding."

The water still runs, but he turns around to me. "What do I have to do to make you understand that I don't want you here?"

I flinch. God, that hurt. But he's injured, and I think this goes deeper than his flesh.

"Give me your hands." I hold out the towel while his blood drips on the white tile floor. Fear has me looking up at him.

A mistake. He's barely containing the darkness that's swirling in his eyes. I drop my eyes and my heart kicks as he places his hands in the towel. I don't waste a second and wrap them and press down. He hisses.

"I'm sorry. Why don't you sit down on the toilet?"

I'm stunned when he follows my suggestion and sits down on the lid of the toilet. I'm standing bent over, holding the towel against his wounds. It's awkward, so I lower myself until I'm kneeling. He doesn't speak and time moves slowly. I'm taking snapshots of his bathroom. The large shower—my mind takes a nosedive into him in it, and I refocus on his hands.

"I'm going to take a look." I chance looking up at him, and his eyes bore into me. He doesn't look as hostile, but he's still not friendly. I take his silence as permission to check.

The inside of the towel is red, making my stomach twist. "Oh, Lucas."

His hands are a mess. I want to cry for him. He must be in so much pain. I want to ask what happened. Maybe his father hurt him. But I don't. Instead, I swallow the tears.

"There's a bottle of whiskey in the bottom drawer on my bedside table." I drink up his words like he's giving me the ingredients to a long life. He's talking to me. I'm off my knees and in his bedroom, opening the drawer. I take out the half bottle of whiskey and return to him.

"A disinfectant," I say.

A ghost of a smile grazes his lips. He reaches out for the bottle.

"I can do it." I don't want him to hurt himself any further. He doesn't answer me but takes the bottle out of my hands. His face scrunches up in pain, but he continues to open the cap and drinks deeply from the bottle.

"Or that," I say as I focus on his hands. A fresh wave of blood drips from them, but the flow has lessened.

How he's holding anything is beyond me; the pain must be horrific. My stomach hollows as I think of all the times he's worn gloves. Was he hiding this damage over and over again? He stops drinking and looks at me now.

"You need to leave." He sounds drained.

"You need stitches." I fold my arms across my chest. I know provoking him is dangerous, but I can't leave him here like this.

He lets out a heavy sigh like he can't be bothered fighting with me. Standing up, he hands me the bottle, and I grab it from him and take a large gulp. It burns.

Lucas's laugh is quick, but I hear it. When I look up at him, he's staring at me. His eyes are a little lighter but also a little sadder.

Another part of me cracks open for him, and something warm sneaks out, sending my heart pounding. I'm falling for him, falling deeper down the rabbit hole, and I know there's no return.

Lucas reaches for his T-shirt, and it slowly rises across abs and tanned skin. I can't look away as he pulls the T-shirt off. My mouth hangs open, and I'm holding my breath as I take in Lucas's muscular chest and wide shoulders. When I feel dizzy, I remember I need to breathe.

"I need to take a shower."

I'm nodding. I can't look away. Another quick laugh has me looking into his eyes.

"You can wait in the bedroom," he says. "Or stay if you want."

My heart trips all over itself as he grins at me. He tugs at the band of his trousers, and I leave quickly, nearly walking into the doorframe. If I stay, I won't be able to stay away from him. The water starts to run, and I try not to picture him pushing down his trousers. He's naked, only a few feet away from me.

I run my hand along his bed, the sheets soft and silky. I keep looking to the bathroom, my feet moving in that direction.

*Don't overthink it*, I tell myself as I step into the bathroom.

# CHAPTER TWENTY-THREE

## LUCAS

I'M ALL TOO AWARE of Ella in the next room. The shaft between my legs is like steel. I tighten my hand around it. The pull on my damaged knuckles is too much.

My father had another man ready for me to beat. This time, I wasn't allowed to wear gloves. I'm not under the illusion that it was my punishment for having him leave Ella alone. I know when he hands that out, it won't be easy.

Every time, I pretend like I'm beating a punching bag. There's no flesh, no face; it's just a bag I can unleash my anger on. This time, I didn't stop.

I'm not sure how much longer I can do this for; it feels like the violence is eating away at me, leaving more violence in its wake. What if I lash out at the wrong person?

What if I lash out at Ella?

My body responds to her name, and I take my cock in my hand again and pull.

"Oh." The small voice has me turning around. Ella's staring at my cock, her mouth forming a little *O*. Now all I can picture is her mouth around me. I have no restraint, and having her look at me like that isn't good.

"What are you doing?" I snap.

Her eyes dart up to mine, her cheeks glowing. She licks her lips. "I don't know."

"Just wait for me in the bedroom. I'll be out in a moment." I turn away. I can't keep looking at her, or I'll drag her in here and take what I want. When I glance over my shoulder, she's still standing there.

"Ella," I warn.

She reaches for her top and pulls it up over her head. My heart beats rapidly in my aching chest. I fight with the last shred of willpower I have as she touches the waistband of her skirt.

"Don't tease me. I can't hold back."

She freezes, and a part of me is happy she's listening, but another part of me takes over when she wriggles out of her skirt. My cock throbs painfully as she walks to the shower in a white pair of panties and a full white bra.

I should tell her to go back. I should stop her right now as she opens the door and steps in. I should really stop her.

*She's fucking gorgeous.*

She stands only a foot from me, and I'm afraid of her, afraid of hurting her. I'm still raging with violence, and she's a virgin.

"I want this. I want you." She's holding her head high, but I can see the tremble in her chin.

"Come here," I order, my willpower splintering.

Her steps are slow, her eyes trailing across my body. She inhales deeply when she looks at my cock. It's hard and throbbing for her.

She steps under the stream of water and I dip my head, skimming her lips before placing a kiss on her cheek and then her neck.

My hands burn as I reach back and unclip her bra before dragging the straps down her arms, then it lands with a heavy thud onto the tiles. Her pink nipples are hard, and I bend down, taking them into my mouth. Ella buries her hands in my hair as she gasps. Pulling my teeth along the nipple has her wriggling against my cock. I groan.

Moving her back, I'm careful with my hands. They ache, but nothing burns quite as much as the want I have for Ella. I want to flip her over and take her hard and fast. I release her nipple once she's against the tiles. Her eyes dart across my face, the lust clouding them. Her small hand reaches down and wraps around my cock. My knees nearly buckle at the touch. She strokes it and I groan. It's so good. She has no idea what she's doing, but her touch is everything.

Her small thumb runs across the head of my cock, and my body jerks. My hands react as I grip her face and smash my lips against hers. The pain is searing, but the want to have her is overriding it. My cock prods against her stomach, and I want to reach down, spread her legs, and slide my shaft inside her. I break the kiss, panting, and she returns to stroking my cock.

"Ella." I lean across her shoulder and hold on to the tiles as her strokes become more sure, stronger and faster. I can feel my release, and I thrust my cock into her hand until my seed pours all over her thigh. I jerk several more times before I'm emptied. The pain in my hands returns with an intensity that has me pushing away from the wall. Ella's looking at her leg, at my cum.

She picks some of it up and leaves me fucking gobsmacked when she puts her finger into her mouth, her eyes focused on my face.

My cock is getting hard again. Her pink tongue flicks out and removes the last bit of my cum from her fingers. I'm imagining her tongue flicking out, licking my cock.

"Ella," I growl.

She could make a saint sin. I don't step away when she reaches up and places a kiss along my jawline. She coats me with kisses, each one sinking deeper under my skin. I know I should stop this, but I can't drag myself away from her touch. She kisses the corner of my mouth, and I turn, planting my lips fully on hers. Her nipples brush my chest, and my cock starts to grow again. I want to touch her, but my hands tingle with pain.

Leaving her lips, I move her back against the tiles and sink to my knees. Her hands instantly sink into my hair. Her white panties join her bra on the shower floor, giving me access to all of her. She parts her legs, and I sink deeper until I taste her. She's so fucking sweet. My cock twitches, and I push my tongue deeper inside her before dragging it out and licking her clit. She jumps and jerks as I suck the bunch of nerves before going back inside her with my tongue. Her legs tighten around me, and I know she's going to come before I taste her in my mouth. I don't stop until all the waves have subsided.

The look of awe in her eyes when I come back up made it all worth it. She's flushed and breathing heavily and it's beautiful. I step back into the spray of water and she follows. I need her again, and I know it isn't fair.

"Take as long as you want," I say and she glances at me over her shoulder. I don't want to leave. Placing a kiss on her shoulder, I leave the shower and wrap a towel around my waist.

I shouldn't have allowed that to happen.

She stays in there for a while. I'm dressed and am considering going in, when she comes out looking sheepish. Her breasts are free, her nipples showing through her top. I can't look away.

She runs her hands self-consciously across her hair.

"You're not wearing a bra," I say.

Her hands cross over her chest. "My bra is soaked." She shrugs. "Are you going to tell me what happened to your hands?"

Hands that I have covered in gloves now.

"No," I answer honestly.

I open my mouth to speak again, and she holds up her hands, stopping me.

"It's okay if you don't want to tell me, but please don't start about how this can't happen again, or how this is wrong." She has her eyes closed as she speaks, and when she opens them, I walk to her and take her face in my hands.

"Okay."

She looks startled but bobs her head. "Okay."

"Okay," I repeat before planting a light kiss on her lips. I was going to tell her this can't happen again, but I feel tired now, and for this moment, maybe I can have her. I can't tell her my date with Sandra is soon. Or that my father has arranged a sit-down meal for Sandra. I'm a coward for not telling her.

"You should be getting back," I say, placing another kiss on her lips.

"I don't want to." Her eyes widen and the sadness leaks out.

"What do you want, Ella?" I ask. Her staying here isn't possible.

She looks away from me, cutting me off, and I don't like it at all. Taking her chin in my hand, I bring her face back to me.

"That's a loaded question." Her smile is sad. "I don't think I can have what I want." She takes a step back.

"Maybe I should go." She's shutting down on me. I clench my jaw. I can't ease this for her.

"Before you go, you should know my date with Sandra is today." I try to keep everything I feel in check.

The color leaves her face. "Oh, I'll let you get ready."

I exhale loudly. "Jesus, Ella, you knew this was happening."

"It's fine." If it's fine, why does she look so crushed? I'm not stupid. I know this is anything but alright. Once again, I have the urge to stop this. She's staring at me.

"If you tell me to leave again, that's it, Lucas. I won't come back." She holds her head high. I see her pulse spike in her neck. She's giving me an out on a plate.

Here is my chance to let her go. She deserves so much better. She's twisting her hands as she waits.

"I'm beginning to understand that staying away from you isn't possible."

Her relief is instant, and she comes back and dips her head while wrapping her arms around my neck. I hold her and enjoy the warmth and softness of her body against mine. My hands rest on her small waist. I have no idea how any of this will work, but letting her go isn't an option.

"But I'll need time, Ella." I make her look at me so she's listening.

She's nodding. "If you don't see me, you can't come looking for me. It's too dangerous."

She nods again, and I don't think she's listening to me.

"Ella," I warn. "This is serious."

"I know it is." There's something burning in her eyes. I pull her in and kiss the top of her head.

We wrap ourselves in silence, but there's such comfort in having her in my arms.

"There was a reason I was looking for you."

She steps out of my embrace, wearing a look of guilt. "The day your father had the... chat with me."

The day he put his hands on her. I grit my teeth. She's being careful with her words.

"I thought he would send me home. I was ready to go, but he said he would keep me here, to keep you in line."

None of that surprises me. What does surprise me is that Ella still doesn't stay away. "Can you not see how dangerous this is?"

Her hand flutters to her throat. "Yes." It's a whisper. She doesn't look away from me. "But I think you're worth the danger."

*No. I'm not.*

# CHAPTER TWENTY-FOUR

## ELLA

L EAVING LUCAS IS HARD. My head is spinning with his touch. I can't leave through his bedroom door, so I sneak out the back. There's a part of me that feels dirty. Pushing my shoulders back, I keep my head high and remind myself that none of this is dirty. The circumstances are just blurred. Things aren't black and white like I expected them to be. God, I feel so naïve when I look back at what I thought this would be.

I'm walking with my arms folded across my chest in case I bump into anyone. I don't want to give them a peep show. Lucas's room disappears as I walk back around to the front of the house. The sheds come into view and my feet slow, my heart picking up into a fast rhythm. The thought of his hands is eating away at me, and the answer just might be in that shed.

I glance over my shoulder, my heart in my mouth, and I try to talk myself out of going in.

The handle turns in my hand, and I step into a large shed. Gray covers are everywhere. I close the door behind me, the only light coming from high windows that I can't see out of. I give a nervous smile, trying to calm my churning stomach. I don't move as I scour the room for anyone. I'm alone.

Lifting one of the tarps, the black wheel of a car has me dropping it carefully back down. There were a lot of cars. At the back of the shed, there are several high steel shelves. I walk back there. There's nothing here, only cars. Scanning the walls, I don't know what I'm looking for—traces of blood? Was he hitting a wall? It was possible with the state of his fists.

I'm like a deer in headlights as a noise to my left has me freezing. I've been caught. I count to ten, and when no one appears, my heart starts to settle. I wipe my sleek hands on my skirt. Cutting my losses and getting out of here sounds like the right thing to do.

As I turn, light glinting off the floor catches my attention. I move around another car, and the light widens and expands until I'm standing at the top of steps that descend under the shed. The light is on, and something tells me not to go down. I bend to see walls made of stone, and lights that are covered with steel are strung along the wall. It looks cold and dark, and something sinister radiates up. That's where Lucas came from.

I hesitate on the first step. What would I see? Is Lucas the bad one in all this? Would I find out something I would have been better off being blind to? My stomach hollows, and I feel like a coward when I turn around to leave.

"By all means, Ella, please go down." Andrew gestures to the stairs behind me.

My stomach plummets. I'm shaking my head. My knees weaken. *Stupid. Stupid.*

"No, thank you, Master Andrew." I take a step away from what feels like doom, but Andrew keeps his eyes pinned on me.

"I insist." His words leave no room for argument. I could beg and tell him I'll never leave my room again. I don't want to go down there.

He doesn't so much as blink, and I feel like I'm looking into the eyes of the devil himself. I turn around and take the first step into the basement. Each step has my stomach tightening. Andrew's heavy footsteps behind me send a wave of trepidation skittering along my spine.

We reach the hallway and I pause. There's a smell of dampness and something else. I don't know what exactly, but it makes me wrap my arms around my waist.

"Thank you for showing me, Master Andrew, but I'd like to go back." I turn to him, and he wears a smile that drains the rest of the warmth from me.

"Follow me." He steps around me, and I keep my arms wrapped around my waist as I follow Andrew deeper into the ground. I glance back over my shoulder and the steps disappear.

"I'm sorry for being here. I thought maybe there would be a bicycle in the shed so I could get some exercise in, Master Andrew."

There are so many doors with so many scary things behind them—that's what my mind is telling me. Is he going to kill me?

He stops suddenly and opens a large white door that looks like a refrigerator door. I don't move. I don't dare.

"Take a look, Ella."

I'm shaking my head. If I look, I can't unsee it. "I'm okay, Master Andrew."

"I'm not asking."

I take a shaky step toward him. I have no idea what I'm going to see, but it might explain Lucas's hands. Bile rises in my throat, and I swallow it as I look into the room. I'm confused at first.

"As you can imagine, feeding six guests isn't an easy task."

I'm staring at a pig hung up on hooks, its stomach slit open and insides gone.

"So we keep the meat down here."

The white door is closed, and I feel weak, like my body is crashing.

"Have you heard the term that curiosity killed the cat?"

A bolt of fear shoots through me as Andrew takes a step toward me. He won't hurt me.

"I was looking for a bicycle, Master Andrew."

He holds me in position with his heavy eyes. All I see is evil, right down in the depths of the blackness of his eyes. I shiver and wrap my arms tighter around me.

"You may leave."

Disbelief keeps me standing in front of him.

"I said leave."

I bend my head as I pass him. I want to get out of here as quickly as possible. Being down here with him is the worst feeling I've ever experienced. I know he watches me, and I tell myself not to run. I keep passing doors, and I think this place is a never-ending illusion. My heart trips over itself until the bottom step finally comes into view. I nervously glance over my shoulder. My mind keeps conjuring up Andrew right behind me, but he isn't. My shoulders lift high like they're trying to protect me.

Blood droplets on the floor have me slowing down. They lead into a closed room. My heart grows frantic, threatening to come out of my chest. The blood is fresh.

I reach the steps and start to climb to the third door. I have no doubt that it's Lucas's blood. What's behind that door? I reach the floor of the shed and weave through the maze of cars. The fresh air is like a blast to my face. I don't pause but race to the side of the shed, where I throw up. My eyes water, and I finally catch my breath. Wiping my face with my sleeve, I gasp for air. The sky is clear. Birds chirp and everything is perfect outside, but down there, it feels like something worse. Death.

Each step I take, I try to push away the terrifying thought that won't leave me. Is Vicky down there? If she is, is she alive?

My stomach turns again with guilt and fear. I swallow the bile that climbs up my throat. I enter the house and nearly walk into Alex. I wobble but manage to stay upright.

"Are you okay?" He reaches out to steady me, but I pull away. I want to ask what he's doing here, but I have no right.

"Yeah." I try to move past, but he stops me.

"Are you sure? You don't look well."

Tears burn my eyes. Does he know what happens in the shed? I look at Alex in a new light. Maybe he's part of this. What this is, I'm not entirely sure.

"Ella." Alex frowns and I move past him.

"I'm fine," I call over my shoulder and move quickly up the stairs. Bernie and Mary linger on the landing. I keep my head down and don't look at them as I make it to my room.

The door closes and my body takes it as permission to shut down on me. My legs lose the power to keep me up, and I slump to the ground. Covering my mouth with my hands, I try to push down the cry of fear that's tearing through me, but I can't. Tears gather on my hands as they stream down my face.

I want to run to Lucas. I want to make him tell me if Vicky is down there, and we left her to die.

My stomach turns again, and I race to the bathroom and empty its meager contents down the toilet.

I sit on the cold floor and try to calm my racing mind. A sob tears from me. I don't know what to do about any of this.

"Ella." I groan internally at Hannah's soft voice.

*Not now, Hannah.*

She's the driving force that has me getting off the floor of the bathroom. I'm quick to get up and pull my clothes off.

"Don't come in. I'm naked," I shout and turn on the shower. I can't let anyone see me like this.

I step into the spray of cold water, not giving it enough time to heat up.

"Ella," Hannah calls again, and I know she heard me. She steps into the bathroom with her eyes closed, her hand outstretched.

"What are you doing?" I shiver as the water turns warm. I wipe water from my eyes as I stare at Hannah.

"I know you said you were naked, but I wanted to make sure you were okay."

I dip my head into the spray of water and visualize it washing today away. "You can open your eyes."

Hannah does and she exhales like she's relieved it's really me. Her eyes narrow.

"Why are your eyes bloodshot? You look like you were crying."

I laugh. "Always jumping to the worst." That isn't true about her at all. She always seems to know. "I got shampoo in my eyes."

"You were gone a long time."

I'm very aware of my nakedness. Hannah clearly isn't, since she sits on the toilet seat like she's settling in for a chat.

"I took a long walk."

"Where?" She isn't believing me.

"Can I finish my shower?"

She gets up. "Of course. I'll wait in the bedroom."

Once Hannah leaves, I stand under the spray of the water and try to wash the horrible feeling from my skin. My mind skips to Lucas, and I allow it to settle there. To settle on his touch, on what we did. His torn-up hands flash in my mind, and I push it aside and picture his face, how he looked when I touched him. That's the image I cling to when I turn off the shower and wrap myself in a towel. I tell myself that I'll be fine. Meeting my eyes in the mirror, I smile.

"You'll be fine," I whisper. But my reflection doesn't believe a word I'm saying.

# CHAPTER TWENTY FIVE

## LUCAS

I HATE THE TUX I put on. It's a reminder of every party I've been forced to go to. Each part I've had to play. I normally can, but this time it feels different. It feels like a betrayal to Ella.

I don't want to step outside my bedroom in case Ella sees me. I can't stand to see any more pain in her eyes. I tighten my fists. Inside, the gloves are clammy and each cut burns. It's a perfect distraction.

The hall where the balls are held has been transformed. Sandra rises from the lone round table that sits in the center of the room. It's surrounded in a circle of candles, no doubt my father's doing. Sandra rises when she sees me. I tighten my fists again. I don't look to George who pulls out my chair for me.

"Master Lucas." Sandra bobs her blonde head. The yellow ball dress is over the top, and I want to turn on my heel. But my father's wrath will surely be unleashed on Ella.

I shut everything off, something I'm grateful for now. I never thought I'd appreciate one of my father's lessons.

"Lady Crowley," I greet her.

"Please, call me Sandra."

I smile. "You look lovely, Sandra."

She doesn't smile, and her eyes narrow. Lovely isn't what she's going for. I sit and so does she. George pushes her in first before assisting me, and the date begins.

"I hope you like my dress," Sandra says while George fills up our wineglasses.

"It's very pretty, Sandra."

"I thought it would be more than pretty, Master Lucas. It is, after all, your favorite color."

I hate that color.

I force a smile. "Of course, yellow is very striking."

She frowns. "I had thought it perfect for my bridesmaids."

I sip the wine. "There's really no need to rush."

Sandra purses her lips and glances to George. "Could we have some privacy?"

George nods and leaves.

"I'm not sure if your father has explained to you how this goes, Lucas."

Her tone and demeanor have changed completely. I can see why my father picked her.

"We *will* get married." She picks up her wineglass and takes a sip before pulling a face. "My father has invested a lot into this marriage, and I intend to make sure he gets his money's worth."

She smiles at me now, like a doting wife. "So why don't we start again."

She picks up a little silver bell beside her plate and rings it. George reappears. That's new. I glance at George to see what he makes of being called on like a dog. His face gives nothing away.

"We will both have the chicken, minimal sauces." She glances at me with a smile. "I'm watching my figure for my wedding."

The silver knife on the table is polished and sharp. How long would it take for her to bleed out on the table if I stuck it into her neck? "There is no need to watch your figure. You're perfect." I smile.

She raises her head in victory. Like it took her two sentences to put me in my place.

"Oh, and take this wine away. I want something older." She shrugs her shoulders. This time, George looks at me, and I give him a nod to do as she says, for now.

My hands are clenched through most of this, and I feel liquid in my gloves. I relax them while placing them onto my lap. The temptation to hurt her is starting to overwhelm me.

"I've been snooping around the house. I'm not exactly happy with all the décor." She shrugs again with a self-assured smile on her face. "Some of it is so outdated. Who was the most recent designer?" She sips the wine that she had George take away, and her face twists again.

"My mother," I tell her.

"Well, it needs a woman's touch."

George returns, and maybe it's a good thing he does. The chicken dishes are set in front of us, and he waits outside the circle of candles. Sandra moves most of her food around the plate, making it look like she's eating. I don't even pretend, and she doesn't notice. She talks about our wedding and the house.

"The attic area is nice, but we need to do something with it."

That gets my attention. "You've been in the attic?"

She tries to look shy, but she can't pull it off. I wonder if she's even a virgin. There's nothing innocent about her. Sandra is sharp and cunning. She could have had her results fixed if she wanted. Money can buy you a ticket at the top table.

"No, one of my friends volunteered to go up and report to me on the décor."

*Volunteered.* Forced would be more accurate. The meal drags, she talks, and I laugh and smile when appropriate. George serves dessert, and I know I'm close to the finish line. I have thought of burning her with the candles, stabbing her, or just gagging her with a napkin so she'll shut up. I've kept myself entertained.

I push in my dessert after a moment and place my napkin on the bowl beside it, ready to end this. Sandra's eyes snap to my bowl and she stands.

"Well, I will wish you a good night, Master Lucas. I'm very tired and will end this wonderful night."

I don't stop my grin as I rise. "I was just thinking the same thing."

She steps around the table, her eyes downcast, trying to look coy. When she reaches me, she looks at me from under her lashes. She's waiting.

"Aren't you going to kiss me goodnight?" She raises both brows now.

"I think we should stick to tradition and wait until our wedding." The lie is delivered easily.

She frowns. "I think a kiss is allowed."

"I'm a stickler for tradition. Good night, Miss Crowley."

Her eyes spark, and I see her peeking at me with all her cunning-ness and sharpness. She curtsys. "Master Lucas." Her steps are filled with a purpose.

I stand for a moment, and George starts to clear the table. "Can I get you anything else, Master Lucas?"

I exhale as I flex my hands. "Yes you can, George."

He looks at me with tired eyes.

"Get rid of that bell."

His smile is quick, and his eyes no longer look so heavy. "With pleasure."

I touch his shoulder gently before leaving the room.

My hands are soaked in blood. I bathe them before wrapping them in white bandages. I think of Ella, holding them carefully in the white towel. She was so gentle, so caring.

Guilt churns in my stomach, and I push it down. I change out of the tux and into black trousers and a shirt before finding a new pair of gloves. It's hard getting my hands into them with the bandages, but I wrapped them lightly enough that I do manage. The pain has me biting the inside of my jaw as I leave my room.

My father is in my study when I enter. He's sitting behind my desk. "I thought you would be here sooner, since your date ended over an hour ago."

I close the door behind me. "I was changing."

"Sandra isn't very happy."

I glance at my father now and can't hide my disgust. "I don't care."

He's standing, his hands curling into fists as he leans onto my desk. "You should. She's worth a small fortune. The merger of our families will strengthen us. Don't be foolish, son." He pushes off the desk and moves toward me.

"This is what you were born for, to rule. You can't rule with softness. You must do so with an iron fist." He clenches his hand.

His eyes are wide and driven with hunger for more power. I used to think I was just like him, but I'm not.

His face softens as he reaches me. "I know you're angry, son." He smiles. "You have a weakness just like me for pretty things, so I have come to a solution for you."

He pats my shoulder hard before stepping away from me and back to the desk. My muscles are taut since I entered the room.

"A solution?"

Pride sparks from his eyes. "Yes, with Ella."

My hands tighten. I hate him even saying her name.

"You can have her."

Everything starts to unravel with hope, confusion, and fear. Is he lying, trying to trick me? My heart pounds.

"I don't have to marry Sandra?" I hate how hopeful I sound.

My father's laughter is cruel as he throws his head back. I have to wait for him to stop, and when he does, it's abrupt, as he pulls the chair in close to the desk.

"You will marry Sandra, but you can keep Ella here as well. I'm sure we can all come to some arrangement. Publicly, Ella isn't to ever come to light."

I hear my father's words, but they sound far off. "Like a mistress?" My tone is flat.

"You don't have to label it, son."

I feel sick. I move toward the desk. "Like an affair. Wouldn't she lose a wedding finger?"

His eyes cut to the bookshelf. "If I knew you wouldn't appreciate my offer, I wouldn't have made it."

"Sorcha Newtown, was she your plaything?"

He taps his fingers on the desk and glances up at me. "Yes." I didn't think he would admit it.

"But don't be foolish like me. I got caught."

My stomach turns again. "What about Mother?"

"She was angry, but she got over it."

I tighten my fists at how dismissive he is about my mother. "Did you lock her away so she couldn't tell people?" Blood roars to life in my ears.

"Don't be daft." My father stands, his eyes narrowing.

"Am I really being daft? Or are you worse than I could have possibly ever imagined?"

"Your mother is locked away because she's a danger. She tried to kill your brother." He sounds so calm.

"Why, because he tried to kill me?" The past was rearing its ugly head.

"Don't start licking old wounds. Children play in gardens. They get lost. It happens." He waves it off like it's nonsense.

"He wasn't a child."

"Are you still going on about that?" His smile is cruel, and I shut down, trying to remove myself from this conversation.

"How did Sorcha die?"

His smile turns into a warning glare. "Your mother killed her."

I'm nodding. "Yeah, because she's a crazy killer."

I see a crack in my father's armor. It's brief, but it's there as he lowers his shoulders.

"My affair resulted in Henry." His words are low, but I hear them. "Your mother was enraged. We couldn't have a child, though we had tried for so many years."

There's something vulnerable in my father right now, like he's speaking about someone else and not himself. Like he pities these people.

"So when she found out about Sorcha, it drove her mad." His eyes meet mine now. "She killed Sorcha and I covered it up."

I move back toward the bookshelves to give myself something to lean against. "You mean you drove her mad," I correct him and he ignores me.

"She cut off Sorcha's finger and hid it. It's something we've never been able to find."

How did it end up in Henry's possession? It's his real mother's finger. Does he know that?

"Does Henry know?"

My father shakes his head. "No."

My father looks at me for a long time. "When you were born, it was like I got my wife back. She was happy with her precious son. So when Henry did..." He waves his hand in the air before placing it back into his pants pockets. "What he did, she snapped, and I had no choice but to have her locked up." He pauses before speaking again. "Now you know."

"Did you kill Declan?"

"No."

I have no reason to doubt my father, but that doesn't mean I should believe him either.

"But he was having an affair with someone since his finger was cut off."

My father looks at me, and I try to keep my own truths in about what I know.

"I don't know who he was having an affair with," he answers.

"So someone is collecting fingers," I state. I have both, and both were found in Henry's possession. Both people were also connected to him.

"The past won't change the present or the future. I would prefer you focus on strengthening your upcoming marriage to Sandra." My father fixes the cuffs of his shirt. "That is why I'm here."

He looks up at me, any earlier vulnerability gone. "I have decided on your punishment."

I nod, actually glad that I'll find out what it is.

"The final ball is in two nights." My stomach rolls, but I don't react.

"You will kiss Sandra in front of everyone."

"No," I say immediately.

My father gives me a bloodthirsty smile, and it makes me nervous. "Yes, you will. It's a kiss that will free Ella from my grasp and also give Sandra the validation she requires."

"This is Sandra's idea?" She must have run to my father after the meal.

"You refused to kiss her, so she wants it publicly now. She has power, and she knows how to use it."

"No," I say again, but I can already feel the defeat.

"That's fine, son." My father steps closer to me.

"I've been understanding. I've given you a choice. To keep Ella safe, you must give one kiss." He holds up his hand. "If you can't, that's fine."

He turns, ending our conversation, and my heart pounds. It's not fine. It means Ella is there for the taking. He'll hurt her and hurt her badly. Maybe worse than before.

It's just a kiss.

One kiss.

"I'll do it," I say.

My father has his back to me and pauses at the door. "I know." He sounds like he's smiling as he leaves my study.

# CHAPTER TWENTY-SIX

## ELLA

"I THINK I KNOW where Vicky is," I admit and both Hannah and Jessie drop the books they're reading. My room has turned into our hangout spot. Hannah is curled up in the window seat while Jessie has made a bed on the floor.

I've been lying on my bed watching the open door, waiting for Sandra to return from her date with Lucas. My stomach curls now as I think about her huge display before she left. She was in a ball gown. She wasn't getting a simple picnic in the garden. She was getting a sit down meal with Lucas.

"Where?" Hannah's legs drop off the chair as she faces me.

"Remember earlier when you arrived and I was in the shower?"

Hannah is nodding eagerly. "I knew it." She stands and looks at Jessie. "I told you, every time she leaves, something happens." Her eyes are impossibly wide. "You're never leaving us again. I don't care, Ella. Wherever you go, we go too."

Jessie doesn't back Hannah up. Instead, she rolls her eyes at me as I suppress a smile.

"Isn't that right, Jessie?"

"Yes, Hannah," Jessie sings, and Hannah takes her word for it while climbing onto my bed.

"Tell us what happened." Jessie joins us on the bed.

"When I went for my walk, I came across sheds out in the back."

Hannah is shaking her head. "I knew you were gone far too long."

"Will you let her finish her story?" Jessie nudges Hannah, who looks ready to pass out.

"I was snooping and got caught by Master Andrew. I tried to leave, but he insisted that I finish what I started. He was trying to prove a point. So he brought me down into a basement under the shed."

Hannah pales further, and now I'm questioning if I should tell them. "There were loads of doors, and one of them had blood going to it. Fresh blood."

Hannah inhales sharply.

"The room he showed me had a pig in it, but it was hung up and cleaned out. So I know the blood wasn't from the pig."

"Did you check?" Jessie asks, and it's like she's holding her breath.

I shake my head. "I was afraid, and he was still there. But something felt so off about it all." I don't mention Lucas. I can't involve him in this.

We all sit in silence for a moment.

"We have to rescue her." Hannah nods while looking from me to Jessie to see if we agree.

I shiver at the thought of going back down, but if Vicky is down there, we need to find out.

"I agree," I say.

Commotion in the hallway has the three of us scrambling off the bed.

Sandra has returned from her date, her cheeks flushed, her hair tussled. She's talking to Bernie and Mary, but her words are loud enough for everyone to hear her.

"He is"—she fans herself—"very... How can I put it? He struggled to control himself."

More giggles.

"From running away?" Jessie says under her breath but loud enough for everyone to hear.

Sandra spins around, her eyes pinning me in place. Hers shine with victory, and my stomach tightens. She turns to Jessie.

"Not running away, Jessie. But that's cute." She sounds like it's anything but cute. "I was referring to him trying to keep away from me." She touches her tussled hair.

"Is he a good kisser?" Mary asks, her eyes greedy for information.

"A lady never tells," she says while staring at me.

My heart beats wildly, and I glance at Mary. "He's a fantastic kisser." There's a loud inhale at my bold statement.

Sandra's nostrils flare, and I feel a sense of victory, but it's brief.

"I second that." She steps away from me, smiling.

I swallow the bile that rises in my throat. He couldn't have kissed her. He wouldn't. She's playing mind games. But I can't stop the rise of pain that squeezes my chest.

"Come on, Ella." Hannah pulls my arm gently for us to go back into the room. I do and Sandra continues to smile. I hear their laughter as I close the bedroom door.

"Never mind her. She's just jealous and lying." Hannah's words have me pushing Sandra's lies aside. It has to be a lie. He wouldn't do that.

I join them back on the bed and try to take my mind off Sandra as we plan our rescue of Vicky.

"So when do we go?" Hannah asks while chewing her lip.

"There's no time like the present."

We all jump as someone knocks on the door. The second knock has me scurrying off the bed and opening the door. I nod at Mark.

"Miss O'Leary, Master Lucas requests your company in the gardens. I will escort you."

I glance back at Jessie and Hannah, both of which are smiling and nodding eagerly. But I think of Vicky and hesitate at the door.

"Once you get back, we'll finish it," Hannah says.

"Go." Jessie widens her eyes, and I leave with Mark.

Mark doesn't speak as he leads me to the gardens. I don't see Lucas, and Mark stops walking. "He said you would know where to find him."

I nod and leave as I make my way to the only place I can think of, the maze. My heart pounds as I get closer. I don't see him. I glance back to see if I can still see Mark, but he's nowhere in sight. Something heavy settles around my shoulders as I stand at the entrance of the maze.

"Lucas," I call and glance behind me. Facing forward, I call his name a little louder. Something is telling me to go back the longer I stand here. I hear the rustle of the hedge, but I don't feel the wind.

"Lucas, are you here?" I take a few more steps but keep the entrance in my sights at all times. As I reach the bend, I stop. There's a second that I think it's Lucas, but it's the shortest second ever, as Henry attempts to smile. He isn't wearing his glasses.

I shake my head and step away. He's quicker than I expected and pulls me back in. His hand immediately covers my mouth, as he pulls me against his chest. Panic overrides all logic, and I reach back and try to claw his face. He roars but his hold tightens around my chest, threatening to crush it.

"Stop moving." His command is barked loudly into my ear. My heart rate won't slow as I try to see past the fog of panic.

"I'm not going to hurt you. I only want to talk." He still holds me, and I try to compose myself.

"I have a deal for you. It's about Lucas."

I'm nodding. I want his hands off me.

"If I let you go, you better not scream."

I'm nodding again, but he doesn't release me. I jerk and he pulls tighter, moving us further into the maze. I kick out, but he's expecting the blow and blocks it easily.

"Would you stop?" His warning is hissed in my ear. I wouldn't have expected his strength.

He releases me abruptly, and I stumble forward only to have him grip my arm. I yank it back, and he blocks the way out. I'm considering running into the maze, but that's the panic talking.

"What do you want?"

He touches his face. "Just to talk." He looks at the blood on his hand. I don't feel guilty at all.

"So you sent Mark to trick me?" He keeps his legs wide so he can shift left or right if I try to get past. Kicking him between the legs is an option. I just need to wait for the moment of distraction.

"Would you have come if you knew I was here?"

"Maybe," I lie, and he hunches forward in that creepy way and half laughs.

"What do you want?" My heart is pumping too fast. I need to calm down. So far, he hasn't hurt me.

"I have a proposition for you." He stands up fully now.

"Where are your glasses?" I don't know why it's bothering me so much. Is he trying to look like Lucas? My stomach churns. He never could.

He takes them out of his pocket and slides them on. "Is that better?"

No. It would be better if I wasn't here.

"Lucas has something belonging to me in his room. I need you to get it."

I'm ready to laugh. Is he crazy?

I shrug. "Why would you think—"

He cuts me off. "I saw you going in and coming out of his room. So let's not pretend you don't have special access to my brother."

"You've got the wrong girl." I take a step toward him, my body repelling the minute he moves and tilts his head.

"I don't want to hurt you." *But I will* is left hanging in the air.

"Hear me out." He speaks through gritted teeth.

I stop moving.

"If you get me the box that I need, I will get you something in return."

He's crazy if he thinks he can give me anything. "Okay," I say, just wanting this to end.

His roar has me backing into the hedge. "Don't lie to me!" He grips his hair, and I'm nodding, staring at him like the lunatic he is. Oh God.

"You have to hear the whole deal."

"I'm sorry. I'll listen."

My words seem to work. He releases his hair and pushes his glasses up on his nose. "Lucas is going to marry Sandra. The contracts are signed. I can get rid of Sandra if you get me the box."

I feel physically sick. "Like, kill her?"

"Is that what you want?" He seems sincere, and that makes this worse.

"No, thank you." A weakness enters my legs as he takes a step toward me.

"She's standing in the way of your future with Lucas. Do you understand?"

I'm afraid to say yes, because I don't. But I don't want to prolong this.

"No. I don't." I'm waiting for the backlash.

"Good. You're listening." He nods and bends his head again. "My father and her father have agreed on the marriage from the start. There's no contest. Her father has the most money."

Bile rises in my throat. *No.*

"I've read the files." He sounds bored now. "I've read yours and know you have no money. Your father left your mother in a right mess."

I tighten my fists. How dare he mention my father. But I also wonder if Henry is telling the truth. I know money wasn't plentiful with us.

"Does Lucas know?" My throat feels dry.

Henry smiles and it chases all the warmth from my bones. "Yes."

He holds up his hands. "In his defense, it was all done without him. But he is aware of it."

"Why would I want to get rid of Sandra now?" My blood roars in my ears. If what he's saying is true, it means that Lucas led me down the garden path.

"Or Lucas?" he smiles again, and a coldness seeps into my skin.

"You're offering to kill your own brother?"

He's more twisted than I expected. "I don't care. Just get me the box."

My heart is still beating too fast, and I keep my hand over it.

"What do you want if not Sandra or my brother?"

I swallow the saliva that's pooling in my mouth. Could I really get him this box? "What's in the box?"

He smiles again. "Trust me, you don't want to know."

"If I say no?"

He's staring at me and not answering, so that's not good at all.

"I'll try," I say.

He shakes his head. "I don't want to hear that you'll try. It's a yes or a no."

"I don't even know where to look. What you're asking isn't reasonable." *You're not reasonable.*

"I know where it is." He's looking hopeful now.

"Where?"

He smiles and bends his head. "In the back of his wardrobe."

I nod.

His eyes widen as he straightens. "Is that a yes?"

"Yes," I whisper, as if I have a choice.

I take a step to leave.

"If you lie to me, I'll hurt your friends. The one called Hannah looks like she would break easily."

I can't back down. I'm so close to him now. "Don't threaten my friends. I'll get you the box."

I'll attempt to find it, but maybe having it will give me power over Henry. I'll see what's inside it.

"What do you want in return?"

Nothing. There is no deal. "I'll think about it." My anger has given me strength and he believes me.

"I'm happy doing business with you." He reaches out his hand, and I walk past it. He doesn't stop me, but his laughter follows me out of the maze.

# CHAPTER TWENTY-SEVEN

## ELLA

I GLANCE BACK OVER my shoulder at the maze, but Henry is no longer in sight. Folding my arms across my chest, I make my way back to the house and the safety of my room. It's the only place that feels normal right now. I try not to think about Lucas actually marrying Sandra. I know she was put forward as the favorite, but to me, it was all in theory, not actually signed on paper.

I remind myself that Henry could be lying. It would have been more beneficial if he was lying. That way, I would have tried to save Lucas. Now he painted Lucas in a bad light.

I check the foyer for Mark, but only George is there. He's coming out of the drawing room and peeks up at me. His smile is instant. "Lady Ella."

I like him. "George." I don't linger but make my way up the stairs. I need to tell Hannah and Jessie so I can make sense of what Henry said. Too much of me is believing him right now.

I twist my hands together as I enter an empty room. I'm ready to leave and go back downstairs. They must be in the drawing room.

A piece of paper is on my bed, an A4 size, so it's hard to miss. I recognize Hannah's writing straight away.

Gone to do some housekeeping. (Vicky)

Hannah & Jessie

She's even done a love heart over the i's like she always does. The page flutters from my fingers. What have I done? I've put both of them in danger. How long ago did they leave? Panic has my feet moving rapidly from my room and down the steps. I need to reach them. I just hope I'm not too late. What if something happens to them? I'll never forgive myself.

My heart rate spikes to an uncomfortable level as the sheds come into sight. I slow down and look around me. I take a walk along the side like I'm just curious. Sweat gathers at the back of my neck. My mind races, telling me to get in there and get them out. I want to make sure we all get out, hopefully undetected. This was such a bad idea.

I walk around to the door, my patience to disguise my reasoning for being here disintegrating quickly. The door opens and I enter, pulling it closed behind me. I let my eyes adjust to the different lighting before I weave through the cars. Blood crashes against my ears as I peek out from behind a car toward the stairs.

I count to ten in my head to try to calm myself before deciding that on the count of three, I'll go down into the basement. One, two—a gloved hand across my mouth has me throwing myself backward and into my captor.

"Ella, be quiet." It takes me a moment to battle through the haze to allow Lucas's voice to settle me. I turn and he releases my mouth instantly.

His jaw is clenched, the warning in his eyes crystal clear as he grabs my hand and tries to pull me from the shed.

"Lucas," I whisper and he spins fast. His anger would normally terrify me, but right now, I can't think about me or the repercussions of what I've done.

"Hannah and Jessie are down there. It's my fault." I need to get them. Even more so as Lucas's face turns pale. It must be bad. A cry wants to erupt from my lungs, but I swallow it down along with my panic.

"We need to get them."

Lucas steps away from me before returning quickly and gripping my hand, dragging me away from the stairs again. I yank hard and he turns with a flash of warning in his eyes.

"I won't leave them." I try to pull my arm again, but his ironclad hold on it isn't budging.

"I'll get them. You stay right here." He sounds like he's talking to a stranger. Anger has a funny way of altering our tone. I don't want to stay, but I nod.

"Don't you dare move." His growl has me moving away from him until I bump into a car. He still hasn't left, and I want to shout at him, ask him what he's waiting for. He's pointing his finger at me as he leaves.

It's forever that I stand there feeling naked. *Please God, tell me they're fine.* I repeat the mantra in my head. My eyes snap open as a scream has the hairs standing on the back of my neck. It's Hannah.

I'm moving, but my foot catches in the tarp and I tumble. My hands take the impact, along with my knees. Pain radiates throughout me, and I'm up and running again.

I'm halfway down the stairs when Lucas looks up at me. His eyes widen before they narrow. I take a peek at Hannah and Jessie behind him, who are both red-faced but look unharmed. Lucas, who had paused, marches toward me, making me climb back up the steps. He doesn't speak, and that's more terrifying.

I've never seen him look so angry. His clenched fists and tight jaw have me looking away from him. We follow him silently out of the shed. I'm waiting for him to turn on us and start shouting, but he doesn't.

"Follow me, the three of you." His words are delivered calmly, and I wrap my arms around my waist. Hannah keeps looking at me, trying to catch my eye, but I refuse to look at her. I'm angry at myself but also angry at both of them for going without me.

We follow Lucas all the way to his office. Once we're all in, he closes the door. His eyes are heavy on me, and I swallow. No one speaks, but we all shuffle. Yeah, we messed up big time.

"I'm sorry. It was my fault," I start the moment he sits down.

He holds my gaze for a second. "Let's start with why both of you were down there," he says, and I know Hannah is glancing at me.

"Because of me," I say, and Lucas's attention snaps back to me.

"Don't speak unless I address you." His anger isn't just peeking out at me; it's jumped into the front seat and taken over. I wisely bend my head and keep quiet.

"We thought Vicky was down there, Master Lucas." Hannah has a soft tremble in her voice, and I want to plead with Lucas to let them go, as this is all my fault.

"Why would you think that?"

Yep, Hannah is glancing at me. I meet her eyes and give a nod.

"Ella was down there..." Hannah doesn't get any more words out before Lucas is standing and marching toward me.

Each step is fueled with rage that he's barely containing. I stand my ground and raise my chin.

"You were down there?" His voice sounds strange.

"Yes, your father caught me." I quickly look at the girls. Hannah is watching me. Her cheeks are ablaze as she chews on her lip. Jessie is facing forward. Lucas grips my chin and pulls my face back to him.

"Why would you put yourself in that kind of danger?" His eyes roam my face like he's searching for an answer that he can't phantom.

"I'm sorry."

He releases me but shakes his head. "No, Ella. You're sorry you got caught."

He goes back to his desk and glares at me. Sweat trickles slowly down my back. I want this scolding to end. He picks up the phone and starts punching in numbers. Fear has me taking a step toward his desk, and his eyes snap to me, freezing me in place.

Is he ringing Andrew? That wouldn't make any sense since he just saved us all. I tighten my hands into a fist, and the sting of my cuts has me breathing a bit heavier.

Lucas's eyes dart to my hands. "Can I speak to Vicky O'Sullivan? It's Master Lucas." He holds the phone slightly away from his face.

"Show me your hands."

I feel like a baby. "It's nothing." I place them behind my back.

"Now, Ella!"

His growl has my face heating up. I glance at Hannah and Jessie, who face forward, not looking at me. I bring my hands out front and show him. He tuts.

"It's nothing," I repeat, but he ignores me.

"Vicky, I have someone who wants to speak to you." He holds the phone out to Hannah. "Talk to her. Confirm she's alive."

I die as Hannah takes the phone and speaks to Vicky. Her eyes dart to me and she nods. Oh God. Vicky is fine. I had sent them on a wild goose chase.

Lucas is standing and walks toward me. "Why didn't you just ask me?" His voice is heavy with disappointment, and that brings a lump to my throat.

"I'm sorry," I whisper.

Hannah clears her throat. "Vicky is fine. She's at home. Still slightly mad about being sent home, but she's fine."

"When you all arrived here, you were told you could only go to designated areas. The three of you have broken that rule. So you will all be punished."

"It was my fault."

Lucas cuts me off with a harsh look, and I sensibly focus on the floor and don't interrupt him again.

"I will decide your punishments. For now, go to your rooms and don't leave them."

The warning is clear. I feel terrible as I turn for the door.

"Not you, Ella." I glance up at Lucas before stepping aside and letting Jessie and Hannah leave. Once it's just me and Lucas, I'm waiting for him to lose it. But he doesn't.

I'm surrounded by his smell and warmth as he pulls me into his arms. "You're going to be the death of me."

I'm pushing him away, fear tightening my throat. "Don't say something like that."

"Why, Ella, because it's true? What were you thinking?" His anger has reignited. He takes a breath.

"It's not safe to talk here. Come on."

We're leaving the study. Lucas looks around corners like someone might be waiting there. I think it's overkill, but I don't want to enrage him anymore than I already have. He opens his bedroom door, and while touching my back, directs me in quickly before closing the door behind us. I'm back in his room, and so many emotions chime together. My eyes dart from the bed to the wardrobe. I was here. This is my chance to get the box.

"You need to tell me everything," Lucas says as he draws the curtains on his windows.

I don't speak until he spins around to face me. "I need to know what happened to you."

"Don't try to put this on me. You endangered Hannah and Jessie. Not to mention yourself."

"I can't say enough that I'm sorry."

He's shaking his head like he's trying to believe me but just doesn't. "You're sorry you got caught."

"Fine. You're right. I'm sorry I got caught. I went in there to find out what happened to you. Because I care about you, and your father found me and brought me down."

All the color leaks from Lucas's face. His chest is still, and I'm wondering if he's even breathing.

"He showed me where you kept the food. But as I was leaving, I saw blood droplets leading to a closed door. I put ten and three together and came up with Vicky being held captive there."

I'm out of breath. I sound so dumb. But the color is slowly returning to Lucas's face.

"So I devised a plan to go and investigate."

Lucas exhales loudly before sitting on his bed.

I stay where I am and finish my story. "I took a walk." I skip the whole Henry thing. "When I got back, they had left without me."

Lucas rubs his face with both his hands, his eyes heavy like I've just taken five years off his life. Guilt churns quickly in my stomach.

"Let's clean your hands" is his answer as he stands and walks into the bathroom. I follow but slow down as I glance at the wardrobe doors. The box is in there. I need to get that box.

# CHAPTER TWENTY EIGHT

## LUCAS

Eᴛᴛᴀ's sᴋɪɴ ɪs sᴡᴇᴀᴛʏ, and she looks like she can't stand much longer. I take out two washcloths and run them under some hot water.

"Sit on the toilet seat," I tell her while I rinse out the washcloths.

She exhales heavily. She has no idea the danger she put them all in.

I squat down in front of her. "Give me your hands." I can't look at her. My anger is still burning through my system.

Her hands are cut. But as I wipe them, I see the cuts aren't deep. "Are you injured anywhere else?" I don't look at her. Being this close has my mind going in a completely different direction.

"My knees."

Which are under her long skirt. I stand and wash out the cloths before running them under warm water. I can hear the shuffle of material, and I glance over. She's pulled her skirt up. It sits above her knees in a bundle of dark material.

I squeeze the cloth out unnecessarily tight before returning to her. Squatting down, I come eye to eye with Ella. "I want to make you promise not to do anything foolish again, but I think I'm wasting my breath."

Her eyes widen slightly, but she doesn't answer me. I can read her so easily, but now she seems conflicted.

I focus on her knees and try not to trail up higher. I rest a hand on her thigh, and she stiffens at my touch. Her skin is warm, and I want to separate her legs and taste her.

"How did you do this?" I ask to distract myself. She's only grazed the skin, but I still dab her knees gently.

"How did you hurt your hands?" she retorts.

Her words grab my attention, and I tighten my hold on the washcloth. Water drips out onto her knee and runs down her leg. I follow it until it hits the floor.

My heart won't slow. "I beat someone." I start from her ankle and run my finger under the line of water, bringing it back up. I can hear her breathing quickening.

"It's how all this works," I say as I run my hand past her knee. Her skin is so soft, and I don't want to stop touching her.

"People who break the rules get punished." I separate her legs, and she opens them for me easily. I still haven't looked at her. I don't want to see what she thinks of me.

"They know the rules. They know the consequences," I say as I push up her skirt. When I place a kiss on her thigh, her hands immediately sink into my hair, and her legs spread a little more for me. Running my tongue all the way to her panties has her wriggling. My shaft grows painfully hard.

I stop what I'm doing and look up at Ella. She's staring at me, her eyes clouded with lust and fear. But lust is winning. Her lips are soft and warm as I take them in mine. I break the kiss while I rise and take her hand, leading her into the bedroom.

I pause, giving her a moment to stop this. Giving her a moment to really let what I just told her sink in. I need her right now. I need to tell myself that she is here and fine. Flesh and Bones.

She moves and grips my face, her lips touching mine, giving me permission. Lowering us onto the bed, I try to silence the want in me to pull off her panties and take her hard and fast. She's a virgin; I need to remember that. I still can't stop the wildness in me as my hands greedily grip her breasts.

Her skirt has fallen down, the material blocking me from entering her. I release her and push down her skirt and panties. Her hands pull at my waistband, and I remove my own clothes. The eagerness in me wants to take her, but I allow her to take me in. Her eyes widen as she focuses on my cock. She pulls her bottom lip into her mouth, and I can't hold back.

I move myself between her legs. I want to pound it in. I want to come inside her, but once again I hold back as she stares up at me, I allow her to stop this, but she pulls me down into a kiss that I greedily take, while reaching down and dipping my fingers inside her. She's wet and ready.

I place my cock at her entrance and push in gently. She groans into my mouth, and it's agony going this slow. I push a bit deeper, and she grabs my shoulders, allowing me to sink further and further into her. She gasps and I groan when I'm fully inside her. As I pull out slowly, she tenses and I pause before moving back in.

Holding myself up with one arm, I use the other to play with one of her nipples. She gasps and I pull out of her before moving back in. She widens her legs and tenses when I'm fully in. I keep the rhythm slow and can feel her relax under me. I move faster but nothing like I want to do.

I break the kiss so I can watch her face. It's ecstasy as her arousal takes over her features. She's grabbing me, pulling me closer, and I move a bit faster and harder, my own release not far away. I roll her nipple between my fingers and she gasps again.

Moving quicker, my release is there, and I can't slow down as flesh slaps against flesh. Ella tenses around my cock, her wetness soaking me, causing my own release inside her. It pulses through both of us, and it feels like we're both coming forever until the waves subside and I slowly move in and out before taking myself out of her completely. Sweat trickles down my back, and she's panting as I look down at her. She opens her eyes and smiles.

The air catches in my chest. She's mine. I will make sure of it. I kiss her lips tenderly.

*She's mine*, I remind myself as I take her face in my hands and kiss her one more time. Her actions were reckless, and I'm starting to think I won't be able to tame the wildness that is Ella. I don't think she sees it herself, how she metaphorically steps out in front of a car, thinking it will swerve and she'll be fine.

"I need you to stay in your room from now on," I say, knowing my words will fall on deaf ears.

"I will if you tell me about your arrangement with Sandra."

I sit up. "Why would you ask me that?" Is my father trying to turn us against each other. Who else could have fed her that information?

She sits up too, and I try not to focus on her nakedness. "Sandra was bragging about having this already signed. Is it true?"

The torture on her face has my stomach hollowing out. This is one situation I need to lie to her about, especially after what we just did.

This shouldn't be a conversation we're having right after she loses her virginity.

A knock at the door has me quickly clamping a hand over her mouth, silencing her.

A second knock has my heart pounding. I grab my trousers and pull them on. Ella's already moving into the bathroom. She emerges with her clothes, and I put on my shirt.

"One moment," I say harshly after the third knock. I'm pointing at the bathroom for Ella to hide in, but she pauses with all her clothes in her hands, opens the wardrobe, and steps in before closing the door behind her. I take one final look at the room once I'm fully clothed.

"Yes, Mark?"

"Your father requests your company, Master Lucas."

"I will be with him shortly." I try to close the door, but Mark puts his hand on the door. "Right now, Master Lucas."

Mark is my father's man, and one day he will be mine. He has kept an eye on Ella, but he is my father's man all the same. I glance at the wardrobe before leaving the room and following him.

"This better be important."

Mark doesn't answer me.

My father is in his own office. The moment I set eyes on him, my anger ignites. "Can't you come yourself?"

He sits back in his chair at my outburst. My eyes skip him and move to the two figures who stand still to his left. I hadn't noticed Jessie and Hannah when I entered.

"Where is Ella?" I take a step deeper into the room and don't look at Hannah and Jessie—both Ella's friends, and both in my father's grasp.

"I don't know. What's this about?" I reel in all emotions.

My father studies me for a moment before speaking. "I saw these two ladies sneaking around in the shed, and shortly after, who followed them? Ella."

"I'm aware. I've reprimanded all the ladies already. This is unnecessary."

"How exactly have you reprimanded them?"

"I haven't decided yet."

"I shall decide for you."

My heart picks up pace, and I'm struggling not to leave the room and find Ella to make sure she's safe. She would hate me for leaving her friends, but her safety is all that matters to me.

"Fine." I turn on my heel.

"I'm not finished." His words are like a hook that reels me in. I take two steps back before spinning around.

My father stands, and in his hand is a small red leather book. A fist tightens in my stomach. It's a book I've read before. Our book of punishments.

He opens it, and his smile is quick as he reads. "The punishment for not taking directions from an elite is thirty seconds in the electric chair."

I swear I hear Hannah whimpering. Over my dead body is he placing Ella in the chair. He closes the book with a bang and smiles at Jessie and Hannah.

"I'm not a monster."

Relief has Jessie's shoulders sagging. She has no idea of the type of monster he really is.

"So I've come up with something different. You may even call it a reward. You will be put forward as an option for Henry to marry because Lucas has already agreed to take Sandra's hand in marriage."

Guilt echoes in my chest as Hannah looks at me with wide eyes. The betrayal on her face has me wanting to explain, and she blinks rapidly with a look of disgust before dropping my gaze.

"So Hannah"—my father stands in front of her—"do you accept your punishment?"

"Yes, Master Andrew." She has no idea what she's agreeing to.

"Jessie?"

Jessie isn't as forthcoming as Hannah. "Can I meet him first, Master Andrew?" She bows quickly.

"There's no need. He's a gentleman. My word is enough."

"Yes, Master Andrew." Jessie gives in, and my father returns to his desk.

"Very good. Another problem solved." He smiles up at me. "You may return to your rooms."

They scurry past me, but not before Hannah looks up at me, her lips narrow with anger. I want to stop her and explain.

I hold still until the door closes. "Ella is off limits. We have already discussed this."

My father moves paperwork around his desk. "That is true, but these are new circumstances, so therefore, new rules."

He looks up at me. "If I were you, I'd go find her before she gets herself into a situation she can't get herself out of."

I curse my father with each step I take back to my room.

When I enter, I hate the small gap I see between the curtains that hang over the back doors. I know she's gone even before I pull open the wardrobe doors. I'm ready to close them when my eyes travel across my clothes. Some of them are ruffled and have been moved. Dread fills each step as I push my T-shirts aside and feel around only to come up empty.

The box with Declan's finger is gone.

# CHAPTER TWENTY NINE

## ELLA

T HE BLOOD POUNDS IN my ears as I hunker down behind the hot tub. I've wrapped the box in a T-shirt. It feels heavy in my hands, and I slowly unravel it. My stomach twists. It's like opening someone else's present. I want to know why Henry offered to get rid of Sandra for this box. Why would it mean so much to him?

I'm examining the outside. There's nothing special about it. I'm prolonging this, I know. The guilty part of me wants to put it back. I feel wrong taking from Lucas, but I also need to protect Hannah and Jessie. If this stupid box will keep them safe, then I hope Lucas will understand. That is, if he ever even realizes it's gone. It could have been something the boys fought over as children, maybe even with some sentimental value to it.

The lid slides to the left, and I push it open. The wood falls from my hands and tumbles to the ground as I swallow down a scream. I'm scurrying away from the finger.

*A finger!* I can't breathe. The air won't fill my lungs.

*Calm down. It could be fake.*

I know it's not. It smells the same as Jack Bradley did. I'll never forget the smell as I stood at our neighbor's coffin. It was like dry earth and raw meat. It was a hot summer and the wake had lasted a week as they waited for the family to fly home. By the time they got there, Jack Bradley had already started decaying. I was only fourteen at the time, but the smell stayed with me.

I glance at the finger that sits on the blades of grass. Leaning against the hot tub, I know I need to pick it up. Shivers rack my body.

*Don't be weak. It's fake. It's fake.*

I crawl over on all fours. I pick up the finger and try not to think as I drop it into the wooden box and close the lid. My throat constrains with a need to cry. I can't take this back to the room.

I'm trying to focus on why Lucas had a finger in his wardrobe. Whose hand had it belonged to? Did Lucas cut it off? My stomach squeezes. He had admitted to beating people who broke the rules. It terrified me that I hadn't run away disgusted. It terrified me that I wanted to help him. What if he's a murderer? Will I still stay?

My mind buzzes with too many questions. I just know I shouldn't take this box back to my room. Bending, I scout the area before standing fully. After lifting the tarp off the hot tub, I place the box wrapped in Lucas's T-shirt on the seat and pull back down the tarp.

Opening my bedroom door, I want to bleach my hands. Bleaching my eyes might help get rid of the image of the finger.

"Jesus." I clutch my chest and then drop my hands. "You need to make some noise," I tell Jessie and Hannah as I close the bedroom door.

"Where were you?" Hannah is standing, and she reaches for my hands.

"Don't touch me," I warn quickly and march to the bathroom so I can scrub a layer of skin off.

"Did Lucas or Master Andrew find you?" Jessie asks from the bathroom door where she and Hannah linger. Both of them look worried, and it makes me slow down.

"What happened?" Apprehension tightens my stomach.

"She doesn't know," Hannah says to Jessie before turning to me. "You need to sit down."

Hannah is seriously worrying me. "Just spit it out." My heart can't take much more.

"Master Andrew called us to his office. He knows we were all in the shed."

I close my eyes briefly, trying to stop the snowball effect that came from my stupid assumption that Vicky was dead.

"What did he say?"

Hannah is chewing on her lip, her eyes clouded. I can't look at her any longer as fear grips me by the throat. "What did he say?" I repeat to Jessie. What did I bring upon them?

"We're all being presented as options for Henry to marry instead of being punished."

Saliva fills my mouth.

"We're okay with that." Hannah smiles, but there's no happiness in it. She looks terrified.

"Have you met Henry?" I ask, but I know she hasn't.

"They've selected you too," Jessie says, and I'm trying to wrap my head around what she's saying.

*I might have to marry Henry?* I turn off the taps.

"Lucas is marrying Sandra," Hannah blurts out.

I look to Jessie, who rolls her eyes. "Very tactful. But yes, it's already been agreed."

The towel on the rail is crooked. I straighten it.

"Ella?" Hannah's soft word has me looking at her. "Master Andrew is looking for you. So is Lucas."

I notice the dark circles under Hannah's eyes. "You need to rest. You look tired," I tell her.

She glances at Jessie before her eyes revert back to me. "Did you hear me?" She chews her lip.

"Yes." I heard her, but I refuse to let those words sink in.

"Excuse me, Lady Ella." A foreboding feeling settles into my bones as Mark calls me from the bedroom.

"They've found me," I say to Hannah and force a smile as I try not to splinter the wall I'm building in my mind.

*Don't think. Don't feel.*

"Master Andrew requests your company."

I move one foot in front of the other. I focus on the back of Mark's head. His hair is peppered with gray. It's brushed perfectly, the lines reminding me of when someone cuts a lawn in vertical lines, leaving the pattern behind. I wonder how many strokes it took to have his hair sit so perfectly.

He turns and opens a door. The first thing I see is rows and rows of books, from floor to ceiling. There must be a ladder somewhere so one can reach the top.

Mark moves aside and a stunning mahogany desk dominates the top of the room. Andrew sits behind the desk, a smile in his eyes when he sees me. The wall cracks as I glance to the left. Lucas is standing with his back to me. He doesn't move a muscle as I walk up to his father's desk. He won't look at me. The wall I've built is cracking too fast, and I can't let it shatter. Not here. Not now.

"Ella."

"Master Andrew." I give a small curtsy.

"I see you've learned some manners."

His words ignite a spark inside me that I jump on. *Don't feel. Don't think.* My eyes keep getting drawn to Lucas, but I force myself not to look at him and just focus on Master Andrew.

The door behind us opens, and bile claws its way up my throat as Henry steps into the room. He doesn't look happy. He looks awkward in his black suit. He no longer wears glasses. His eyes land on me and he smiles. I swing around to find Andrew watching me.

"You are familiar with Henry?" he asks.

I peek at Lucas. Nothing. Henry steps to my right.

"Ella and I have met before," Henry confirms.

Andrew cuts him a look before returning his gaze to me. "I asked you a question."

"Yes, Master Andrew. I am familiar with Henry."

His brows rise. "Good, this will be a lot easier. You have been given the honor of possibly being Henry's wife."

He stands now as I try to swallow around a lump in my throat. He places his hands into his pockets. "To be honest"—he moves around the desk, and he's too close to me—"I think you might be the one."

He pushes off the desk and walks over to Henry, fixing his tie like he's a child. I glance at Henry, and he's starting to hunch forward.

"Stand still," Andrew barks and Henry's spine follows the order.

He glances at me, and my stomach twists. He looks so much like them now—a younger version than Andrew, but an older one than Lucas. I glance over at Lucas, studying his side profile. A part of me wants to reach out. Maybe if I touch him, he'll snap out of his frozen state.

"You should congratulate Lucas on his upcoming wedding to Sandra."

Too many cracks coat my wall at Andrew's words. I need to leave.

"Congratulations, Master Lucas," I say and I see a slight reaction in Lucas. His jaw tightens, but I look away as my heart beats too fast in my chest.

My legs grow weak as I stare into Master Andrew's eyes. The devil's eyes. I want to ask him why he hates me so much. I want to shake Lucas and tell him to do something. This can't be real. I find my body leaning toward Lucas. I need something from him.

"Lucas." I say his name with all the pain that fills me, and he finally looks at me. His stare nicks my heart and penetrates right through me. I'm a stranger in his eyes.

"It's done now. We had fun and it's over." His cold words have me stepping away from him. My vision wavers. I'm shaking my head. "No."

His smile is a mirror image of his father's. It's cruel and I recognize this person, the one I first met. The one that would go to the bone just to get a kick out of hurting you.

"You can have her." His eyes have skipped over me as he speaks to Henry like I'm something that can be passed around.

I focus on the floor, my face ablaze with hot humiliation.

"You can leave now." Andrew's eyes are filled with victory.

His image wavers and I bow. "Thank you, Master Andrew." I turn toward Mark, who's ready to escort me out. I can't breathe as I quicken my pace from the room.

The moment my feet touch the hall, I'm running. Running from a barrage of emotions that demand I release them.

I can't.

I won't.

The air outside doesn't help my starving lungs. I run until I crumble to my knees. I want to scream. Covering my mouth with my hands, I try to control the flow of pain that oozes from me. When I feel like I won't scream, I dig my hands into the grass and let myself cry.

Voices not far away have me sniffling and coming out of the black cocoon of pain that I'm wrapped in. Through the flower beds, I see George talking to a blonde-haired lady. Their words don't carry this far. Both of them look up at the house and then they disappear, leaving quickly. I can hear the footfalls behind me, and I know I can't take much more.

"Ella." Lucas's voice has everything in me stiffening, and I don't move a muscle as his voice dismantles the wall completely.

# CHAPTER THIRTY

## LUCAS

"Ella." She's kneeling on the grass, her shoulders shaking with silent sobs. I hate what I had to do to her. I needed my father to think he had won. That he had finally bent me to his will.

"I want you to go away." Her words are controlled and that frightens me. I'm afraid to go any closer. Anyone could be watching.

"I can explain."

She's shaking her head. "Please, Lucas. Just leave."

I tighten my hands into fists. The pain in her voice has me nearly undoing all my work and reaching for her. I remind myself that I'm doing this for her, and in the end, she'll understand.

I leave her, and each step I take kills me. She's hurting so bad, and I put all that pain on her.

\*\*\*

Over the next few days, I keep my distance. Hannah never leaves her side, and her loyalty to Ella is unshakable. I admire her every time she sees me and cuts me with a look like I'm the devil himself.

The ball has been moved to tomorrow night. My father had a matter to deal with that he wouldn't discuss with me. I wasn't naïve to think that I could freely move around the house without every move I made being watched. So I continue to play my part.

Henry is lying out on the rug on the floor, his chest still. I don't move away from the stairs as I stare at him. Is he dead? I take two steps toward him, and he lifts his head.

"What do you want?" He pushes himself fully up on his elbows. "Well, I do have something you want now." His grin has me stopping.

"She's pretty," he teases, and for a moment I'm ready to throttle him, but I refrain from acting out.

"You're gay, Henry. She'd hardly be of any interest to you," I say with my own smirk.

He doesn't like that at all and hunches his shoulders like a wounded animal. There's a fleeting moment that I feel so sorry for him, and for the first time, I wonder why he is the way he is.

"The day you took me to the maze, why did you do it?" I'm the one feeling vulnerable now. I'm talking about something that eats away at me. That can happen when your brother tries to kill you.

He shrugs. "They loved you and hated me," he says like it's logical.

"I was eight," I remind him.

"Maybe." He sits up now and shrugs.

"There is no maybe about it. I was eight and I was terrified."

Henry has the audacity to laugh at me. Why did I even come here?

"You have no idea of true terror."

His words have me looking at him again.

"They never left me alone." His eyes are wide, and he wears a far off look. I think he's finally lost it completely.

"At me and at me and at me." He stands now, breathing heavily. His eyes swing to me. "Don't talk to me about fear."

Did someone hurt him? "Who?"

He scratches his brow and hunkers. "George and her. I think she's back."

Disbelief in his words has me smiling. "George hurt you?" I make sure each word is clear.

"He hates me. They all do." Henry points at me now. "You hate me."

Nothing he says is making sense.

"You tried to kill me, Henry," I defend. "My mother is locked up because of you."

I take a calming breath. I didn't come here to start this. I don't want to hurt him when he looks so wounded already.

He's laughing maniacally, and I think leaving now would be for the best.

"Locked up. They can't keep her away from here."

I turn back around, and my heart starts to beat rapidly.

"They can't keep her away from you."

"What are you talking about?" Irritation ripples through me. Is he really losing it?

"It doesn't matter. They took Declan from me. Now, I just need to keep Alex safe."

I step into the room and stop only a foot away from Henry. "Stop talking in fucking riddles. Are you trying to tell me that George"—I point at the stairs—"as in George, who works for our family, that little old man, killed Declan?"

"I don't want to answer you," Henry starts.

I clear the distance between us and grab him. "I'm not eight anymore. I will fucking beat it out of you. Tell me now."

"Yes, that George." He pulls himself out of my hold, and I release him, my fingers going slack.

"He found out about me and Declan. I know to be careful around him, but he sees everything. I'm sure it was Mother's orders." He rolls his eyes at the word *mother*, and I'm questioning my own sanity of standing here and listening to this.

"George left that finger up here to taunt me. To let me know they would keep taking from me, because I tried to take you from them." He looks very far off, like he's halfway to a padded cell.

"When I was eight?" I ask, and I'm aware of how gentle my voice is. I'm not buying into this madness, but a part of me sees the damage. If it's real, what he's suffered at their hands...

If it's not, then my brother needs help.

He looks at me now and rolls his eyes again before pushing his glasses up on his nose. "Are you going to keep bringing up one little mistake I made?"

"I wouldn't call it little, Henry. You built that maze to trap me."

He's admitted that before.

He shrugs. "I built it to trap us all."

"What does that even mean?" My voice rises, and he blinks like he sees me for the first time.

"I want you to leave now."

He glances to his left, and I follow his gaze. A gray top hat sits on the floor beside some vinyl disks.

"That's Alex's hat?" I ask, walking over to it. He races over and picks it up, not allowing me to touch it.

"Are you...?" My stomach twists. He has no idea who Alex is to him. "Are you...?" I can't finish the sentence.

He shakes his head, but I see it in his eyes. It's always been there. He loves him.

"Henry." I don't even know how to finish my sentence. What do I say, don't sleep with him, as he's really your half brother?

"He's safe." He says it quietly while ducking his shoulders, and now all I see is a very sick individual.

"Did you do something to him?"

Henry won't meet my eye, and when he does, they're blurred with tears. "How do I know you aren't working with them?"

"With who? George?"

"And Mother."

I place a hand on each of his shoulders, and he hunches further, making me feel like a monster. "Henry, Mother isn't here. I think you need help."

"You're so blind." He pushes away from me, and irritation has me following him.

"You are working with them." He says it like a statement as he continues to rotate Alex's hat in his hand. He smiles at me.

"For you, Lucas, I'm going to make an exception."

He's making no sense. He's changing every few seconds, and I can't keep up with all the Henrys.

"I will try with Ella. Maybe your and Sandra's children can play with Ella's and mine."

My control slips. My hands are around his throat, and his face turns red.

"That's it, Lucas. Kill me."

I release him. "You're rotten to the core."

He laughs. "Yep, Mother sure made me suffer."

"She's not your mother. Your mother is Sorcha Newtown, who had an affair with our father. My mother is Elizabeth. But she's not your fucking mother, so stop saying it."

My lungs burn painfully once I have all the words out. I don't regret them. Henry is staring at me, and not with outrage, but it's like a light bulb just went off over his head.

"That's why she hates me." He starts to laugh. "I've always wondered. I never thought *you* would solve the mystery."

He's scratching his arm as he looks far off with a smile on his face. "It all makes sense. She hated me because I was a reminder of the other woman. Was that the other finger?" He looks up now, but he's still scratching his arm in the one spot.

"Yes," I answer as I watch him piece this together.

He's like a kid with a puzzle as he paces. "So she was killed for the affair. Mother's doing..." He holds up a hand. "I mean Elizabeth's doing?" He's back to scratching his arm, the skin turning red.

"Yes," I answer.

"So she must have been very angry with me and Declan." He's giggling now.

I want off this crazy train. He needs help. So much help.

His arm starts to bleed, and he doesn't stop digging his nails in the one spot. "They left the fingers up here to blame me for Declan's death so they would finally get rid of me."

Is he talking sense? I scratch my neck as I watch Henry.

"Your arm is bleeding," I point out.

He stops digging his nails in. He looks at the blood and shakes his head. He won't stop smiling.

"I really appreciate you telling me all this." He's looking at me like he genuinely is grateful.

I think of the rest, and he needs to know about Alex before he does something that's illegal.

"There's more."

He's nodding and giggles. "This is Christmas."

I need to get out of here. "Sorcha isn't just your mother. She's Alex's."

His smile disappears and he hunches, backing away from me with a snarl on his face. His eyes dart to Alex's hat, and he's shaking his head.

"Did you…?" I can't finish the sentence. How do I say it without getting sick?

"Get out." His bark is fueled with rage, and I want to tell him to calm down, but he's marching toward me.

I'm ready for him, but he walks past me and down the stairs. I'm confused for a second. I follow him. He won't slow down.

"Henry, what are you doing?"

He doesn't pause or answer me. He's half jogging all the way to our father's office. I don't stop him as he pushes the door open. I'm about to tell Henry that father isn't here, but he's sitting behind his desk on the phone. His eyes snap up as we enter, and he ends his call.

"You're back?" I say the same time Henry starts.

"You should have told me about Sorcha."

My father looks at me, and I have nothing else to do but shrug. This is a train wreck, and I'm not driving.

"I should have, but you have a tendency to overreact."

Henry walks in a circle. "I don't overreact."

"Henry." The warning in my father's voice has me standing straighter.

Henry stops pacing. "She's back, isn't she?"

"Yes."

"Are you talking about Mother?" I feel like someone just punched me in the stomach.

"The time I left you in charge, I got a call," my father informs me. "She had broken out. She's still missing."

"She wants to hurt me." Henry's cries are alarming, and what's more alarming is my father hugging him.

"There is no need to worry. Didn't I save you the last time?"

Henry looks up at him and nods. "Yes, Father."

My skin is crawling. My father is doing equal amounts of damage to Henry with his manipulation.

"No one needs to be alarmed. We will find her and have her back in the hospital in no time."

Henry looks calmer for a moment. "But what about Alex? You told me I could have him."

"I meant as a friend, Henry. You have Ella to think of now." My father goes back to his desk.

The mention of Ella's name has the shock evaporating.

"So I can't have him?" Henry pouts.

"No." He shuffles papers before looking back up at us both. I've never felt more like a child.

"Both of you on different occasions have barged in here, with absolute disrespect, and you will have to be punished for your behavior."

He looks from Henry to me. "I'll let you know when I decide what your punishment will be. Now leave."

We turn to leave.

"Oh, and Henry." We both stop, even though he's only speaking to Henry. "I found Alex."

I glance at Henry, who looks sheepish, and my stomach twists painfully. What did he do?

"He's upset, but he won't tell anyone what you did," Father says.

"He's upset with me?"

My father releases an exasperated breath. "You tied him up and left him in the refrigerator."

"Only to hide him from George and... Elizabeth."

This is all too crazy, all too much.

"There is no need. I have everything under control," my father reassures him, and Henry seems happy with that.

I follow, feeling like a ghost listening in on a conversation I shouldn't be privy to. My stomach twists, and I know one thing for sure. I need to get Ella out of here.

# CHAPTER THIRTY-ONE

## ELLA

A FTER LUCAS TORE OUT my heart, I can't seem to piece myself back together. I haven't moved from my bed. Hannah draws the curtains open, and the light burns my eyes. A part of me wants to go home and tell my mother everything.

"Why don't we take a walk today?" Hannah smiles down at me. It's been three days. The ball has been canceled until further notice. Each day, I'm waiting to hear that it's soon so we can leave this place. Maybe they'll give us a chance to see our families before we start this nightmare all over again with Henry. I shiver and Hannah sits on the side of the bed.

"Ella, who isn't Bella. Get up." Hannah's flushed cheeks and worried eyes have me obeying.

"I'm fine," I say, with no truth in my words. My unwashed body and crumbled clothes can confirm the lies.

Jessie is sitting at my dressing table. She's facing us. Her eyes don't hold the sympathy that Hannah's does. But Hannah wears her heart on her sleeve, while with Jessie, you need to scrape the surface to see it.

"We got word that the dates start with Henry today," Jessie states before running her hand across her ponytail. A trait I've learned to associate with her nerves.

Hannah is chewing her lip. I'm unsure how she has any skin left. I take her hand, getting her attention.

I've never allowed myself to imagine having a friend like Hannah. Friends are the real fairy tales I never got to read. So that is what I will take from this place—friendship. My heart pangs, reminding me of my loss, and I focus on the flesh in my hands.

"We're going to be fine," I say.

Hannah nods unconvincingly.

"Do you want to know why?" I glance at Jessie too. "I've never had friends before. Now, I have you two." I look back at Hannah, who's smiling widely. "We have each other."

Hannah's hug is the warmth that makes your body sag and take a breath. It also allows the emotions that are just under the surface to stir. I break the hug.

"We will be fine."

This time Hannah's nod is convincing. "Yes, we will be. Now you need a wash. You smell."

"Since you're going on the first date with Henry," Jessie adds.

Hannah rolls her eyes. "You can't just blurt it out."

I climb out of bed. Henry's name is making me twitchy, but I want this done and over with.

"She's right. I better get showered."

Surprise flitters through Hannah's eyes at my quickness to shower. I need to get that finger out of the hot tub. I shiver again as I strip. If I was to do anything right, it would be to protect Hannah and

Jessie by giving it to him so they would be left alone. They might have a chance of going home and finding their happy endings.

The burn across the bridge of my nose has me jumping into the shower without letting it heat up. I need to run from the thoughts that are demanding to be listened to.

***

It's warm outside today. My stomach won't settle every time I think of 'the date' with Henry. But it's an opportunity to make the deal with him. Guilt churns heavily in my stomach, and it feels sour as I reach the hot tub. I'm not sure how long I have before Hannah notices I'm missing. I can see her having a fit with worry, but I need to make sure the finger is still here.

I can't stop myself from glancing at the double doors that I know lead into Lucas's bedroom. My mind snaps to Sandra in there and Lucas touching her. A fire rages through me at the thought. Sandra was upstairs lounging while Mary fanned her down. Her glory of winning Lucas's hand hadn't helped the last few days. Gripping the tarp, I steady myself.

"Ella."

I spin around so fast I nearly fall. Lucas steps to help me, and I move back, nearly falling backward. Gripping the hot tub's edge, I manage to steady myself. My heart is beating heavily against my chest.

He looks so good. A hand tightens around my heart.

"What are you doing?" He stuffs his hands into his trouser pockets, causing the muscles on his arm to bulge. Do they always bulge like that? I want those arms around me. I want him to tell me he's marrying me.

I want him.

I'm so pathetic after everything he did. "Nothing," I manage to squeeze out between my pounding heart and aching chest.

"I'm glad you're here." His eyes bore into me, and I tell myself not to waver.

"Are you? Or maybe you were expecting Sandra?" I don't want to sound so jealous, but jealousy doesn't come close to what I feel for him.

His lips tug slightly like I'm amusing him. My throat burns. Does he care that he hurt me? Humiliated me?

"I'm happy to see you." He exhales loudly and removes his hands from his pocket. He glances around him quickly before folding his arms across his chest.

"I better get back." Standing here and pretending everything is fine is too much for me. Maybe he can do it, but I can't.

I pause, not wanting to walk any closer. He's in my way. "Move," I order and his lips tug up higher.

"You're sexy when you're angry."

His words cause a tide to rise inside me. He thinks I'm sexy? The one emotion that's rising the fastest is what he thinks is anger.

"Angry? Have you any idea of how much you hurt me?" Pain explodes and burns my eyes.

His smile melts from his face. "Ella, I did it to protect you." He unfolds his arms and takes a step toward me.

"Do I look like I'm protected?" Everything hurts and I don't want to do this with him. I don't want him to give me hope only to take it away again.

His jaw clenches. "You just need to trust me."

Tears fall and I don't want them to fall. I wipe the treacherous tears away. "You had my trust. I gave you the best of me and you humiliated me."

Lucas takes another step. It's controlled, almost measured, like he wants to come closer but can't. "I'm sorry. I really am."

"Are you calling off the wedding to Sandra?" The small part of me that's clinging to hope pleads with him.

"I can't." His growl has me knowing I need to leave before I shatter at his feet.

I move past him. He grips my wrist, stopping me. He doesn't face me as I glance up at his side profile. His fingers burn into my skin, and it's like Lucas has a direct link to my heart, the one he's breaking even further.

"Please trust me, Ella."

I pull my arm out of his grasp, unable to bare his touch any longer. "I hate you." The words drip from my lips, fueled with all the pain, and he glances at me. I can see the hurt I've just inflicted on him.

Good. He might understand what I'm feeling. I try to look less like I'm falling apart as I return to the house. I'm no further on without the finger. But I know where it is, and that will have to do for now.

"I hope you weren't pining after my husband." Sandra's voice grates at me as I clear the last step.

"Give it a rest, Sandra." Hannah glares at her before that glare is focused on me. I can see the question in her eyes. Where was I? Why did I go? What trouble have I gotten into now?

"He's all yours," I tell her.

Her sneer has me looking up. "I clearly remember you saying that to Vicky, and then you threw yourself at him."

My heart thrashes against my chest like a trapped animal.

"You're just jealous because we can all see how he looks at Ella." Hannah speaks up for me, and I'm so tired. Her words aren't true.

"Yes, Hannah, I will admit I'm not blind."

Sandra stands now, Mary and Bernie mimicking her movements. "He looks at you with lust, but he looks at me as an equal. As his wife. His love."

Saliva pools in my mouth. Is she right? Was he with me just so he could sleep with me, and now I'm disposable? Pain tears through me at how naïve I've been.

"Lady Ella."

I turn to Mark, unsure how long he's been standing there listening to us.

"She's hardly a lady." Sandra's words are low, but I hear them and now I wonder if Lucas told her I'd slept with him. My face grows hotter by the second.

"Henry is ready for your date." He gives me a look from my toes to my head. I'm wearing a simple white summer dress and flip-flops. I'm not dressed for a date.

"I'm ready," I say, wanting to get away from the carnage of this conversation with Sandra.

My date with Henry is surprisingly in the gardens too, only he's set his up at the mouth of the maze. He's facing the maze, his back to me as Mark leads me right up to the blanket.

"Sit." Henry points at the space across from him. I do and am aware of how boxed in I feel to have the maze at my back and Henry in front of me. He smiles, but I can't return it.

"Eat, Ella." He chews on a sandwich, but my stomach is too sour. I pick up one small one and just hold it in my hand.

"I'm going to pick you because I feel like we already have a connection." My hand tightens around the dough. This is what I wanted for Hannah and Jessie so they could live their lives. But being tied to Henry while I watch Lucas with someone else is a new kind of pain.

"Don't look so sad. It's an honor." He smiles and my fingers touch one another as they break through the bread. I release the squashed sandwich and swallow the pool of liquid in my mouth.

He eats several sandwiches, and I hate the sensation I'm feeling of falling. Like the ground is shifting under me. I steady myself with one hand before filling up a glass of water. My hand shakes. If Henry notices he doesn't say.

"Now with the matter of your friends, I still need that box..." He moves his head from side to side. "Or I'll hurt them," he settles on.

How much more could they suffer? They still had to go on a date with him. Isn't that torture enough? I keep my words to myself, but I want to lash out and hurt him.

"I have the box," I say.

Surprise flitters across his eyes, which already dance with madness. "Where?"

It's my turn to smile. "It's safe. That's all you need to know." I want to ask a hundred questions about the finger, but I don't want to look eager or he will surely use it against me.

"Don't play games with me." He flips easily, just like a switch. He's hunched, his lips tugged down into a frown. It feels like a long bony finger moves up my spine, causing me to shiver.

"If you test me, I will make our wedding night very painful for you."

It's like I've been slapped. Did he just threaten me with rape? My chest burns.

He smiles in victory. "I will only be taking what's mine." He sounds so smug.

My heart slams against my chest as my anger boils over. "You're too late. Your brother already had me, so I'm soiled goods. Second best for you, Henry." I slam my hands across my mouth once the words pour out. I've made a terrible mistake.

One that I can't take back. One that I will pay for if I base the outcome on the look that Henry sears me with.

I'm aware of Mark standing close to us. No doubt he heard me, and I need to take it back. I need to make this right.

"I didn't..." I'm shaking my head.

Henry's face is red. Every part of it looks like he's going to explode. He reaches out and grips my arm before dragging me to my feet.

"Henry," Mark calls and Henry doesn't hear him as he drags me away from the maze and toward the house. His grip is like iron, and fear tightens across my chest.

What have I done?

# CHAPTER THIRTY-TWO

## LUCAS

I DON'T MOVE AFTER Ella leaves. I try to control the need to chase after her. I didn't think she would be that angry. I knew it would hurt her, but deep down, I thought she would see past my words and remember what we had together. She looked so innocent and beautiful in the white dress.

I move around the hot tub, wondering what she had been doing out here. At first, I had been overwhelmed with relief when I thought she had come to speak to me, but that faded quickly when I could see her eyes. I stand where she had. She was touching the tarp. I lift it and look in.

I don't know why I'm smiling as I lift out my black T-shirt. I feel the box before I see it. I knew she had taken it. But why is my real question, and why is she getting it now? What trouble is she in?

I take the box back into my room. I can only hope she hadn't opened it. Placing it on a different shelf, I lean my head against the shelving.

Having Declan's finger doesn't really matter. Do I really care who killed him? A part of me wants to take it back and wait to see when she returns, what she intends to do with it. I leave the wardrobe and the finger in it. George is someone who I haven't seen much of, and I need to ask him of his involvement in all this. I'm avoiding it; I don't want Henry to be right.

My bedroom door bursts open, surprising me.

I reach for George. "What's wrong?" He looks ghostly white.

"Henry has taken Ella to your father. You need to get there." I'm moving through the halls. I can hear Henry's hysterical shouts as I enter my father's lair.

"I want her strung and quartered." He's pointing at Ella, who's kneeling on the floor, her head bent. I'm beside her and squat down, not caring anymore about who's looking. I'm praying that he hasn't hurt her.

"Look at me." Dread plunges into my stomach as Ella looks up. I'm searching her face, and she seems unharmed. Her eyes are wide and filled with fear. I touch her face, and she leans into my hand, like it might take this all away.

"Get away from my wife." Henry's words bounce off me. I'll deal with him in a moment. Right now, I need to take this pain away from Ella. Her eyes stare up at me.

"I'm so sorry." Her voice wobbles with fear. Shaking my head, I force a smile. I want her to know it will be okay. I will fix this. I stand and help her rise slowly. She leans into me once we're standing, and I look up and into my father's eyes. He shows no emotion as he stands and stares at us.

"Get your hands off her." Henry is still wailing, his voice shrill with rage.

"That's enough, Henry," my father barks, and silence falls across the room. Ella's tremble shakes her body, and I tighten my hold on her.

"Let her go, Lucas." My father speaks carefully, and I know that taking my arms from her is wise. He's beyond angry and that's dangerous. I release her but don't move away. My body can't seem to distance itself any further. My father seems satisfied.

"He defiled my wife." Henry is calmer, but his voice is high pitched with anger I've never heard before.

"Is the accusation true?" my father questions.

I tighten my fists. I don't dare look to Ella. "She's not his wife," I state.

My father nods in agreement. "She's not yours either."

"Does it matter if she's my wife? Can't I have my fun just like you, Father?" I'm crossing a line with both my father and Ella. She wasn't just fun, but I need to drive my point home that this is unnecessary. We don't have to entertain Henry just because he isn't getting his way.

My father's stare is heavy until he turns his back on us. I'm not sure what's happening until he starts to give us a history lesson.

"Generations of the O'Faolains have led this community. We rule tens of thousands of people. Year in and year out, it grows. We follow simple rules. If we start to bend and break them, chaos will prevail. The system will crash and we will have nothing left. I have bent these rules for both of you, and it has done no good. In fact, it has harmed our family's reputation."

He turns to us. "That ends now. I was given two sons, two possible leaders, and so far you are both a disappointment. I blame myself." He takes a step toward us.

Ella is still trembling beside me, and I want to comfort her, but my touch will bring her too much pain.

"I spoiled you." My father stands in front of me. "I allowed this"—he points at Ella without looking at her—"to go on for your pleasure, but it needs to end now, and you will take your rightful place at the head of this family, with Sandra Crowley at your side."

I don't let his words sink fully in, but I see the truth in his eyes. "You can't outrun this. You can't leave. It's really a pity you boys didn't educate yourselves better on our ways."

My father turns to Henry. "Henry is correct. To not be a virgin before your wedding night to an elite is punishable by hanging."

My stomach twists painfully as Ella whimpers. My father returns to me, his eyes glowing with the power of this moment. "To walk away from this community, son, is death." He delivers each word like a blow. I can hear Ella's breathing become labored.

Death sounds more pleasurable than this. My father holds up a hand. "Of course we aren't barbaric." He moves to Ella. "I won't have you hung, but I have overlooked too much for you. This is where it ends."

I want to stand in front of her and stop this, but any power I felt I had is dwindling fast. If I do anything, I could make this worse.

"That's not fair." Henry's whines are ignored by my father as he keeps his focus on Ella.

"You will be locked up until I decide your fate."

Ella's head snaps up.

"Master Andrew, I'll take her place." I take a step forward, and I'm ready to beg.

His eyes meet mine, the hardness in them unshakable. He walks past me.

"The only thing that isn't fair, Henry, is that I was given a gay son." Henry flinches at my father's tone. "One who is a half-wit."

Henry flinches again. "I can't keep protecting you. Not when you disregard my authority."

"I didn't do anything wrong." Henry points at me. "He always takes what's mine."

My father's hand connects with Henry's face, and the sound bounces around the room. Henry recoils from my father while holding his face. "Don't ever speak out of turn again."

My father walks back to his desk. "This disregard ends here and now. No one will speak unless they are spoken to. My word is final." He's staring at me as he speaks.

"Mark." I half glance over my shoulder as Mark steps up between me and Henry. I hadn't known he was here. I turn again and see George never left either. His eyes clash with mine, and he slowly backs out of the room.

"Take Ella to the guard house." My heart slams heavily against my chest.

It takes everything in me to stand still as Mark takes her out of the room. She doesn't fight. Once they're gone, my father steps back up to me and Henry.

"This is the final time I'm giving you a choice, son. You either marry Sandra and take your place as the leader, or you will be banished from this community with a bounty on your head."

I've never wanted to kill someone so much. He's everything that's wrong with this world. He is all my violence and hate rolled into one. There is nothing left in my father.

I would take the banishment if it meant Ella was safe, but she wouldn't be. She would be locked up here, and I would have no power to save her. Staying here means I could at least try.

"I'll marry Sandra."

My father smiles and pats my shoulder. "Good choice."

He exhales and turns to Henry, who shrinks away from him. The pity I feel for Henry is short-lived when I think of the situation he put Ella in. The truth is, I put her in that situation. I had no idea it could lead to this. My father is right about one thing. I had no idea about our history or our rules. That is something that will change. Now I need to find a loophole in all of this.

"I can't keep allowing my love for you to cloud my judgment, Henry." My father touches Henry's face, which is red with the print of his hand. He has no idea what love is. He's cruel and cold and incapable of such a feeling.

He exhales heavily again and releases Henry's face. "You will have to marry one of the other girls. Ella is no longer an option."

"Yes, Master Andrew." Henry's voice is small.

"I still need to punish you. You don't go around airing our dirty laundry." His eyes flicker to me before returning to Henry. "You could have come here calmly. But I'm sure everyone heard your shouts. So Alex is not allowed here anymore."

"Please, Father, don't take him away."

This time, the sound of flesh connecting with flesh has me biting down on the inside of my mouth.

"You keep talking out of turn." My father half laughs like he can't believe how stupid Henry is.

Henry holds his face with two hands, and for the first time, I see anger flash in his eyes. My father acknowledges it when he places his hand on Henry's shoulder.

"I'm only trying to protect you from yourself."

I'm as confused as Henry as my father steps away from us.

"Any more problems, come to me directly. We need this house to be in order. You're dismissed."

# CHAPTER THIRTY-THREE

## ELLA

THE SLAM OF THE door seems so final, and I can't move. I can't look around the small space that I'm now confined to. The door has a small window of bars on it. I shuffle forward, and my fingers wrap around the cool steel.

Is this really happening? The tremble that had entered my body still hasn't subsided. When Henry stated that I should be hung, he almost had me laughing—until I looked into Master Andrew's eyes. Everything in me grew cold, and I was staring death in the face.

I bow my head and take in calming breaths. Peeking under my arm, my chest feels tight as I see the small bed and a steel bedside table.

This isn't real. I need to wake up. This is too much.

The blood roars in my ears as a large sound bounces around further down the hall. My face is glued to the bars as I try to see, but the lights don't continue the whole way down. I try to listen beyond my pounding heart.

"Hello." My voice sounds hoarse. No one answers. Sweat soaks my hands, and I release the bars. The image of a furry rat banging into a tin can has all my nerve endings on fire. I still can't turn around and face this reality. If I stay by the door, someone will open it. They can't leave me down here.

I swallow the emotion that bubbles up my throat. A sob erupts from me when I think of Lucas. He had arrived, helped me up, and at the moment, I had been weak with relief. I really thought he would make it all disappear, that Henry's outburst would be stopped.

The wooden door has been repainted too many times. Bubbles of paint are rough under my palm. I trail my finger the whole way to the keyhole. One turn and it would end this madness. I don't deserve this fate.

My heart pangs when I think of Hannah and Jessie. I think everyone heard what I did. Henry roared from the gardens and all the way through the house as he dragged me to his father. It was a walk of shame.

*Humiliating.*

I swear I hear footsteps. I grip the bars and try to see as my heart pounds in my chest. I see a shadow and move back as it continues to move toward me. Black hair and inky eyes, his sculpted face is normally filled with an unshakable confidence. I hate the look of devastation in Lucas's eyes.

This is bad.

Him being here brings so much to the surface. Everything in me is fighting and scrambling to get to the top.

"Please, let me out," I whisper as my lips tug down and I try not to cry. I don't want to speak too loudly, but I need him to get me out.

"Ella."

The way he says my name has me stepping back away from the door. Away from him. "You can't, can you?"

He's shaking his head.

I turn and stare at the space that feels smaller. Covering my heart with my hand, I beg it to stay in my chest. "I'm going to die?"

I can't face Lucas.

"I won't let that happen." His words sound fierce, and if he keeps fighting, then I need to keep fighting as well.

"What's going to happen to me?"

There's a lull before he speaks. "Please look at me."

My stomach roils, and I'm terrified in case I throw up. I turn and meet his dark eyes.

"I'm going to fix this." His large hands grip the bars as he begs me to believe him.

I can't answer him.

"I was never going to marry Sandra. You have to believe me."

I bite the inside of my jaw until a metallic taste fills my mouth.

"I thought if I pushed you away, I would keep you safe." He holds my stare.

I release my jaw from between my teeth and swallow my blood.

"I didn't know that you could be punished like this." His knuckles are white as he grips the bars. "Ella, please say something."

"I'm standing in a cell, in a white summer dress, as I wait for my fate." My lip trembles again. I've never felt so naked.

"I'm going to make this right. I just need time."

My head snaps up and I'm shaking it. I'm moving, my hands wrapping around his. "You can't leave me down here."

A surge of panic rips through me. To hear that's it, not just this moment that I'm down here, that it could be longer, raises another layer of this reality.

"I will make sure you have everything you need."

A hiccup of tears has me bowing my head until my forehead rests on my hands.

"All I wanted was to marry you." I'm thinking of that moment in the car. Larry was driving, and my mother was beside me. The smell of polish from the car's recent cleaning was heavy in the air, along with my mother's perfume.

"All I wanted was you." I look up at him now as tears stream down my face. "Then I met you and you were so horrible." Salty tears escape into my mouth. I half smile. "All the stories at bedtime were lies and it hurt."

"Ella." Lucas's voice is haunted with pain.

"Then you kissed me, and each kiss healed everything in me, and I got more than some story. I was living it." I take a breath as I control the wave of emotions.

"I don't regret it, Lucas. I don't regret you." *No matter the outcome.* I don't say it out loud, but it lingers between the bars and hovers over our joined hands.

"You caught my attention on the first day. It was your eyes. You reminded me of a deer. You stood so still staring at me. I might not have known it at that moment, but you captured me." Lucas presses his lips against my fingers, and a kink in my armor, which is barely hanging on, snaps.

"I really thought you hated me, and the more you pushed, the more I wanted you. Did I tell you you're sexy when you're angry?" His smile has my laugh mingling with my tears.

"Yes." I swallow more tears as he places another kiss on my hands.

"You, Ella O'Leary have dismantled all my walls." He's staring at me and I see them, the gold flecks floating in a mass of space. I'm rooting for their survival.

"I'm going to climb the tower and rescue you." The heaviness in his eyes has me crying again.

"No, that was meant to make you smile."

I laugh into our hands. "You don't even know what story that's from," I say, looking up into his stunning eyes as they chase the cold away, forcing it into dark corners to give way to his light.

"*Cinderella?*"

"It's *Rapunzel* and I've never really liked that story."

"Which one is your favorite?"

I swallow tears as I think of all the bedtime stories. I'm smiling before I even say it. "*Beauty and the Beast.*"

He laughs, and the sound warms my heart. "What a fitting story for us."

*Us.* I like the sound of that.

"You are hardly a beast."

"A beast who has fallen in love with his beauty."

My nerves are flooded with signals that have my mind pausing and needing to take in what he just said again. My stomach erupts, and I can't look away from his dark eyes. Oxygen grows thin, and my hands grip his tighter.

"I love you, Ella."

Tears come quick, and I take in a lungful of air.

"Please don't be upset."

I look back up from him and shake my head, like it might shake the overwhelming feeling away. "I'm not. I'm just happy."

He raises both eyebrows and I laugh.

"It's just..." I swallow. I could keep saying it, but I don't think Lucas would understand that I had dreamed of this moment since I was a little girl.

I wasn't standing in a cell when my prince declared his love for me. When the prince told me I had his heart, I was in a ballroom filled with spectators who couldn't get over my beauty. But the real Lucas isn't some paper version of what I had built in my head. He's layered and confusing, and I love him for each fiber that makes him up.

"You don't have to say anything. I just need you to know that I'm going to make this all right."

"How?" How could he possibly make this right? The coolness at my back has me pushing my body against the wooden door. I want to be in his arms. I want to feel his warmth.

"I don't know yet, but I promise I'll find a way."

His honesty calms me. I have to keep strong. I need to trust him.

He kisses our entwined fingers again, and I focus on the feel of his soft lips against my skin. I've been in here for less than an hour, yet freedom feels like a dream. My stomach tightens when I think of Hannah and Jessie again and what they must be going through.

"Hannah and Jessie," I start and Lucas smiles at their names.

"I will let them know you are fine."

I nod. "Lie to them. Don't tell them I'm down here. Hannah will try to break me out, and I'm sure she'll end up in more trouble."

"Don't try to make her out to be the troublemaker. That's you."

I can't defend myself this time. I do have a tendency to get into trouble.

"She's a good friend. I'll make sure she's okay."

I swallow around the lump in my throat. "Thank you," I whisper as a fresh wave of pain erupts inside me. I want to claw and kick my way out of here, but I try to settle the panic in me that keeps swelling and deflating.

"Tell me what you need." Pain and more pain—that's all I see in Lucas's eyes, and I want to reach in and ease it for him.

"Just you." I smile.

"You have me. But can I get you some books?"

I wasn't going to be able to read for one second, but I didn't want him to know that. If it eased him into thinking I was sitting here reading, then that's what I would do.

"Lots of books. Maybe some blankets."

His eyes grow brighter.

"I do like really red apples, so red that they almost look like wine. Also some warmer clothes."

He's nodding voraciously. "I will get all that."

He seems more content. "Oh, and a tie for my hair."

His laughter warms me again. "Aren't you demanding?"

I shrug and my stomach twists as I sense his departure.

"I'm going to get everything for you, okay?" He kisses my hands again, and I tell myself it isn't a goodbye; it's a see you soon.

"Lucas..." I want to tell him I love him, but I decide that once I'm out of here, I will. It's what will keep me going.

"Be safe," I whisper.

"You too." His body is moving, but I'm still gripping his hands.

*Let him go, Ella.*

I release him and hold my breath as he steps away from the door. I want to scream, "Don't leave me!" but I drop my eyes so he can't see me. His broad back disappears, and I hear his footfalls. Turning to the bed sets me off, and a sob mixed with too many tears from me, and for this moment, I allow myself to break.

Alone, in a cell, but with Lucas's love embracing me. That's what will piece me back together.

# CHAPTER THIRTY-FOUR

## LUCAS

I CAN'T LEAVE HER. So I sit on the cold floor and listen to her cry. Each tear burns me, and I take the punishment for what I have done to her. Her sobs are fast as she gasps for air. I tighten my hands into fists as she continues to cry. I would give up my soul to silence her pain. The sad part is, if I was given the choice to go right back to the moment she looked up at me in the drawing room, on her first day here, would I have looked away and ignored her if that had saved her all this pain?

The answer is no. I couldn't give her up. The most defining moment for me was when she protected Alex. He didn't deserve her protection, but against all the odds that stood in front of her, she never left him. She stood up to me when no one else had. I'm smiling at the memory, but my smile dissolves as I allow her cries back in.

I sit here in her circle of pain until her sobs subside, and I wonder if she's fallen asleep. I know I should go and start figuring out how to get her out of here, but leaving her alone is tearing at me. She's moving and I listen as she moves around. A sob erupts every once in a while, and soon she settles again. The creak of the bed has me using the noise to stand.

I get up carefully, so as not to draw attention to myself, and climb the stairs reluctantly.

The air feels different as I step into the foyer. The house seems like a different place altogether, even a different time period. My hand won't release the knob; closing the door on her makes me feel like a monster. She shouldn't be down there. Someone behind me clears their throat. I look over my shoulder and see George watching me.

"George." I close the door and face him. I can assume he's waiting for me. I'm staring at him and wondering if Henry was telling the truth when he said George killed Declan. It doesn't take strength to flip a switch, stopping the electrical current from turning off. But it takes a sharpness I just don't see in George. He doesn't look like a killer to me.

"Master Lucas, I'm so sorry. How is Ella?"

"I need you to bring her some things quietly. I don't want anyone to know, so be discreet."

He nods. I tell George about the list she had asked for. "As for how she is..." How would anyone be? I don't finish that sentence. "Tell Ella I will get back to her as soon as I can. I need to find a way out of this."

I'm opening the floor to any suggestions, because right now, I have no idea how I'm getting Ella out of that cell. And I do get her out, then how can we be together without being banished and hunted down by my father?

"If I think of anything, I will let you know, Master Lucas." There's an uncertainty in George's eye that vanishes when he bobs his head. I don't stop him as I spot Hannah and Jessie marching toward me. Hannah's mouth opens wide, and I grip her arm and steer her into a sitting room directly beside us. She releases a squeal as I push her in. Jessie is staring at me.

"Get in now," I order and she quickly joins Hannah, whose hands are fisted on her hips. Her cheeks are red with anger, and her being friends with Ella makes sense. Both of them are passionate and fiery. It isn't the best combination at all in a dangerous place like this.

"You both can't be marching around demanding answers. Ella would be so angry if she knew you were putting yourselves in danger."

"Where is she?" Hannah doesn't take in a word I just said.

"She's safe." The only plus to this is that she can't get into trouble while she's down there. I don't have to worry about what she's up to.

Hannah is shaking her head. "I want to know where my friend is." Hannah chews her lip.

I can go two ways with this. I can reason with them or frighten them. Frightening them seems more appealing, but I think of Ella and what she would say to me for frightening them.

"My father had her locked up," I answer honestly.

Hannah's eyes grow wide, her hands leaving her hips. I glance at Jessie, who's slowly sitting down.

Both girls look devastated, and I stand awkwardly.

"What are you going to do about it?" Hannah asks.

I can't stop the smile. "I'm going to get her out."

She bobs her head several times. "What's the plan?"

"Plan?" I have no plan; that's the problem. But they don't need to know just how clueless I am in all this.

"Yeah, how are we going to do this?"

I shake my head. "There is no we," I tell Hannah.

She glances at Jessie as if I hadn't just spoken. "You told me once that you can pick a door with a bobby pin."

I'm ready to interject, but Jessie rolls her eyes. "No, I said I think I could do it. That's how the agent did it on TV." She shrugs. "It just looked easy."

"I could try," Hannah says before chewing her lip.

"No one is picking locks. I just need the two of you to act normal and stay out of trouble."

"Where exactly is she being held?" Hannah's earlier feistiness returns.

I run a hand across my face. They don't get it. So I have to go for option B. I don't want to, but we're going around in circles, and I don't have time.

"Sit down!" I bark, and Hannah moves backward and lands right beside Jessie.

"Ella broke the rules, so she's in serious trouble. This isn't that she might get a slap on the wrist. This is her life we're talking about." I'm firm with my words.

Two sets of eyes fill with tears, and I take my tone down a bit. "But don't worry, I'll get her out."

Hannah nods and tears fall.

"She will be okay," I try to reassure them.

It works as Hannah smiles. I don't want her smiling.

"But this is serious," I reinforce and her smile wavers.

I'm thinking about locking both of them in their rooms. "Now, if I can at some point, I will try to let you see her. But right now, you need to stay in your rooms."

They'll never see her down there, but they don't need to know that. I just need to give them something to hold on to.

I glance from one watery face to the other. I've never felt so out of my comfort zone as I am while they stare up at me like I hold all the answers.

"You really hurt her," Hannah states while looking at me from the corner of her eye.

I shift. "I know."

She sniffles. "Like, really hurt her."

"He gets it." Jessie nudges her and I suppress a smile.

I retrieve a box of tissue from one of the reading tables and offer them one each. Hannah takes three while Jessie takes one. I have to stand while both girls clean their tears.

"Okay, you need to go to your rooms, and I'll try to figure out a solution." That weight on my shoulders feels heavy.

Both girls rise, and Hannah pauses in front of me, no doubt ready to deliver a warning.

"I will have her back in no time," I say and that stops Hannah from speaking. Jessie shoves her out of the room. I didn't believe they would stay put, but right now, they're the least of my worries.

I leave the sitting room and make my way into the basement that holds the archives to our history. I should have done this from the start. Well, before the ladies arrived. Knowledge could be powerful, and I hope I'll find something down here.

I pass the glass box; the room has been set up again for a meeting. I'm not aware of one happening soon. I pray it isn't a vote on Ella's punishment. I glance at the box again and picture Ella strapped to the chair.

*Over my dead body.*

A small voice in my head tells me that's exactly what it might take. As I pass the wall that divides this side of the house from the other side, where Ella is, I'm tempted to touch it and tell her to hold on. I tighten my fists as the room that I hope holds answers to get me out of this mess comes into view.

The room looks the same as it always does. Rows and rows of books coat the top half of the wall, and below them is filled with rows of filing cabinets. The room holds only one large table that has a reading lamp on it. It's normally free of anything else, but right now, a red leather book sits in the center. I step back out of the room and listen, but no one is here.

Someone had been, though. I close the door behind me and sit down, picking up the book. I open the book, where the red ribbon lies. There's the smallest of stars on the left of the page. I glance up again before I start to read.

*The power that's invested in the leaders is divided equally between a husband and wife. No one person can have full control unless:*

*1. A spouse is deceased. Remarriage is highly recommended at this stage.*

*2. A spouse suffers a brain injury or a psychological breakdown. A divorce and remarriage is highly recommended at this stage.*

*If a spouse receives an injury that has them hospitalized for longer than three days, they may nominate someone in their place.*

The list goes on, but I go back up to the star. Someone left this book out for me to find. They had starred it at this particular line. I close my eyes. What does it mean? My mother had fifty percent power in her marriage, but she had a breakdown so my father should have remarried. But he didn't, so...

I stand up, feeling irritated. Is that something I can use? It doesn't say it makes him powerless; it just states that he would be recommended to remarry. But he didn't *have* to.

What if my mother never had a breakdown? She would still hold fifty percent power. But she did nearly kill Henry. I saw her beat him. She had killed Sorcha, and Henry said they taunted him and killed Declan, too.

I return to the book and flick through it, but nothing else stands out. As I flick again, a piece of paper sticks out along the edge. I'm careful not to lose the placement as I open the page. My heart pangs as another small star is beside a line.

*If a male individual of the community commits sodomy, the penalty is death by hanging.*

I read the line three times, and it's still the same. The rules are barbaric and were never updated over the centuries, but they still stand.

So Henry should be hung for loving Declan? That's so wrong. But I try to push the inhumane aspect of the rule aside and focus on the knowledge that I could demand Henry be hung for being gay. My father already knows this.

A second thought starts to drip into my mind. What if my father left the book here to send me on a wild goose chase? I slam the book closed, my irritation growing. I think about breaking down the door and getting Ella out. But then what? We run and can never settle down? I sit back down with the book and try to find something that can save us.

# CHAPTER THIRTY-FIVE

## ELLA

T HE TEARS FINALLY DRY on my cheeks, and all I want to do is scrub my face raw. The bed creaks under my weight as I draw my knees up to my chest. I rest my cheek against my knee and close my eyes.

I pretend I'm at home, surrounded by all the things I had taken for granted. The small beaded bag that held my collection of cosmetic jewelry I could only wear in the comfort of my room. The box under my bed where I kept my journal of all the places I would visit when I was married. A tear leaks from the corner of my eye. My mother's scones and creamed coffee. My mouth waters now, and my stomach growls. I sit up and wrap my hands tighter around my stomach. I focus on Lucas's words.

*"A beast who has fallen in love with his beauty."*

I can hear movement again and scoot off the bed. My heart pounds. It can't be Lucas; he left a short while ago. He couldn't possibly be back so quickly. Footsteps continue and I half approach the door, weary, until George's smiling face appears between the bars.

"Lady Ella." His soft voice has me forcing a smile. He raises a bundle of things for me to see. It's what I requested Lucas get for me. I'm disappointed that Lucas didn't bring them. "I will push each item through."

It takes us a bit of time, but we manage to get the clothing and books through the bars. The blanket is the hardest, but with a bit of pulling and back and forth, it finally fits through. The only thing that won't fit is the apple.

"It's okay, George," I say.

He shakes his head. "Where there is a will, there is a way. I'll be back in a moment."

He disappears and I push my face against the bars, looking out of the corner of my eye so I can see his back. "Be careful," I call.

I didn't even want the apple or any of these things. It was just to keep Lucas busy, not get anyone into trouble. God only knows what would happen if poor George got caught.

I step back from the door, and when I face the bed, my throat tightens again and I busy myself stacking the books onto the bedside table before spreading the blanket out across the bed. A cardigan that isn't mine doesn't offer much warmth, but I still wrap it around my cold shoulders.

The sound of footsteps again has me moving close to the door. It's George. He holds up the apple, a half in each hand.

"The wonders of a knife, Lady Ella." He easily passes it through the bars.

I accept. "Thank you so much." I clutch the apple, and there's a moment of hesitation in his eyes.

"Master Lucas will be here later."

I want him here now. I nod. "Thank you."

He still hesitates. "Can I get you anything else?"

"A key would be nice. One that would fit a keyhole like the one on this door."

His smile wobbles. "I'm sure Master Lucas will have you released in no time."

My stomach twists. I don't think George is sure at all.

"Can I get you anything else besides a key?"

I force a smile. "No, thanks. But thank you for this, George." I hold up the apple.

He bobs his head before finally stepping away from the door. "You are very welcome, Lady Ella."

I listen until I hear a door close in the distance. My stomach growls, and I remember I haven't eaten anything at all today.

I take a bit of the apple and chew slowly. It has no taste. The apple fills the void in my stomach, and I climb back up onto the bed. The light from the hall continues to glow, but I have no idea if it's day or night. I pull up my knees again and rest my cheek on my legs.

I know I'm drifting when my body slumps to the left, and I wake up, catching myself before I fall. I shuffle closer into the corner of the bed and resume my position.

I dream of poisoned red apples and Sandra's smiling face. It's all meshed together, and when I wake up, I know something is wrong. The cold wall at my back and the hard bed under me reminds me I'm in a cell. But it's the lack of lighting that starts my heart pumping fast. A drumming sounds in my ears, and I'm not sure if it's the hum of my body or an actual sound.

"They took Alex away from me."

Fear grips me by the throat as my eyes dart around my small cell. My back pushes harder against the wall. The fabric of the blanket under me is fisted in my hand.

"They took you away from me."

Where is he? I'm searching the dark space, but I can't figure out where his voice is coming from over the pounding of my heart. My breath comes in short spurts, and the buzzing noise grows louder.

"They're going to hang you."

A whimper escapes my lips, and I swear I hear him laugh.

*Calm down. Calm down.* My heart slams against my chest painfully, and I rub the spot, trying to calm it down.

"What do you want?" I manage to squeeze out.

"It's like a broken love story, me and you. I find my wife, only my brother has slept with her, and now my father removes her from my grasp and sends her to the gallows." He sounds so pleased with his words. Like it's poetic somehow and not twisted with lies and dipped in madness.

I release the blanket as my temperature spikes, sending a cold sweat down my back.

"What do you want?" I ask again, and the blood doesn't thrash so hard in my ears now, and the humming sound has lessened, but it's still there.

"Can't a broken man come see his wife?" His voice is to the right of me and sounds distant. I try to think and know I hadn't heard the door open. So at least he isn't in here with me.

I use that nugget of information to calm myself. To tell my body it's okay. He can't hurt me. He can't get to me.

"I'm not your wife." I feel a bit braver now as my body starts to slow down.

"We really could have been something." He doesn't seem to hear me as he continues to speak. His laughter is shrill. "Can you imagine Lucas's face when he sees us walking down the aisle? It really will be justice. Take him down off his high horse. He always thought he was better than me."

He grows silent and I'm listening, trying to hear movement. But there's nothing.

"You're not very talkative, are you?"

I stay still and listen. I still can't figure out where he is exactly, and there's that voice in the back of my head that tells me he's in my cell and at any second he'll pounce.

A bang rips a squeal from me, but it doesn't stop at one.

"Answer me." The bangs continue, and I shuffle deeper into the bed as Henry beats the door in a frenzy.

"Go away." My roar bounces off my cell but stops his onslaught on the door.

His laughter feels like it's everywhere. I want to cover my ears with my hands and bury my head in my knees until this ends.

More silence follows, and I'm really starting to think he has left.

"A boy broke into our gardens once and got lost in the maze. I found him, of course, because I did design it." He's still here, and he sounds so proud.

"It took me a long time to build it, nurture it and help it grow." He shifts. "That takes patience, Ella. Real patience."

I hate how he uses my name like he knows me or has a connection with me.

"So this boy who I found in my maze wasn't scared of me. We would have both been around sixteen. He thought he was better than me, just like Lucas does. Both turned out to be very wrong." Henry sounds far away, and dread curls in the pit of my stomach. I don't want to know about his twisted maze or his crazy thoughts.

"He had no idea how creative I was." He trails off, and I just want him to leave. "How long do you think you can go without sleep?"

I glance at the door. I can't see anything, but now I'm wondering if that's what's happening here. Will I be tortured by Henry's voice keeping me awake?

"The boy started to hallucinate after only three nights of keeping him awake. Honestly, Ella, between me and you, I had such fun. He was a hoot. He was trying to climb the walls, shouting about sheep."

Tears burn my eyes. He's sick.

"Maybe his father was a farmer? Who knows, but he kept me entertained for hours."

"Is that what you're going to do to me?" I sound so small and I hate it, but I'm exhausted. My brain can't process all he's saying. I don't think I'd be as strong as the boy and last three nights listening to Henry.

He laughs. "Hardly. This structure isn't designed for sleep deprivation. But don't worry. I will come visit each night."

I bury my head back into my knees. Maybe I am still dreaming.

"I wish I could sit beside you."

My heart slams against my chest. My head rises.

"I heard you move." He sounds like he's smiling. "Maybe I could get a long stick and poke you." He's laughing again, and I see how unstable he is.

I clench my fists and keep quiet.

"You're just like a dog. Lucas's pet. Lucas actually had a dog. It always barked at me, and I hated it. Woof woof, yip yip. Annoying creature." He moves again and exhales loudly.

"He didn't last long with me. You should have seen Lucas's face when he saw his dog dead. He was crying and yapping, just like the dog." He's laughing again.

I feel sick. "You're a monster, Henry. *You* need to be locked away, not me." I'm off the bed, shouting at him. "Go away."

Over the beating of my heart, I listen to the silence.

"I only came to keep you company." His words are low, like I've actually hurt his feelings. "I only came to check on my wife." He sounds like he's moving, and for one perfect moment, I think he's finally bored with me and has decided to leave.

Everything in me freezes as I hear the click of the door. I'm shaking my head while stepping back.

*No. No.*

The creak of the door warns me of his arrival.

I don't stop moving until my back hits the wall.

"I can hear you breathing so fast."

I hold in a cry as he steps into the cell.

TO BE CONTINUED

Get A Cruel Confession Now! HERE

# About The Author

When Vi Carter isn't writing contemporary & dark romance books, that feature the mafia, are filled with suspense, and take you on a fast paced ride, you can find her reading her favorite authors, baking, taking photos or watching Netflix.

Married with three children, Vi divides her time between motherhood and all the other hats she wears as an Author.

She has declared herself a coffee & chocolate addict! Do not judge
Social Media Links for Vi Carter

Website

Facebook Reading Group

Facebook Author Page

Printed in the USA
CPSIA information can be obtained
at www.ICGtesting.com
LVHW042231280224
773119LV00004B/48